ISBN: 979-8-9870879-1-6

Acknowledgments:

Shout out to my beta readers, who can read between the lines, even when the words don't make sense.

Big thanks to Peggy Stautberg for her professional feedback, and always pointing me in the right direction.

Thanks to Lorraine Davis for her beautiful art and for appreciating crazy when she reads it.

Thanks to Jodi, who lets me talk endlessly about people who only exist in my mind.

This book is dedicated to my tea fairy.

# Danish Jubilee

A Jewel Journal Adventure

By Kristel Beck

Prologue

The ginger-haired man waited behind the warehouse door. The meeting spot had been prearranged, just like every detail of this job. It pleased him. For a caper like this, there was so much to think through, and his employer had anticipated each step down to the last detail. Everything was supplied from the panel truck to the uniforms—even a synchronized watch to keep things on schedule. He took another look at the three crates on the box cart. His role would be complete when the packages were handed off.

As he glanced at his watch, he heard one of the large bay doors opening, and a breeze off the Mississippi River wafted past. He could smell the water. He could almost taste it. He watched as a black limousine entered the warehouse and slowly drove toward him before stopping a few feet away.

A hulking figure exited the limo wearing a chauffeur's uniform as the back window lowered just a few inches.

"Mr. Chauvin," the ginger-haired man said to the person behind the glass. "You're right on time."

The chauffeur went to the trunk, pulled out a crowbar, and then walked to the crates. He pried the lids off of the boxes, one by one. The wood groaned as the lids gave way.

Once the lids were off and the protective packing removed, Chauvin climbed out of the limo and personally examined the contents of the crates. A smile of triumph slid across his face.

"Load them up," Chauvin ordered.

The ginger-haired man and the chauffeur repacked the crates, and stowed them in the trunk of the limousine.

"We're good, right?" the ginger-haired man asked.

Chauvin nodded in agreement.

"Then where's my money?"

Chauvin leaned against the limo.

"Pay the man, Landry," he instructed the chauffeur.

"Do you have any other jobs for me, Mr. Chauvin? I really like working with you rich types. You think of everything," the ginger-haired man said, but his sentence came to an abrupt halt as a knife plunged deep into his abdomen. He looked down in shock as Landry twisted the knife.

The man wanted to scream. His mouth opened, but only his ragged breath escaped. He ripped his shirt open to expose the wound. He watched in horror as Landry pulled the knife free.

"Landry, don't toy with him. Just finish it," Chauvin said.

The ginger-haired man fell to the concrete floor. He grabbed the wound as blood poured from the cavity the knife left behind. He made only a whimper as he felt the air escape from his lungs.

Landry knelt with a syringe, grabbed the man's arm, and plunged the needle into a vein. Within a moment, the man relaxed. Euphoria passed through his body. He looked at Landry and Chauvin with glassy eyes.

"Now, isn't that better?" Chauvin asked. "You did a great job, and it was a pleasure doing business with you. I hope there're no hard feelings about my killing you. I can't have loose ends."

The man started to convulse and his eyelids fluttered.

"I know the heroin overdose alone would've been sufficient. But Landry here, has different tastes," he said as his nose wrinkled in disgust.

"Let's go, Landry. I have a meeting in thirty minutes," Chauvin said as he climbed back into the limousine.

The ginger-haired man felt his head forcefully turned until he could see Landry's face in front of his eyes. Landry wore a crooked smile as he reached out with a quick movement.

The ginger-haired man felt the sting of the knife as it passed across his throat. He watched as Landry returned to the limousine and drove away, and then he saw nothing.

Chapter 1
Barring Murder, it was Great


Jewel joined the crowd jockeying for position in line at Malpensa Airport, Milan. After traveling by train and bus from Venice, she was already exhausted and didn't look forward to spending the next thirteen hours in flight. She cursed her frugal nature for choosing the cheap flight from Milan rather than paying twice the cost and taking a direct flight from Venice.

Sounds echoed off the high ceiling causing every movement to be amplified. The man behind Jewel was talking into his phone. Although she didn't understand Italian, it was obvious he was arguing with someone. She tried to block out all the sounds around her and focus on getting through customs.

She stepped forward and presented her ticket and passport to the clerk. After studying the passport, the clerk looked up at Jewel, and then beckoned two men that were standing a few feet away. One of the men took Jewel's passport, and the other approached Jewel.

"Miss Townsend?" he asked.

"Yes," Jewel said in a small voice.

"I am Signore Bucci with the Regional Police. I need to ask you a few questions."

The man's English was excellent. He was in his mid-fifties and balding. He stood a foot taller than Jewel and hunched his shoulders slightly.

Jewel's chest constricted and her heart raced at the word "police". She looked from Signore Bucci to the other man. He was burly and resembled a toad with heavy eyebrows. He had a puffed-up look about him as if at any moment his tongue would shoot out and catch an unwitting insect. The toad was tapping Jewel's passport in the palm of his hand.

"I have a plane to catch," Jewel said to Bucci.

"We have made arrangements. It will be possible for you to take a later flight if it is necessary," he said, leading her out of the line and through the bustling crowd.

Jewel could feel her heart pounding and placed her hand on her chest to keep it from bursting through her ribs. She had every worst case scenario running through her mind.

*Crap! What did you do, Jewel? Was it jaywalking? Littering? No, Jewel, you didn't do those things. Seriously, is this because I tipped the cab driver? No, idiot that is not against the law . . . or is it?*

She looked into the sea of her fellow travelers trying to find a sympathetic face, but there were none to be had. The policemen guided her to a hallway and then through a series of doors and into a windowless room that contained a table and four chairs. Her body trembled in response to her fear. She selected a hard plastic chair and sat down. The toad closed the door and leaned against the wall beside it.

"What's going on?" she asked.

"Miss Townsend, don't be alarmed. We just need to ask you a few questions. Can I get you anything? Some water perhaps?" Bucci said, then turned to the toad and spoke in Italian, which prompted the man to leave the room immediately.

"Please tell me what this is all about," Jewel pleaded.

"Just a moment, I must wait for my colleague to return," he said while using a handkerchief to wipe his tanned brow. Under the intense fluorescent lighting, he looked stressed and his eyes had a permanent squint about them.

Jewel looked at the cheerless white walls, whose only adornment was a clock. In the strained silence the clock's ticking was menacing and added to her discomfort.

The toad returned with two bottled waters. Jewel took a bottle and set it on the table in front of her, unopened.

"Miss Townsend, do you know a man by the name of Brogan Walsh?"

"Yes," she answered feeling relieved and confused at the same time.

"When was the last time you saw Signore Walsh?" Bucci asked.

"Yesterday . . . last night."

"Do you remember the time?"

"Um . . . about seven, seven-thirty. Why?" Jewel asked.

"Miss Townsend, I regret to inform you that Mr. Walsh is dead."

"What? What do you mean, he's dead? How?"

"He died, last night, about ten o'clock," Bucci said, placing a newspaper down in front of Jewel. She picked it up to read then shook her head.

"I can't read Italian."

"*Mi scusi*. I'm sorry," Bucci said, taking the paper from Jewel. "There was a fire last night at the Hotel Alexa in Venice. The fire was started in Mr. Walsh's room. What was left of him was found in the bed, burned quite badly, I'm afraid."

"Oh," Jewel said. She felt herself shake as tears welled up and rolled down her cheeks. "How horrible. What happened?"

"It appears that he was murdered. His body was doused in petrol and lit. I'm very sorry to be the bearer of this news, Miss Townsend," Bucci repeated as he twisted the cap on his water bottle.

*Murdered? Murdered?*

Tears streamed down Jewel's cheeks. She wasn't sure why it affected her so mightily. She kept thinking about the wonderful time she had had the evening before. She thought of the last kiss and the hope of a future relationship. Hope was something she hadn't felt in a long time. Bucci offered her a tissue. She accepted it and dried her eyes. Once she had composed herself, he continued.

"Miss Townsend, do you have any information that could help us in this investigation? Your cooperation is vital," Bucci said, which to Jewel felt like a threat.

"Surely, you don't suspect me of . . . of . . . this," she clamored.

She discovered that she couldn't say the word *murder* while it was so fresh, as if it would be disrespectful to the dead.

"I only met him yesterday. I really didn't know him."

7

"No, you're not a suspect. Your alibi is confirmed," he said, opening a notepad and looking. "A Signore Marzio Porto, a resident in your sister's building, tells me that you returned to your sister's flat at a quarter past seven last night. Also the Hotel Alexa clerk states that he saw you and Mr. Walsh in the lobby of the hotel at about five in the evening, but Mr. Walsh returned to his room at a quarter to eight and had no visitors." Bucci laid the notepad on the table and looked at her expectantly.

"I'm not sure what I can do to help you. Like I said, I only met him yesterday," she responded. She stared down at the condensation ring that was forming on the table where the bottle of water stood.

"What can you tell me about him? What was your relationship?"

The word *relationship* poked at Jewel's heart. She had been elated since her day with Brogan. She thought of his throaty laugh, vivid green eyes, and large smile. She shook the image out of her mind.

"I met him yesterday at the café across the canal from my sister's apartment. We spent the day together sightseeing, we had dinner, and I told him goodbye," Jewel said, picking up the water and breaking the seal. She reached into her pocket and produced a medication bottle. As she opened it, Bucci pulled her hand to examine the contents.

"It's just medication. It's for anxiety," Jewel explained.

Bucci released her hand and nodded his head.

"We found your card in his wallet. Did you plan on seeing him again?"

"Yes, well . . . he told me he'd be in the U.S. on business soon. We were going to get together," she responded as she shook a pill out of the bottle and popped it into her mouth.

"When?" he asked. He held her gaze as he searched the breast pocket of his blazer and pulled out a box of cigarettes. There was a moment of silence. Jewel grew aware of the hammering of the clock on the wall, and felt that it matched her beating heart.

"Do you mind if I smoke?"

Jewel looked at the cigarette and shook her head.

"When were you to meet Mr. Walsh?" Bucci continued.

"We didn't arrange a time or date, he just said he would call me when he came to the States."

"Did Mr. Walsh give you an address where he could be reached?"

The flame shot out of the lighter and caught the tip of the cigarette.

"No. Didn't he have an address in his wallet?"

"Yes, but the address appears to be incorrect," Bucci replied quickly, with a gust of smoke. "Do you know where Mr. Walsh lived?"

"No. He was Irish, but he said he travels a lot," Jewel said between sips of water. She noticed goose bumps on her arms as she set the bottle down. She was unsure if they were caused by fear or cold, but she rubbed her arms for stimulation.

"Did anyone else accompany you on your sightseeing?" he asked, with cigarette laden breath.

"No," she said. "Wait . . . there was a man that approached Brogan at dinner when I was in the restroom. When I came back to the table they were talking in some foreign language. I could tell it wasn't Italian, so I asked him about it. He told me it was French. I wasn't introduced to the guy, and I didn't really get a good look at him," she said, her last words trailing off as she realized how useless the information was.

Bucci said something in Italian to the toad, who mumbled in response. Jewel glanced at the toad and then to the clock.

"Do you think you could describe this man?" Bucci asked.

"No. I don't think I would recognize him if I saw him again."

"What was your business in Venice?"

"No business. I was visiting my sister, she lives there," Jewel responded, as she put the tip of her thumb to her mouth and began biting her nail.

Bucci looked around for an ashtray, but saw none. He mumbled something in Italian, dropped the cigarette on the floor, and stepped his foot atop it.

"Yes, a couple of our officers are talking with your sister now."

*Oh, poor Jane. She'll be freaking out. But she always handles things better than I. She's better at love, at money, at life. She can handle a police interrogation.*

"Where in the U.S. were you supposed to meet Mr. Walsh?" he asked, as he sat on the corner of the table.

"I told you we didn't make any plans. He was going to call me when he was in the U.S. and we were going to get together," Jewel repeated.

"Do you know where he was going in the U.S.?"

"No," Jewel responded sharply.

*Keep it together, Jewel. Don't lose your temper.*

"Do you know what business Mr. Walsh was in?" Bucci asked, picking up his notebook.

"He told me he was in art acquisitions," she responded, as she began gnawing on the pinky nail.

"What was he doing in Venice?" he asked, writing in the notebook.

"I don't know. I didn't ask him," she said, her voice rising as her anxiety was reaching its boiling point.

"You spent the day with him, but the topic never came up?" he asked, continuing to write.

"No. I guess it never came up."

"Miss Townsend, did you go anywhere or speak to anyone, other than your sister, after you returned to her flat last night?" Jewel thought about the question for a moment and shook her head.

"No."

The toad shifted his weight and Jewel saw her passport in his hand. Her body was hurting from the tense state it had been in since meeting the two policemen. Jewel's gaze returned to Bucci and she found he was watching her closely.

"Do you have an address or telephone number where Mr. Walsh could be reached?" Bucci asked.

"No. I already told you. No. Look, I'm really tired and I just want to go home. Are we about done here?" Jewel asked. She was trying to calm herself by regulating her breathing.

*In through the nose and out through the mouth. I think I might vomit.*

"Yes, soon. Where did you and Mr. Walsh have dinner?"

"I don't know," Jewel stated.

*Breathe, Jewel, breathe.*

"You don't know where you ate dinner last night?"

"You make it sound so suspicious. We were walking and we wandered into this restaurant. It was open air . . . you know with tables outside. It wasn't on the Grand Canal, but it was near it," she said, rubbing her forehead as if to massage the memory from it. "Oh . . . the restaurant had two big blue pots or vases holding the doors open."

Bucci said something to the toad and both men snickered. Jewel bit her lip at the rudeness.

"Where are you headed?" Bucci asked.

"Home to Houston, Texas."

11

"Can you think of anything else about Mr. Walsh that may be helpful? Bucci asked.

Jewel shook her head then looked at the clock. She was wondering if she could make it in time for her plane when she remembered something.

"No. Wait . . . Brogan said that the guy, you know the French speaking guy, well Brogan said he was an associate of his . . . that's all I can think of," Jewel said with a shrug.

Bucci said something in Italian. The toad produced a sheet of paper and set it on the table.

"Is this information current?" Bucci asked, pushing the page in front of Jewel.

She read. It was a profile containing the information found on her driver's license and passport.

"Yes, it's correct."

"Thank you, Miss Townsend. If we have any further questions, we will be in touch," he said, taking the page from her. The toad dropped her passport on the table.

"Am I free to go?" she asked, standing.

"Yes. I apologize for the delay," Bucci responded.

Jewel grabbed her passport and hurried to the door. She felt relieved, but couldn't shake the knot that had taken up residence in her stomach. Feeling like it was too good to be true, she stopped with her hand on the doorknob and looked back at the men.

"I can go?" she repeated.

"Yes. I hope you enjoyed your stay in Italy."

She smiled involuntarily. In her moment of relief, she let her thoughts spill out.

"Barring murder, it was great."

Chapter 2
A Social Moron

*Jewel Journal:*

*It has been two days since my return home from Italy. I feel like I have changed somehow. I know this journal is supposed to be for me to record my emotions, but I have so many thoughts swimming around in my head. Dr. Wright told me that if I continued writing down my emotions and write what I expect my emotions will be then I will have clarity and understand myself better and blah, blah, blah. Dr. Wright, I'm glad I don't see you anymore. I paid you eighty dollars every week and I'm still angry at my ex-fiancé.*

*Jane has been worried about me. After her interrogation by the Italian police she called and spent thirty minutes telling me that I have to be careful. I'm the big sister, but it never feels like that. Well, she will be out of touch for the next three weeks. The company is sending her to the Amazon jungle. Ugh! I wish I could travel as much as she does. But I chose to be a librarian, and I love my books. I wonder if there's a traveling librarian job. Note to self . . . research traveling, international librarian jobs.*

*My current emotions: I'm sad that one of the most amazing parts of my trip was meeting Brogan Walsh and now he is dead. I haven't even told Mary about Brogan. I just feel like I can't talk about it. When she asked about my trip I simply said, "It was fun." I feel like Italy has changed the way I think. I'm just different. I feel like my normal routine of going to work at the library, and then sitting at home mocks me now.*

*Now for my emotions forecast: Cloudy with a chance of more sadness.*

Jewel sat in a lonely corner of the tiny library. She was sorting books on a cart and found herself flipping through pages, checking her watch, and wishing she were someplace else.

"Are you daydreaming again?" Mary asked.

"What? Oh, I guess so," Jewel replied, looking up from her seat on the floor. She smiled at her co-worker.

"You certainly are moving slowly today," Mary stated as she loomed over Jewel.

"Yeah . . . well, maybe my heart just isn't in this job anymore," Jewel said, dropping a book onto a stack.

"You can't say that. You've only been doing this for six or seven years. Wait until you've done it for eighteen years like I have," Mary said as she took a seat on the floor across from Jewel.

"Haven't you ever wanted something more? You know, like adventure. I'm not saying that being a librarian isn't amazing, because it is. I just. . . I just need to get back into the swing of it again," Jewel said forcing a smile as she continued to work.

Mary watched Jewel closely, waiting for their eyes to meet.

"Are you all right, Jewel?" Mary asked. Her warm brown eyes took on a look of concern.

"Yes, I'm fine," Jewel said, trying to reassure her friend.

Mary picked up a stack of books and ran her finger down the spines noting the colored tags, but continued stealing glances at Jewel.

"You've been a little off since you came back from your trip. I thought you would've returned all refreshed, but you look like you have the weight of the world on you."

"I'm fine. I'm just …"

Jewel was looking for the words to describe her feelings, but the search was coming up empty. She ended her statement with a shrug of her shoulders.

"You know what I think you need?" Mary said as she placed the stack of books on her lap.

"Don't say it, Mary," Jewel warned, with color rushing to her cheeks.

"You need a little romance in your life. You need to get back out there and start dating," Mary said, as she pulled her grey-streaked hair behind her ear.

"I told you not to say it. I can't do it, Mary," Jewel said, trying to keep her temper in check.

"You're still young. You're only thirty-two years old. It's silly for you to give up altogether. So you've had some bad luck in the past, that doesn't mean that it's the end of your love life," Mary continued.

"Why are we talking about my love life? Why are we always talking about my love life?" Jewel could feel the blood in her cheeks and hear her heart beating in her ears. "Why do you think that's the cure-all remedy for me? I'm not going to subscribe to some antiquated idea that I need a man in my life to be complete."

"I admit that you've had some bad luck in the love department, but you need to just get back out there," Mary continued, undaunted.

Jewel shook her head in anger.

"I was left standing at the altar, Mary. The guy vanished. He sent me a text message to break up with me. He took the living room furniture, and the bedroom furniture, and the patio furniture, and my mother's tea set while I was waiting for him at the church. Who does something like that? You call that bad luck?"

Mary opened her mouth to respond, but Jewel never gave her a chance.

"I'm done talking about this, Mary," she said, getting to her feet and storming away. She stopped and turned to face her friend. "I am a strong, independent woman," Jewel stated with clenched fists at her side, then turned and continued her trek to the restroom.

"You say that, but do you actually believe it? Life goes on," Mary continued as she watched Jewel disappear behind the door. "That was two years ago, Kid. It's time to let go," Mary said to no one.

Jewel washed her face and looked in the mirror.

"I'm a strong, independent woman," she said to her reflection. She started to repeat the mantra, but stopped and studied the image before her. Her cheeks were red and blotchy from her emotional outburst. Dark brown frizz framed her head like a fuzzy corona. Her hair fell to her shoulders as she released the pins holding it. She brushed her hair with her fingers, twisted it into a bun, and secured it. She studied her reflection and felt overwhelmed with sadness.

*I'm over being me. I'm over being scared. I'm tired of watching everyone else live their lives while I sit on the sidelines.*

Jewel understood that something needed to change. She needed a major change, not just a new hairstyle or a new shade of lipstick. She needed something drastic.

She walked out of the bathroom to find Mary sitting on the reference desk with keys in hand.

"I didn't mean to upset you, Jewel. I just want to see you happy. I haven't seen you happy in a long time. I miss that gal who would get bubbly about the latest novel she was reading, the gal who would go to the movies every Friday night, the gal that would get totally stoked about the rodeo every year. You haven't been to the rodeo in two years, have you?"

"I know. I've just lost my drive to do things."

"I know that guy was a piece of shit, but he had us all snowed. I thought he was great. I guess you really don't *know* someone until they let you know who they really are," Mary said.

"Are you seriously trying to steal and corrupt a Maya Angelou quote? 'When someone shows you who they are, believe them the first time'."

Mary tilted her head in thought. "Humph, I guess me and Maya Angelou both know a thing or two," she said with a wink. "I just want my best friend back, but I don't want to make you angry. I guess I just piss everybody off. It comes naturally," Mary said with a smile. "Hell, the day I stop making you angry we may need to start reviewing my choices in life."

"I'm not angry with you, Mary. Speaking of life choices, has your sister found a job and moved out, yet?" Jewel said as she walked around the desk and picked up her purse.

Mary made a growl deep in her throat.

"No. I suspect Theresa and the *banditos* will be with me for another two or three months. I'm not sure how long my husband will put up with it. Seven people living in a two-bedroom house with one and a half bathrooms is not smooth sailing. If it wasn't for the half-bathroom, I probably would have peed myself at least a dozen times since they moved in. Seriously, what kind of woman leaves her husband and moves out with four children without having a solid plan?"

"We can't all be as efficient as you, Mary," Jewel joked.

The two women stepped outside. They were greeted with Houston humidity. A tow truck was parked on the street and the driver was securing a vehicle in place on the back of his truck. The short hairy driver gave Jewel a wave and a smile as he got in his truck and pulled away. As he drove off, Jewel saw a blue sedan parked across the street. She had noticed the vehicle earlier in the day.

"Do you have plans this weekend?" Mary asked as she locked the library door.

"Oh, you know the usual action-packed weekend: read, watch television, write in my journal," Jewel replied as she continued watching the car. "Hey Mary, did you notice that car earlier? I think it's been sitting there all day."

"Where?" Mary asked, looking around.

"Don't look! You make it too obvious. I noticed the car when I was at lunch and I think there was a guy sitting in it. Is the car empty or is someone in it now?"

"You sound paranoid. They're probably just waiting for someone," Mary said with a shrug then walked to her own car. "I'll see you Monday, Kiddo. Enjoy your weekend off." Mary waved to Jewel over her shoulder.

"Sure," Jewel said as she watched the blue sedan while searching her purse for her car keys. She lost her grip and the bag fell, spilling its contents onto the sidewalk. She quickly gathered her things while covertly watching the car. She detected a small flash of light from the interior, followed by what looked like a tiny red eye staring at her. Jewel felt the hair on the back of her neck stand up as she detected the red glow of a cigarette inside the car. She grabbed the last of her possessions from the sidewalk and scurried to her vehicle.

∞   ∞   ∞

Since her return from Italy, mealtimes had become problematic. Jewel missed the Italian belief that mealtime was a social celebration and not just a necessary function for survival. In Italy people rarely ate dinner alone. They ate with friends, family, or even neighbors. Jewel had no friends or family nearby, with her sister living on the other side of the ocean.

*I guess eating in a restaurant full of strangers is better than dining alone at home.*

It was seven in the evening when Jewel was ready to leave her house. She wore the same brown skirt and white sleeveless blouse she had worn to work that day. But when she opened the door to leave, she found herself looking into vivid green eyes. She took a step back.

"Brogan?" she whispered.

She felt her cheeks warm from her blush as she realized the man before her was not Brogan Walsh. He looked uncannily like Brogan, but he lacked the charming smile.

"No," the man said. "You must be Jewel Townsend. My name is Michael Walsh. Brogan was my brother."

*Of course he's not Brogan, you idiot. Brogan is dead.*

"Oh," Jewel replied, taking in his features.

Michael's build and bone structure were the same as Brogan's, but a noticeable difference was the nose. Brogan's nose was slightly crooked, whereas Michael's nose was long and straight.

"You look a lot like him," Jewel said.

Michael Walsh tensed at the statement.

"I was wondering if I could speak with you about Brogan."

Jewel paused for several seconds. She wondered if he was the man in the blue sedan that had been parked at the library. She looked past Michael into the driveway, but instead of a blue sedan she saw a small white compact car.

Michael followed her gaze, and then looked back at her with a furrowed brow.

"Is something wrong?" he asked.

"No. Come in, please," she said, stepping aside for him to enter. Jewel normally wouldn't invite strangers into her home so freely, but this man was obviously Brogan's brother. The term "dead ringer" had popped into her head.

He wore khaki pants with a pressed white shirt and walked with a stiff reserve. His hair was shorter, slightly darker than Brogan's, and meticulously groomed.

"I'm sorry to bother you like this," he began.

Jewel could detect only a hint of his Irish accent.

"It's not a bother. Can I get you something to drink?" she asked.

"No, thank you," he said, as he continued to stand in a stiff military manner.

"Please, sit down," she said, indicating a chair.

He picked up the lace-covered pillow from the chair and sat on the edge of the seat. He eyed the yellow flowered wallpaper and collection of Hummel figurines that lined the bookshelves.

Jewel watched him as he took in his surroundings. She realized how painfully feminine the room was. From the ruffled curtains to the lace trimmed doilies, the room was undoubtedly decorated by a woman. It had never occurred to Jewel how deep she had fallen into the stereotypical role of an old spinster. She wondered if Michael was thinking the same thing.

*Great! I just need six or seven cats to stroll into the room.*

She grabbed the pillow from him.

"Thank you," he said, relinquishing the lacy poof. He waited for Jewel to take a seat then continued. "You knew my brother, right?" It sounded to Jewel more like an accusation than a question.

"Yes."

"What business did you have with him?" he asked in a sharp tone.

"I didn't have any business with him. We just spent some time together."

"Oh, I see," he said, smugly.

Jewel immediately suspected that he believed her relationship with Brogan had been sexual, and he did not approve. She squinted and studied him critically. She wasn't sure why, but she didn't correct his inaccurate assumption. With her new adventurous attitude she didn't mind having a stranger think she was a woman of loose morals.

*That's right. I'm bad.*

"The Italian police told me that Brogan spent his last day with you. Is that true?" he continued.

"Yes."

"Miss Townsend. Did my brother give you anything?"

*Give me anything? Crap! Did he have some venereal disease? We kissed. I could have oral herpes. I'm so glad I didn't risk having sex with him. Wait, Jewel, that's not what he's talking about. That can't be what he's talking about.*

"No," Jewel responded quickly. "Was he supposed to?"

Michael sighed, and rubbed his forehead. His tension and exhaustion were visible.

"I'm really sorry for your loss. I'm sure your family is very upset," Jewel said to comfort the man.

"I'm the only immediate family Brogan had. We have an aunt that we were both close to and a couple of distant cousins, but that's all," he responded.

"You must have been very close to him," Jewel stated, thinking of her own sister, Jane, and their weekly phone calls, that is when her sister wasn't jet-setting around the world.

"No. Actually, we've not spoken in six years," Michael said not making eye contact.

*Six years? There is definitely a story here.*

"Oh," Jewel said, "Would you excuse me for a moment?"

Michael nodded. Jewel hurried to her bedroom and peeked out the window. She noted the white compact car on the driveway, but no sign of the blue sedan. She wasn't sure why that blue sedan was still bothering her. She wondered if perhaps she was being paranoid like Mary had suggested. She took a moment to review the few words that had passed between her and Michael Walsh and wondered why the man was in her home. She set a determined march toward her guest. She entered the room like a woman on a mission.

"Tell me again. Why are you here, Mr. Walsh?" she said with resolve.

"Because I would like you to tell me about the last day you spent with my brother," Michael stated as he got to his feet.

"Okay," she said. "Are you sure I can't get you something to drink. Perhaps you would like some lemonade or something a bit stronger," she offered.

"Don't assume, ma'am, just because I'm Irish or just because my brother was a drinker that I too follow that path," Michael snapped while towering over Jewel.

*Holy crap! This guy is tense.*

"I . . . I wasn't assuming anything. I was offering you a drink," Jewel said, shocked by the man's sharp tone. She returned to her seat and eyed Michael with curiosity.

Michael paced while Jewel watched.

"Miss Townsend, do you know who or what 'The Dane' is?" he asked.

"No. Should I?"

Michael sighed and shook his head.

"Do you have any idea what my brother was doing in Venice or where he was heading?"

"No and yes."

Michael stopped pacing.

"Well?" he said, impatiently.

Jewel felt her hackles rising and clenched her teeth in response.

"I feel like I'm being bullied by you, Mr. Walsh, and I don't like it," Jewel stated. She was feeling empowered and a spark ignited in her gut that made her want to take control.

*You are a strong, independent woman.*

"Bullied?" he asked in surprise.

"Yes, bullied," she said, getting to her feet. "And I'm going to ask you to leave now," Jewel said as she started walking to the door.

"W . . . what?" he sputtered, his face taking on a look of disbelief.

"Leave," she said opening the door. "I find you rude and, frankly, meeting you is ruining the fond memory I have of your brother," she said as she gestured the way out.

Michael Walsh stood, perplexed, then exited as asked. Once outside he turned to protest, but Jewel shut the door on him.

Jewel knew it had been a long time since she'd stood up for herself like that, and it felt good.

*Hot damn! I am making changes. But, wait . . . you threw him out too quickly, idiot. You could have had a dinner companion, but just how much of a companion would he be?*

She went into the bathroom and applied fresh lipstick. Turning off the lights and stepping out the door, she made her second attempt to leave for dinner. She walked to her car to find Michael Walsh standing beside it.

"Miss Townsend, I'm afraid we got off on the wrong foot. Please accept my apology." Jewel considered him for a moment with skepticism.

*Can I trust this guy? Should I trust this guy?*

"If you promise to be polite, you may join me for dinner."

*Better than eating alone.*

"Sure. Absolutely. I'll drive," he said.

Jewel looked at his car, then to her own car. She had a moment of panic.

*Jewel, do you really want to get into a car with a stranger?*

Michael walked to his rental car, and opened the passenger door. As Jewel approached, she studied him through narrowed eyes; she stopped beside the door, and looked up into his face. He took her hand to help her into the vehicle. She paused, studying him.

*Should you really trust him? You should be screaming "stranger danger".*

"Is something wrong?" he asked, noting her pause.

Jewel look up at his face. He was very tall, but from Jewel's five foot stature most men were.

"Are you a creeper? Is this a human trafficking thing?"

Michael took on a look of surprise then a line formed between his brows.

"No," he said with a hint of irritation in his voice.

After a moment of hesitation, Jewel got in to the car.

The only verbal exchange that took place during the drive was Jewel's directions to Lo Ming's, a local Chinese restaurant. They entered, took their seats, and ordered drinks without a word to each other.

Lo Ming's was a quiet family restaurant. On this particular evening only two other tables were occupied. The drinks arrived. Michael's attention was captured by the red and gold painted dragons on the walls. Jewel watched him while removing the paper from her straw.

"I hope Chinese food is okay with you," she said, dropping the straw into her iced tea.

He grunted as he continued looking around the restaurant. He was interested in the gold Chinese characters that decorated the edge of the table. After passing his finger over the decorative symbols, he rubbed his thumb and forefinger together then wiped them on his napkin with a grimace.

"So, tell me about yourself, Michael," Jewel prompted.

"What would you like to know?" he responded stiffly, as he looked up to face his companion.

"Well, what do you do for a living?" she asked.

"I teach art history at the University of Florida."

"Oh . . . well, that's nice. Art must run in the family," she said, emptying a packet of sugar into her iced tea.

"Yes. Both my mother and her sister taught art history in Ireland. So, I guess you could say it's in my blood. And you? What do you do?"

"I'm a librarian," she replied.

"Really, that's unlike Brogan's usual taste," Michael said.

*What is that supposed to mean?*

"I'm sorry if I don't live up to the standard," she replied.

"The standard wasn't that high," he mumbled while looking into his drink.

"Umm . . . Are you trying to be rude?" Jewel asked.

Michael's head snapped up to look at her.

"No. That didn't come out the way I meant it. Sorry."

The waitress returned and took their order. They sat in silence. Jewel was thinking of how different her encounter with Brogan was compared to the one she was having now. She looked at Michael to find him staring at her. She reached up and touched her hair to make sure it wasn't poking up.

"How did you meet Brogan?"

Jewel smiled at the memory. She enjoyed the reminder of that encounter.

"He rescued me," she said.

Michael raised one dark eyebrow in interest.

"Please, go on," he urged.

"I was in a café, and this guy was pestering me. Brogan saw what was going on, so he pretended that he knew me and that we had a previous engagement. He just walked up, grabbed my hand, and dragged me away. It was really funny," she said, grinning at the memory. "That poor guy didn't know what was happening. He just stood there, perplexed." She started to laugh when she looked up to see Michael's face. He sat, expressionless, watching her. He reminded her of a *Moai* statue from Easter Island, the stone face with the long, straight nose.

"What?" she said. "Does it bother you for me to talk about Brogan?"

"No. That's what this is all about. I wanted to talk to you about his last day. I want to know if anything peculiar happened."

The food arrived. Jewel looked down at her Mu Shu chicken with zeal. Michael poked his noodles with his fork as if he were looking for hidden objects.

"The food is really quite good here," she assured him.

He raised a noodle-covered fork to his nose and sniffed it cautiously before tasting it.

They ate in silence. Jewel glanced up a few times to find Michael watching her with what she was sure was revulsion. Many questions swam around in her mind. She worked up her courage and asked the one question she was most curious about. Six years was a long time to not speak to your sibling. Jewel thought about her relationship with Jane. They were very different people. Jane was a civil engineer and had spent the past two years working in Italy. Her job kept her on the move. Jewel tallied that Jane had lived in three different countries since she became an engineer. Whereas Jewel had stayed in the same town she was born in working as a librarian. No matter how different the two women were, Jewel couldn't imagine going more than a month without speaking to her sister.

"Why hadn't you talked to your brother in six years?" she asked.

"An old disagreement. And it is one that I would rather not talk about," he replied without looking up.

"Oh . . . What was her name?"

Michael stopped eating, put down his fork, and took a long drink of his iced tea.

"I don't see how that is any of your business, Miss Townsend," he replied, pushing his plate to the side and lacing his fingers.

*Oh, I hit a sensitive nerve.*

"Sorry," she said sheepishly, embarrassed by her curiosity. Reaching for her glass, she misjudged its distance and knocked it over. The iced tea dribbled over the edge of the table onto Michael's pant leg.

"I'm so sorry," she said.

*Karma baby!*

She hid her smile as she sprang to her feet and grabbed the glass. A waitress appeared and sopped up the liquid on top of the table.

Using his napkin, Michael tried to repair the damage to his pants.

"I'm really sorry," Jewel repeated, but she felt a little humored by the accident.

"It's okay," he said, as Jewel returned to her seat.

"On my brother's last day, were you and he alone?" he asked, with irritation, returning to the purpose of the dinner.

"Yes."

"The whole day?" he prodded.

"Why are you so interested?" she asked, wondering about the man's goal of this meeting.

*There is more going on here than I know.*

"I have my reasons," he said, dropping the wet napkin on the table.

"You haven't spoken to your brother in six years. Why are you suddenly interested? Why do you want to relive his last day? What made

28

you come here to talk to me? I mean, you could have just called me on the phone," Jewel said.

"I have my reasons, and they're really not your business," he replied.

*Umm, what?*

"Oh, but they are. You have made them my business when you showed up on my doorstep. You're asking me for information, but you haven't said or done anything to inspire me to be cooperative," she replied, feeling confident.

They stared at each other, both in evaluation of the other.

After a long pause Jewel answered the initial question.

"Yes, we were alone. But when we were at dinner I went to the restroom and when I returned Brogan was talking to a man. They were speaking in French, and the man didn't look happy. Brogan told me the man was an associate of his. So, I guess he was some art guy," she said.

"Art guy?" he asked, sitting up straight. "Why do you say that?"

"Because I assumed he worked in art acquisitions with Brogan," she replied, stirring sugar into her fresh tea.

"Is that what my brother told you? He said he worked in art acquisitions?"

"Isn't that what he did?" Jewel asked before sipping her tea.

"My brother was a treasure hunter. Yes, he would mediate the acquisition of art, but it wasn't always on the level," Michael stated with venom.

Jewel paused. She realized that she didn't really know Brogan, but she was not going to let Michael believe he had the upper hand in this conversation.

"Well, then he didn't lie to me. He was in art acquisitions," Jewel said, eager to defend Brogan.

Michael snorted and shook his head. Jewel was angered. *This guy is an ass.*

"I certainly hope it was worth it," Jewel snapped.

Michael looked confused.

"What was worth what?" Michael asked.

"Whatever you and Brogan quarreled about six years ago. I hope it was worth the hatred you obviously harbor for your dead brother," Jewel stated, hoping the words stung. Jewel could see Michael's jaw tighten as his teeth clenched.

"Don't fool yourself, Miss Townsend. Don't fool yourself into believing that you knew my brother, because I doubt you did. I'm sure you were just one of his distractions; one of his *many* distractions," he snapped.

Strained silence followed. Jewel could not argue this point. Michael was correct. She didn't really know Brogan. Sorting through a list of dark pasts that Brogan could possess, she thought of their first meeting. It was odd how she trusted him so easily, but she attributed it the adventurous nature that Italy instilled in her. It was what she considered the "the mystery of Italy".

"Was there anything else remarkable about the man you saw speaking to my brother?" Michael asked, stirring her from her thoughts.

"No, and I'm not answering any more questions until you stop speaking to me in that tone," Jewel snapped. "Mr. Walsh, perhaps you're not accustomed to social graces, but people like to be spoken to in a kindly manner." She studied his face. Her words didn't appear to distress him. "I bet you're a real hit with the art history students," Jewel said, as she waved to the waitress, and ordered a cup of hot tea.

The pair sat in silence for several minutes.

"I'm sorry," Michael said, letting out his breath. "I'm not trying to be rude."

"Wow, just think what you could accomplish if you were trying."

Michael looked surprised for a moment, and then let out a small laugh. He was transformed by the laughter. When he smiled, he looked a lot like his brother.

*There's Brogan. Now I can see him in the man before me.*

"Who was older, you or Brogan?" Jewel asked.

"He was. By three years."

"What do you . . ." Jewel started.

"Wait, it's my question," Michael interrupted, holding up a hand to stop her.

"Okay," she said, pulling the tea cup closer as the waitress set it down.

"Where did Brogan say he intended to go when he left Venice?"

"Germany," she answered, and realized that she hadn't mentioned that to the police in Italy.

The waitress cleared the plates and placed the bill upon the table. Jewel reached for it, but Michael snatched it up.

"Please, allow me. It's the least I can do," he said, as he pulled a wallet from his pants pocket.

His wallet had an ornate Celtic knot embossed upon it. Jewel studied the crossing pattern.

"Why was Brogan's accent so much stronger than yours?"

Michael shifted uncomfortably with the question.

"I left Ireland several years ago."

"Yeah, but Brogan traveled all over the place. I would think that your accents wouldn't differ that much. I can barely detect yours."

"Good," he replied.

"Good? Why is that good? I think it's lovely."

"I think the preconceived stereotypes people have about Irishmen don't reflect well upon me. Brogan, on the other hand, played the role of an Irishman to the hilt," he said, placing cash atop the bill and pushing it to the edge of the table.

"You're not proud to be Irish?"

"I'm exceedingly proud to be Irish. I've just assimilated well into American culture. Are we ready to go?" he said, rising from his chair.

"No, not yet," she said, lifting her half empty teacup. He settled back onto the chair and looked at the red lantern that hung above the table.

"Are you married?" She spoke into her cup as she peered over the rim.

"No," he responded, still looking at the lantern.

"Have you . . ." she continued.

Michael held up his hand to interrupt the question. He fixed her with his green eyes.

"My question . . . did Brogan say where he had been before he went to Venice?"

"No."

Jewel felt like there were two different conversations taking place at the table. She was determined to have a pleasant interaction, which was proving difficult as the man appeared to be a social moron. She set her cup down on the table, drained of all its liquid.

"Are we ready now?" he asked with a hint of condescension in his voice.

"Yes."

She collected her purse and led the way to the door.

## Chapter 3
### You've Got Some 'Splainin to Do

Rain greeted the pair as they stepped outside. They dashed to the car, dodging puddles as though they were land mines. Michael unlocked and opened the door for Jewel. She hopped in, leaned over, and unlocked his door. He hurried into the car and wiped the rain off his face.

"Where did that shower spring up from? I didn't see anything like that in the weather forecast," he said.

Jewel noticed his Irish brogue was much stronger in this unguarded moment. She chuckled to herself. His smile faded and the atmosphere became tense once again.

"I should get you home," he stated in a low voice.

Jewel didn't direct him back to the house, and was impressed that he remembered the path. They dashed to the cover of the awning. She was shaking the rain from her hands when Michael grabbed her arm. He pointed to the door. It stood slightly ajar. She looked up and gaped.

"I didn't leave that op . . ." she started.

"Stay here." He stepped up to the door and quietly entered the house.

Jewel reached into her purse and pulled out her phone to call the police. She reviewed the actions she had taken when she left the house earlier, and was certain that she hadn't left the door open. As she stood with the phone in her hand ready to dial, she noticed the wet footprints on the porch. There was a terrible leak where the awning met the house and the top step to the door always had a puddle of water. Jewel noticed that there were two sets of footprints. Two sets of footprints entering the house, but none exiting. Panic slithered through her limbs as she realized that Michael was going to come face-to-face with whoever was inside.

"Michael!" she yelled. At that moment a loud crash erupted from the dark interior. Jewel charged over the threshold. Running through the living room, she tripped and stumbled on something. She tried to keep going but her foot caught and she fell over. While on her hands and knees someone slammed into her side, knocking her over onto her back. She heard the person grunt, fall, get to his feet, and run for the exit. In the minuscule light from the street lamps Jewel watched him disappear out the open door. "Michael?" she called out to the fleeing figure.

She got to her feet only to be knocked over by another charging figure. This time she yelped in pain as she fell over what felt like the coffee table. The figure dashed out the door, but soon returned and stood panting.

"Michael?"

He fumbled along the wall, and with a click the room filled with light. He blinked to adjust before locating Jewel on the floor. He took in her absurd position and shook his head. Jewel's legs lay atop the coffee table while the rest of her body was on the floor. Her skirt was pooled around her waist exposing her pink panties. She shielded her eyes from the overhead light.

"You certainly lack stealth," he said, reaching a hand to help pull her to her feet.

She rubbed her ribs where she had been hit and sucked in air when she touched a tender spot.

"Are you hurt?" he asked.

"Just bruised, I think," she said as her hands moved to her posterior. "That was really stupid. Why would you go barging in here? What kind of macho crap is that?" She looked up at him. "You have some . . . blood, right there," she said, indicating his cheek.

He reached up, touched his temple, and discovered a trace amount of blood.

"Are you all right?" she asked. "And why would you put yourself at risk like that? Do you have some kind of death wish?"

Michael shook his head faintly.

Jewel looked around the room for the first time and her lower lip quivered at the sight. The room was in chaos with overturned furniture and pillows ripped apart. Her collection of Hummel figurines lay in pieces on the floor.

She turned and ran down the hallway. The other two rooms looked much like the first. Her bedroom, however, appeared untouched with the exception of a broken bedside lamp and an upended wastebasket. She turned back to the hallway in a panic. Michael was standing near the doorway. She blinked several times as tears spilled down her cheeks.

"What happened?" she whispered.

"It appears someone was searching for something."

*He seems pretty casual about this.*

She watched Michael through tear-filled eyes.

"When I came in this room there was someone going through your nightstand drawer. I was sneaking up on him, when *someone* yelled my name. I'm not exactly sure what happened after that. I grabbed the person. We started struggling, and then I believe he hit my head with something," he said as he reached up to touch his temple again.

Jewel had a fleeting moment of guilt, but she was overcome again with suspicion.

"What was he looking for?" she demanded.

"How would I know?"

She tried to piece the events together. She rubbed her chin as she watched him lean down and pick up the lamp. The wooden base was still attached to the shattered remains of its ceramic body. Several of the pieces were held together by the cord that ran through the center of the lamp. It reminded Jewel of a human spine framed by a mangled body. Jewel felt exposed and naked. Someone had been through her house, her private sanctum. Her sanctuary had been violated. She continued to watch Michael. He picked up the wastebasket and was collecting the ceramic shards from the lamp.

*Whoever did this must have been watching the house or knew I would be out.*

"Was it your job to get me out of the house?" she asked in an unsteady voice.

"I'm not sure what you're talking about," he stated without looking up.

"What was he looking for, Mr. Walsh?" she demanded. "See . . . I find it terribly suspicious that my house gets ransacked the same day you arrive on my doorstep. You say it's to learn about Brogan's last day alive, but I don't understand why you would be so interested in the demise of a brother you so obviously hated." Jewel's voice had risen and her body was stiff with anger.

Michael stood straight at the last word and stared down at Jewel. He didn't betray any emotion. His eyes were distant and glassy.

"I didn't have anything to do with this," he insisted, waving his hand around the room.

"What was he looking for, Mr. Walsh?" Jewel asked, staring fixedly into his green eyes.

"I don't know what he was looking for. I can't even tell you what *I'm* looking for," he said.

Jewel's brow furrowed at his statement.

"I came here because of something my brother sent me. I thought he may have told you about it. So, maybe I haven't been completely up-front with you, but I had nothing to do with this," he said, setting the wastebasket on the floor.

Jewel stared into his green eyes seeking the truth. She noticed the trickle of blood on his temple, but still wasn't convinced she should believe him. Her eyes moved to his shoulder. Large crimson shapes had bloomed on his white shirt.

"Is your shoulder hurt?" she asked.

He looked at his shoulder and touched it.

"No," he replied. He touched his temple once more and moved his hand behind his ear. "But my head is," he said as he moved his hand into his field of vision and the color drained from his face. He swayed. "I think I'd better sit down."

Jewel rushed to his side and tried to steady his huge form. Helping to support his weight, she walked with him to the bathroom. The contents of the bathroom cabinet were strewn upon the floor. She kicked them aside and led Michael to sit on the toilet.

"I'm all right," he reassured her. Jewel grabbed a towel and pressed it against his head. After a few moments of pressure on the wound, she inspected the towel. A crimson blotch the size of a softball covered a section of the dainty towel. She tilted his head toward her chest and inspected the cut.

"It's not too bad. It's actually rather small," she said. "Hold this firmly on it for a few more minutes to stop the bleeding."

She leaned against the wall and looked at her personal effects on the floor. She spotted some feminine products that normally would have embarrassed her, but in her current disorientation, she ignored them.

"Do you need an ambulance?"

"No, I think I'm fine," He lifted the towel and looked at it. "See, it stopped. How about you? Are you okay?"

"I'll be fine. I'm going to go call the police," she said and turned to leave the bathroom. Michael began to stand. Jewel spun back around.

"No. You stay here," she demanded, pointing to the toilet. "After I deal with the police, you have some explaining to do," she added while exiting.

*I'm getting good at taking control of my life. Now that it's in pieces, I hope I'm as good at putting it back together.*

∞    ∞    ∞

Jewel stood on the front steps, rigid with anger, as she watched the police car drive away. Her jaw muscles hurt from clenching her teeth. When the police officers found that nothing had been stolen, they called in to check Jewel's criminal background. The officers assured her that it was "just procedure." She watched the police car taillights disappear at the end of the street before she entered the house.

Michael had righted the couch and coffee table. He sat with the bloody towel in his lap. The couch cushions had been cut open and now were bleeding white fuzz. The couch and the blood-speckled man were well-matched. Jewel took a deep breath and shook her head.

"I need a drink."

She went into the kitchen and returned with two glasses and a bottle of whiskey tucked under her arm.

She sat beside Michael and examined the bottle. She knew it well. It was one of the many gifts from her wedding—the wedding that never happened. She had tried to return the presents in the weeks following that disastrous day. Many of the gifts came right back to her citing reasons for their return: lost receipt, don't need it; you should give it a good home. Jewel took them for what they were—pity gifts. This bottle was one of those many pity gifts. It had sat in the cabinet above the refrigerator for the past two years collecting dust. She smeared the dust across the label with her thumb then began picking at the seal. She opened it, poured two glasses, and slid one into Michael's hand. He sat dazed and staring off into space. She set the bottle on the table in front of them.

"Lucy, you've got some 'splainin to do," Jewel said with a forced accent.

After a pause, Michael's brow furrowed and he looked at Jewel strangely.

"You know Ricky Ricardo? The *I Love Lucy* show? Jeez, how long have you been in this country?"

Michael shook his head.

"Yes, I know who Ricky Ricardo is. I was just thinking. Your intruder didn't find anything."

Jewel blinked at him over the rim of her glass.

"And Brogan didn't give you anything," Michael said.

"Nope. Just a wonderful time. I get the idea that you, however, know more than you're saying." She pulled her knees up to sit on her legs, and sipped her whiskey.

"You're right," he said, setting his glass on the table, standing, and walking out the front door.

*Well, crap.*

Jewel sat staring at the closed door with wide eyes.

*Yep, I just have that effect on men.*

She put her whiskey glass on the table and started to rise when the door opened again, and Michael returned.

"This came three days ago," he said, handing a postcard to Jewel. One side of the postcard displayed a scene of the Grand Canal in Venice, Italy. She turned the card over. In a short slanted print Jewel read: *"I have found The Dane. I need your help."* It was signed simply "B."

"What does it mean?" she asked, rereading the card. She noticed something written in the corner. "Wait, this says, '19/03'."

Jewel was vaguely familiar with the European format for date writing; writing the day before the month.

"This was written back in March, right?" Jewel said, pointing to the numbers scrawled in the corner.

"Yes, I noticed that too," Michael agreed, leaning over Jewel's shoulder to look at the date.

"But you just received it three days ago?"

"Yes. And the next day I had word that he was dead," Michael replied, his voice growing quiet on the last word. "Apparently it took them some time to find his next of kin."

Jewel took a sip of her whiskey and leaned back on the oozing cushions.

"Are you sure it's from Brogan?" she asked.

"He always signs his missives to me with a 'B'," Michael said, rubbing his fingers through the hair on the undamaged side of his head.

"Wait, you told me that the two of you haven't spoken in six years."

"Well, we . . . haven't spoken, but he has written to me now and then. He usually dropped me a word every few months," he said, taking the postcard and staring at the picture.

"Well, that was nice of him. Did you ever respond?" Jewel asked, taking another sip.

He shook his head while he continued to look at the postcard.

"So, he wrote it back in mid-March, but you received it three days ago. That sounds typical for the U.S. postal service."

"But look, the postal date stamp is only a week old," he said, tapping the card with his finger.

Jewel shrugged. "So, what is 'The Dane'?" she asked, repositioning herself on the couch.

"I don't know. I came here, hoping you would know." He sat down and looked at her with anticipation.

"You came all the way here from Florida because of this?" she said, snatching the postcard.

"Well, yes. He asked for help," Michael said, rubbing his hands on the tops of his thighs.

She watched Michael for a moment, and then looked at the postcard.

"If he were still alive would you help him?" She knew her question was cruel, but she wanted to better understand the relationship Michael had with Brogan.

Michael tensed. Jewel noticed his hands whiten as he gripped his legs tightly.

"I don't know," he said quietly.

Jewel felt guilty for being so direct. She could see that Michael had regrets.

"So, do you think this Dane thing had something to do with his death?"

"Yes, I do."

"Do you think this Dane thing has something to do with my house being destroyed?" she asked, feeling anger rising in the pit of her stomach.

"Yes, of that, I'm fairly certain," he replied. "Unless you're involved in other things that would provoke a search of your home," he said, lifting one dark eyebrow.

"You sound like the police officers that just left. No, I'm not involved in anything . . . including this. Brogan didn't give me anything and I want no part of your little mystery," she said, handing the postcard to Michael.

"I'm afraid someone believes you're already involved," he said, waving his hand indicating the chaos around the room.

"This is your fault. If you hadn't come here then none of this would have happened."

"My fault? Miss Townsend, you were the last person to speak to my brother. If anyone were following my brother's trail it would lead them right to you. Don't be so naive as to believe that I have brought undeserved attention to you."

Jewel grabbed the bottle from the table and poured herself another drink. She sipped the brown liquid silently staring at the pile of shattered figurines in front of the bookcase. Michael was correct, but Jewel was looking for someone to blame and Michael was conveniently present.

"So, what are my options?" she asked, her eyes still fixed on the rubble.

"I'm not sure," Michael responded, turning the postcard over in his hand. "Whoever was here tonight, will probably be back."

"What? Why?"

"They didn't find anything. If they're determined enough to break into your home to search it . . . I just don't think they'll give up easily," he said.

She looked around the room. Her home had been invaded. She became fearful and angered by his words.

"Do you have a friend or relative you can stay with?" Michael asked, getting to his feet. "I don't think you should stay here."

*Yeah right. There's Jane in the Amazon Jungle, or Mary with all her banditos and the one bathroom.*

"No. Wait! You aren't going to leave me. How do I get these people off my back?" she said, setting down her glass and sitting up.

*I don't want to be alone. I'm scared. Someone defiled my home and now I won't feel safe here. I'm not sure I'll feel safe anywhere.*

"Once I figure out what they want, they'll probably be more interested in me, and leave you alone," he said, stuffing the postcard into his pocket.

Jewel sprang to her feet.

"You can't just leave me like this. What if they do come back?"

"That's why I think you should go stay with a relative," he said, turning to the door.

"Whoa, whoa, hang on," Jewel said, grabbing his hand. "The Walsh family got me involved in this mess. I'm coming with you."

"With me?" he spat, shaking his hand free of her grip. "I don't think so."

"I don't have anywhere else to go. I can't sit around here hoping you'll figure this thing out . . . pardon my candor, but I don't have that much faith in you."

Michael looked down at Jewel in evaluation.

"Perhaps you should come with me," he said.

Jewel was set for a fight and was surprised when he relented so easily. She stared into his deep green eyes processing his reply.

"Really?" she asked.

"Yes. I would worry about your safety if I left you here alone. Besides, you may think of some significant detail about your time with Brogan."

"Umm . . ." Jewel thought for a moment and wondered if she felt safe with Michael. She looked around the room and knew she didn't feel safe in her house and she didn't feel safe alone.

"You should pack lightly, and don't forget your passport," he said, as he sat back down on the couch.

Jewel studied him. She debated his motives. She wondered what Michael had to gain by her accompanying him. Then she wondered if this was a bluff.

"Okay, I'll go pack," she said, watching his response critically.

"Would you like me to help you pick up before we go?" he asked.

She tore her eyes away from him and followed his gaze around the room.

"No. If they come back and do more damage, I'll have to re-clean." She started down the hall, but stopped midway.

"Mr. Walsh, where are we going?"

"Italy."

Chapter 4
I Swear, Woman, You Need a Babysitter

*Jewel Journal:*

*I have had some unexpected events. I am now travelling with a man who is practically a stranger to me. He is arrogant, rude, and has the charisma of a tick. As soon as we got on the plane, he closed his eyes and went to sleep. I already had a sample of this man's personality during dinner. Conversations with Michael Walsh are about as enjoyable as a tax audit. When I first saw him, I thought he reminded me of Brogan. Boy was I wrong. He is so different from Brogan that it's hard to believe the two men are even related.*

*So, I am now on a plane headed back to Italy. Actually we are headed to Washington D.C. We have an eleven hour layover then on to Venice. It is weird to be going back to Venice so soon. I really hadn't thought this through. I just packed a bag and followed along with this plan. I may have been hasty in my decision.*

*My current emotions: scared and vulnerable.*

*Now for my emotions forecast: What in the hell am I doing?*

Jewel wrote the last line in her journal, shut the notebook, and shoved it into her purse just as the fasten seatbelts sign came on and the pilot made the announcement to prepare for landing in Washington, D.C.

Jewel continued thinking about the last thing she wrote. She reached into her purse, pulled out a small medication bottle, and shook a tiny white pill into her hand. She turned and looked at the man beside her with resentment and then popped the pill into her mouth.

As the plane bounced on the tarmac, Jewel continued to reflect on the actions that led her to board a plane to return to Italy. She wasn't the sort of person to run headlong into a situation. Jewel's brain was trying to process her emotions. She felt like the feeling of vulnerability had pushed her into this decision. And as for Michael . . .

*He didn't give me any reassurance. He's the reason I'm on this plane and yet there he sits sleeping like a baby while I'm stressing out.*

The plane landed at Dulles Airport and the other passengers swarmed the aisle to retrieve their bags from the overhead bins. Michael opened his eyes.

"I can't believe you slept through the whole flight," Jewel sneered.

"Well, it's all about clearing your mind and . . ."

"Yeah, yeah, yeah," Jewel cut him off.

Their seats were near the rear of the plane. The passengers began exiting. Most had disembarked before Michael moved into the aisle and Jewel followed behind him.

As soon as she stepped off the plane she was lost in her thoughts and feeling uneasy. The crowds were contributing to her feeling of unrest. She had hoped the fresh air outside the plane would comfort her, but that was not the case.

"Do you have any idea how large this airport is?" Jewel asked the tall figure in front of her.

"Fairly large, why?" he responded over his shoulder.

"I was just wondering if we can walk to a hotel or if we need to take a cab," she said.

Michael froze in his tracks causing Jewel to run into him. He turned to face her.

"Why do you need a hotel?" he asked.

Jewel stared blankly at him for a moment. The buzz of the crowd around her made her thoughts foggy.

"I'm not sitting around the airport for the next eleven hours."

"Considering that you have to arrive three hours early for international flights, it's more like eight hours. Do we really need to spend money on a hotel for such a short stay?" Michael asked.

The crowds passed around them like water rushing around boulders. Jewel kept feeling bumps as people brushed past her, which only added to her anxiety. She studied Michael's face as she chewed on her lip. A passerby bumped her hard enough to knock the duffle bag off her shoulder. She pulled the bag back upon its perch as her gaze dropped to the floor.

"I'm not really sure what I'm doing," she said, her voice barely audible.

"I didn't think we needed to spend the funds. I was thinking that we could get some dinner and just wait it out in the airport," Michael continued, not detecting the transformation taking place in front of him.

Kristel Beck

Jewel was feeling short of breath. Her heart was racing. She rubbed her eyes frantically with both hands and made a low growling sound.

"I have no idea what I'm doing," she roared as she walked past Michael. She began mumbling unintelligibly as her pace quickened. She was familiar with this feeling, as she had dealt with it for months after she was jilted. She recognized the signs. She was heading for a full-blown panic attack.

"Miss Townsend, are you all right?" Michael asked, trailing behind Jewel.

"Yes, I mean no. I mean . . . I can't believe I'm running across the world because some guy broke into my house. I think I've made a huge mistake—a *huge* mistake," she said, rubbing her face with both her hands.

*Keep it together, Jewel. Just breathe.*

Michael continued to follow, but offered no words of comfort.

"I think that in my desire to make a change in my life, I have made a foolish decision," she said, making a sharp turn and walking over to a bench. She sat down and leaned over, resting her head upon her knees. Tears filled her eyes. There was no sobbing, but tears pooled up and were immediately soaked into her skirt.

Michael followed her. He stood in his stiff manner looking down at the small trembling woman.

"Have I done something to upset you?" Michael asked.

"Ugh," Jewel exclaimed, looking up at Michael with her eyes already swelling from the burning tears.

He was a bit shocked at the change in her visage, and backed a step away from Jewel. She continued sitting on the bench with her body folded in half. Her hands had moved up to cover her ears. Michael watched her rapid breathing. He dared not touch her.

50

*I wish I was alone. I wish the people would go away.*

"Miss Townsend? Are you unwell?" Michael asked.

*I wish he would go away. I need to change my fabric softener. This skirt should smell better.*

Jewel's head popped up, she got to her feet, and grabbed her duffle bag.

"I'm going to get a hotel room, take a hot shower, and then catch the next plane home," she said, as she turned and headed for the exit.

"Miss Townsend, perhaps I've missed something. Why have you become so emotional?" Michael asked, trailing behind Jewel once again.

Jewel groaned in response and quickened her pace. She cut a path through the crowd and made her way to the exit. She followed the signs to a line of taxi cabs. She selected an available cab. The driver was standing beside the vehicle and opened the door as the pair approached. Jewel tossed her duffle bag onto the back seat. She turned to find Michael standing on the curb behind her.

"Look, Mr. Walsh, I think I'll go it alone from here," she said, looking up at the man.

He stared blankly at Jewel for a moment before replying.

"Well, I . . . would like to see you to your hotel," he said.

Jewel considered his request for a moment. She was feeling extraordinarily foolish, and didn't like it. She especially didn't like to appear foolish in front of her smug companion, but that's all she had shown Michael: weakness and fear. She racked her brain trying to find a good reason to say no.

"Please," Michael added.

Jewel sighed heavily, climbed into the cab, and slid across the back seat to make room for him.

The cab smelled like tuna salad and cigarette smoke.

"What's your destination?" the cabby asked.

"The cheapest and nearest hotel," Jewel said.

"Are you here for Virginia or D.C.?" the cabby asked.

"Huh? We just need a room to wait for another flight," Jewel responded.

"Gotcha," he said, as he urged the car away from the curb and followed the stream of vehicles leaving the airport. Jewel was deep in thought while staring out the window. She wanted some peace and quiet and an opportunity to clear her mind. A few hours earlier at her house it seemed perfectly logical to go on a crazy adventure with this stranger, but now she felt foolish. She looked over at her companion.

*He has the warmth and personality of a frozen fish stick.*

The cab approached the front door of a hotel.

"I'll check for a vacancy," Jewel said, as she opened her door.

"I'll check," Michael said, as he opened his door and hurried away.

Jewel was going to chase after him, but looked down at the two duffle bags on the back seat. She didn't want to lug them both with her, but didn't trust the cabby enough to leave them there. After a moment, Michael poked his head out of the door.

"They have a vacancy. You take care of the cab fare and I'll take care of the room," he called before disappearing back into the lobby.

"Wait, I . . ." Jewel yelled, but her words didn't reach the retreating figure. "Crap," she said under her breath. She wanted to regain control, and Michael wasn't making things easy. She paid the taxi driver and pulled her duffle onto her shoulder. She tried to pull Michael's bag onto her shoulder as well, but discovered she couldn't handle both bags. She entered the lobby dragging Michael's bag behind her like a dead dog on a leash.

The lobby was lovely with a high glass sloping ceiling and a baby grand piano. The atmosphere was soothing. Jewel realized that she should have clarified her definition of a cheap hotel to the cab driver. This was not her idea of cheap.

Michael was standing in front of a large counter. He turned and glanced at Jewel. She thought she detected a small flash of a smile when he looked at her. He approached and took his bag.

"Our room is on the second floor," he said.

"*Our* room?"

"Well, I thought I would stay for a little while and relax; if that's okay with you. I don't want to impose. I just thought I could . . ."

"Well, you thought wrong," Jewel spat. "I just want to be alone."

Michael furrowed his brow and his lips tightened.

"Okay, here is your key card," he said, placing the small envelope with the key card in Jewel's hand. "The room number is on the envelope," he added. "I would like to say it has been a pleasure, Miss Townsend, but I think we both know better."

Michael took a step or two away and shifted the weight of his duffle. He glanced at her once more then exited.

Jewel watched him standing outside. She had a moment of guilt for how she treated him and then the moment was gone.

The elevator was extremely slow. Jewel watched the glow of the number two button and was tempted to tap it again. She found her room. She noticed it had two double beds.

*At least he had honorable intentions.*

She locked the door, dropped her duffle bag on the floor, and lay across the bed. Slowly, she felt like control of her life was inching back into place.

∞    ∞    ∞

*Jewel Journal:*

*I'm on my own now. That guy was really stressing me out. I don't know why he has to be so difficult. This crazy adventure has ended and I don't have to see Michael Walsh ever again.*

*My current emotions: I feel stressed, but I'm beginning to calm down. I used redirection to avoid a panic attack. I keep trying to remind myself that I am a strong independent woman; sometimes I get tired of trying to convince myself.*

*My emotions forecast: I believe I'll be more positive once I'm back home.*

A hot shower worked like a healing tonic for Jewel. She pulled on a cotton dress and studied her appearance. She decided to wait until after dinner to change her plane reservations. As she exited her hotel room and pulled the door shut, a flash of movement caught her eye. She looked down the hall, but saw no one. She took the elevator down to the first floor and wondered if the stairs would have been faster.

Jewel entered the hotel restaurant and was seated at a table for two. She cringed as the hostess removed the second place setting. The china and silver sounded an alarm announcing that someone was eating alone.

It was early for dinner, but two other tables were occupied. A family of four sat near the windows. The mother was correcting her two sons, while the father read a newspaper. A couple was seated at a table near Jewel. She watched them for a moment. They sat side-by-side and held hands. The man was speaking softly into the woman's ear, as the woman laughed lightly. Jewel had a sick feeling in her stomach.

*Get a room.*

She thought about how she had behaved with Michael and felt a twinge of guilt. For a moment she wished she hadn't sent him away until after dinner so she could have a dinner companion, but then felt more guilt at the thought of using him in that fashion.

"Don't you hate dining alone?" a voiced asked.

Jewel turned around to see a man sitting directly behind her. The man was not there when she took her seat, and had arrived silently. He was in his mid-forties. His dark eyes were deep-set and fringed with dark lashes. His brown skin contrasted with his white button-up shirt. Jewel was considering his ethnicity when he surprised her with a question.

"May I join you for dinner? So neither of us has to eat alone." His smile displayed straight white teeth.

*India . . . his features look Indian.*

She was jarred by the request, but pleased by the prospect.

"Yes, that would be very nice," Jewel said with a wave of her hand to indicate the chair opposite her.

The man joined Jewel at her table. She smiled nervously.

"Jewel Townsend," she said, extending her hand in greeting.

"Suran, Jason Suran. I am pleased to meet you Miss Townsend," he said, accepting her hand. He didn't shake the hand, but bowed over it briefly.

Jewel noted a hint of a British accent.

"What brings you here Miss Townsend; business or pleasure?"

Jewel's smile faltered, and she shifted in her seat.

"I'm not sure . . . let's just call it a flight of fancy."

"I see," he said, settling down in the chair. "Do you travel much?"

"No. I just came back from Italy, though."

"Was that trip business or pleasure?" he asked with a smile.

"Pleasure," she responded as she took a sip of water.

Suran hailed the waitress and also ordered a glass of water.

Jewel studied him briefly. He had a medium-sized frame and warm eyes.

"What did you do in Italy?" he asked, as the waitress set a glass of water in front of him.

"I spent a week in Venice. It was wonderful," she said as she watched the doting couple stand up and leave the restaurant. "How about you, Mr. Suran, do you travel much?"

"Yes. I enjoy traveling which is a good thing, because my job requires it," he said as he gingerly wrapped his beverage napkin around his sweating water glass. "Did you meet any nice people in Venice?"

Jewel paused and looked at his smiling face. The question wasn't terribly odd, but something about it didn't feel right.

"What brings you here, Mr. Suran?" Jewel asked, redirecting the conversation.

"Business," he responded.

"What kind of business are you in?" Jewel asked watching him critically.

"I am in art acquisitions," he said, then took a slow sip of his water while watching Jewel.

A lump formed in Jewel's throat. She looked around the restaurant. The family near the window was laughing and the waitress was nowhere to be seen. Jewel smiled weakly.

*Red alert! Red alert!*

"Would you excuse me for a moment, Mr. Suran?" she said taking pains to keep her voice steady and her face devoid of any emotion.

"Yes, of course," he said rising from his seat.

Jewel stood, walked out of the restaurant, and into the lobby.

*This cannot be a coincidence.*

She went to the elevator and pressed the button. She held her breath until the doors closed and the elevator began to move. She began tapping the number two button several times hoping it would make the elevator move faster, but knowing it was futile.

*Damn it. Why didn't you take the stairs, Jewel? You idiot. I just want to be in my room with the door locked.*

"Come on," she said, reaching out and pounding the button multiple times.

She stepped out into the second-floor hallway. She looked both ways, and then quickly walked in the direction of her room. She turned left down the next hallway and was almost to her room when a hand covered her mouth and yanked her back. She let out a yelp of panic, but the sound was muffled by the attacker's hand. She felt the burn of a pointy object in her ribs. Her breath became rapid and she let out a whimper as she realized her nose and mouth were both covered and she couldn't breathe. She reached up and tried to pull the hand from her mouth, but the pressure on the knife increased.

*Reserve your oxygen Jewel. Don't panic. Don't panic. Oh, hell yes, I'm panicking.*

The attacker sounded like he was trying to catch his breath.

*Why is he breathing so heavily? Is he getting turned on by this? Oh crap, I'm being attacked by a pervert.*

"Miss Townsend, please don't draw attention. I don't want to hurt you, but rest assured that I will if I must," he said near her ear as his breath began to slow.

57

*Suran!*

Jewel's heart was racing. Her eyes darted side-to-side in hopes that a hotel guest would come to her rescue, but the hall was empty and quiet.

*Now what, Jewel? Now what? You're running out of air.*

Jewel began trying to suck air in through her nose and mouth at the same time, but it was pointless.

"Miss Townsend, let me cut to the chase. I'm seeking an item that I believe you possess," he said in a low voice, then loosened the hand over her mouth. Jewel breathed in the air greedily.

"I don't know what you're talking about. I don't have anything," she said, trying to fill her lungs before he covered her mouth again, but left her nose uncovered.

Suran pushed Jewel the ten or so feet to the door of her hotel room.

"Open it," Suran demanded.

Jewel did not want to go into the room with the man. She knew once the door was closed, she would be completely alone with little chance of getting help. Suran applied more pressure to the knife and Jewel let out a gasp. She reached into the small purse that hung across her body and retrieved the key card. She slid the card through the slot and the green light glowed. Suran nudged her. She turned the handle until it unlatched. Suran pushed her through the door. She was about to spin around and make a run for it when she saw something that stopped her. On the floor beside the bed, there was a duffle bag. Although it was not hers, she recognized it.

The door clicked shut behind them as Suran pushed past the threshold. Just as they passed the small entryway Michael lunged at Suran. Jewel was prepared. She threw herself forward, and away from the knife. She got her footing and spun around.

Michael and Suran fell to the floor in a struggle for possession of the knife. Jewel felt helpless as she watched. Michael had Suran's knife-hand turned away from him. Jewel ran up and grabbed for the knife. As the two men struggled she pried Suran's fingers off of the hilt and pulled the weapon free. She held the knife in her hand, ready to strike out with it. She was going to plunge the knife into Suran's back. She stepped forward ready to part his flesh with the blade, but found that she could not do it. Finally, she shoved the knife into her small purse and ran forward to assist Michael.

The men were locked in a wrestling match. Michael held Suran's wrists, but Suran was getting the upper hand. He slammed Michael against the door frame of the bathroom. Michael grunted with the blow. Jewel leapt onto Suran's back and put her arms around his neck. She was squeezing as tightly as she could.

Michael took advantage of Suran's momentary loss of balance. He released Suran's wrist and aimed a blow straight for his chest. The blow pushed Suran and Jewel against the wall. Upon impact Jewel lost her hold around the man's neck and fell to the floor. She sprang back up and hopped onto Suran's back again. This time Michael's fist made contact with Suran's face and Jewel's along with it. Jewel dropped to the floor in a daze. She could hear the scuffle continue as she tried to regroup. Michael fell on the floor in front of Jewel as Suran bolted for the door and disappeared.

"Are you all right?" Michael asked. His Irish brogue was heavy in the heat of the moment. He got to his feet.

"I . . . I . . ."

"Good, you should grab your things and get out of here," he said, as he pulled her to her feet. He then ran out of the room.

Jewel shook her head to regain her senses. She rushed into the bathroom and snatched the few toiletries she had removed and tossed them into her duffle bag on the bed.

Michael returned, panting, and shut the door.

"Who was he?" she demanded.

"How would I know? You're the idiot who invited him to your table," Michael spat, his cheeks red with anger.

"What? You were watching me? How dare you!"

"Oh, how dare I? Well, if I hadn't been watching you, I wouldn't have been able to spare you from whatever that guy had planned. I saw you get up and head for the elevator. As soon as you did he jumped up and I could see what was going to happen. I raced up the stairs just in time. I heard him below taking the stairs two at a time to beat you to the second floor. I was only trying to help you. You were the fool who invited him to join you."

Jewel's teeth were clenched in anger. She was breathing heavily through her nose as she stared at Michael. She didn't care if she looked crazed.

"How did you get in here anyway?" she demanded.

"I paid for the bloody room. The clerk gave me two keys. I kept one and I'm glad I did, because it saved you from your own reckless nature. I swear woman, you need a babysitter."

They glared at each other. Michael noticed the red area on Jewel's cheek had begun to darken.

He calmed himself. His breathing steadied.

"I'm sorry you got hurt. Are you all right?" he asked, anger still deepening his voice. He reached up and touched the injured area of her cheek.

She slapped his hand away. A look of shock crossed his face and his eyes narrowed.

"You go wait in the lobby while I call the police," he ordered.

"The hell I will. I'm not leaving," she said, folding her arms.

"Fine," Michael said, turning and walking to the hotel room phone. He called for police assistance, and then turned back to Jewel.

"Do you have all your things?" he asked.

"Yes. Why?" she asked, with arms still folded.

"I just think it best for you to be out of harm's way. You should go wait in the lobby."

"Why are you so eager for me to leave?" she asked with narrowed eyes and a tilt to her head.

"I just want you to be safe. Someone has obviously targeted you . . . wait, you believe I had something to do with this?"

"No. I just, well. . ." she stammered, shifting her weight.

"You are unbelievable," he said, shaking his head.

"I don't think you had anything to do with this . . . well, maybe I did for just a moment, but it wouldn't make any sense."

Michael shook his head and began speaking rapidly under his breath. Jewel concentrated on trying to understand what he was saying, but quickly realized that he wasn't speaking English. She sat on the bed with folded arms and quiet disdain.

"Can we call a truce for now?" Michael asked.

Jewel studied him for a count of six then agreed.

Chapter 5
Really Tall Blondes

The police had come and gone leaving Jewel angrily pacing the hotel room.

Michael watched as she cleared the short distance from the door to the window yet another time. "Why are you so upset?"

"Did you hear what that cop said? Domestic disturbance! He thought I brought that guy up to my room and then he and my boyfriend got into a fight. As if the idea of me bringing some random guy to my hotel room wasn't enough, the cop thought you were my boyfriend. You!"

Michael sat stiffly on the end of the bed and continued to watch Jewel pace.

"Well, after you gave them Suran's knife they seemed to be more open to the truth," he said.

"Yeah, but it's a shame I put my fingerprints all over it," she said, as she stopped and turned to face Michael.

He rotated his shoulder and winced in pain.

"Are you okay?" she asked as she stepped in front of him.

"I'm fine."

She sat down on the bed beside him. He looked at her, noting again the bruise on her cheek.

"How about you?" he said reaching up and gently touching the bruise.

She stared into his green eyes and was touched by his gentle concern.

*Damn, his eyes are beautiful.*

For just a moment she liked him. For just a moment she felt like he was a warm human being that she could care for, but that moment was fleeting.

"Why in the bloody hell would you invite some stranger to dine with you?" Michael asked.

She slapped his hand away, and moved to the other bed.

"We need to figure this out," she said. "This whole situation. Who or what is 'The Dane'?" She stood and began pacing again.

"I don't know. But I do know we need to get out of this hotel," Michael said, reaching for his duffle bag.

"Why?"

"Well, Suran was not the guy that broke into your house. This leads me to believe you have more than one person looking for you."

"I thought you said you didn't get a good look at the guy who broke into my house," she said, spinning around to glare at him.

"I didn't get a look at the intruder's face. However, I can tell you that Suran has a wiry build. The other guy was shorter and rounder. Since they tracked us so easily, I suggest we find an ATM and operate on a cash-only basis from now on so we don't leave an electronic trail. We should stay away from airports, too."

"Huh! You sound like you have some experience in this cloak and dagger stuff," she said, eyeing him with suspicion.

"No, it's just common sense," he said, then caught sight of her narrowed eyes. "Miss Townsend, if we are going to work together then you will need to ease up on your outrageous suspicion of me. We're on the same side."

Jewel continued studying him silently.

"I'm not some spy and I'm not your enemy," he declared.

"That is just what a spy would say," she countered with a snap of her fingers.

He unwillingly smiled at the retort. The appearance of his rare smile caused Jewel to return the kindness. She gave Michael a genuine smile— dimples and all. Michael froze in his movement and locked eyes with Jewel.

She became uncomfortable, but couldn't turn away. For just a moment Jewel felt like they were two people in a normal conversation about normal stuff, but then she remembered that there were crazy events and crazy people she needed to deal with. Jewel closed her eyes and sighed heavily.

"Okay. Lead the way," she said.

∞   ∞   ∞

They caught a taxi to a local sports bar, and sat as far from the televisions as possible. Jewel ordered iced tea and a cheeseburger. Michael ordered water and a tuna melt. When the drinks arrived, Michael pulled out a small notebook and pen. At the top of the page he wrote "The Dane" and underlined it. He looked up at Jewel.

"So, do you have any ideas?" he asked, tapping the ink pen on the page.

"Well the obvious answer would be a Great Dane dog. Your brother didn't have a strange Scooby-Doo fixation, did he?"

Michael stared at Jewel, completely devoid of expression.

*Yeah, I deserve a look like that.*

"Well, the only other Dane I can think of is Hamlet," Jewel said.

Michael shrugged then wrote "Hamlet" on the paper.

"There's Henry Heerup," he said.

"Who's that?" Jewel asked.

"An artist," Michael said adding the name to the list.

"Okay, there's Hans Christian Andersen. Oh, and Kierkegaard, he was a Dane," she said.

Michael jotted the names down and stared at the list with furrowed brow.

"There's Wilhelm Marstrand. He's another artist," he said writing the name as he spoke. He shook his head. "I'm not sure we're heading in the right direction."

Loud cheers roared from the bar where two men sat watching highlights from a baseball game. A portly man in a suit entered and sat at the bar. He appeared to be in his mid-fifties and had male pattern baldness. He sat and immediately opened a newspaper. Jewel smiled to herself as she had an immediate thought of the three stooges.

"Something funny?" Michael asked.

Jewel shook her head in response. The waiter set their sandwiches down in front of them. Jewel picked up her burger and took a bite, and returned her attention to the list.

"Well, if you had to guess who the Dane is, who would it be?" she asked.

"I don't know," he said, setting down the pen and steepling his fingers.

"Well, let me see," she said pulling out her phone. "Famous Danes," she said as she typed with one finger. "Viggo Mortensen? Doubtful," she said as she scrolled. "Brigette Nielsen? Did your brother have a thing for really tall blondes?" Jewel asked. She looked up to find Michael watching her with an unreadable expression.

"Well, since you are neither tall nor blonde then I would think not."

"Come on. He was your brother, you have to have some idea how his mind worked," Jewel said, as she put her phone down, picked up her burger, and took another bite.

"He was your lover. You should have just as much insight as I," Michael said. "In fact you should have more." Michael's face remained expressionless.

Jewel swallowed down the bite she was chewing. She took a sip of her tea.

"Umm, Michael, I . . ." Jewel began her confession that she and Brogan were mere acquaintances.

Michael looked up at her with cold eyes. She was shocked by the look on his face. He almost looked angry.

"Never mind," she said, turning away from his cold stare. "Maybe we're over-thinking this. Maybe it's a place. Was he in Denmark recently?"

Michael shrugged while he ate. He wore a look of concentration as he grabbed the napkin off his lap and wiped his mouth. He leaned over, rummaged in his duffle bag, and retrieved a small stack of postcards. Flipping through the stack, he removed one and set it on the table.

"This was the last postcard I received before the one from Italy," he said.

The front of the card displayed a picture of a strange sculpture in the middle of a small pool. Jewel turned the card over to read the hand-written message:

*"I'm amazed to see that there is still damage from both Hurricanes Katrina and Ida visible in this city. I have discovered some good finds. Some of these beauties, you would be interested in."*

Like the Venice postcard this one was signed with a "B". Jewel read the printed information on the card twice.

"This is from New Orleans, Louisiana," she said.

"Yes, and it's dated March first."

"So, on March first he sent you a card from New Orleans, and then on March nineteenth he sent you one from Venice," Jewel recapped.

"Which is odd in itself. I told you he would send me a card or note every few months. I usually got about three or four cards every year. I have never gotten two in the same month," Michael said leaning forward to look at the postcard.

Jewel took the Venice postcard from the stack and placed it next to the New Orleans one and examined them. She finished her sandwich and pushed her plate to the side.

The television near the bar was playing interviews with sports figures. The sports fans were still watching and chatting, but the pudgy man was reading. She could see the reflection of light as it caught his bald head over the newspaper.

She sipped her tea and turned to find Michael watching her. He quickly looked away. She studied Michael for a moment. His strong squared jaw was so like Brogan's. She bit her lip as the memory of Brogan's death resurfaced. The brutality of his murder made her aware of how much danger she was facing.

"What kind of help would Brogan ask of you? I mean . . . what would he call upon you for?" she asked.

Michael considered the question. Jewel watched as he removed the napkin from his lap, folded it neatly, and set it beside his empty plate.

"He could have needed money or legal help. I told you about his unscrupulous business dealings."

"Yeah, but this doesn't sound like that. You're his brother, so he would ask you for . . . what? . . . A kidney?" Jewel sighed in resignation. She was staring absently at the list. She noticed that her contributions were writers and Michael's were artists. They each had their areas of expertise. She smiled as she was struck with an idea.

"Art is your specialty, Michael," she said.

He looked at her with a cocked eyebrow.

"I mean, if Brogan is asking you for help, then it may be help that only you can give, or someone like you. Art is the thing that you and Brogan had in common so it makes sense that 'The Dane' has something to do with art."

Michael looked at the list on the table and slowly shook his head.

"That may be true, but I still have no idea who the Dane is."

"Well, I'm out of ideas," she said, leaning back in her chair.

Michael sat straight-backed staring at the postcards. He picked up the New Orleans postcard. He turned it over twice and tilted his head in thought.

"What?" Jewel asked.

"This postcard is from the New Orleans Museum of Art."

"So?"

"Well, Brogan wasn't the type to go to a museum unless he was robbing it," he said.

Jewel's mouth dropped open in shock.

"No, I have no proof that he ever robbed a museum. I just find it strange that he would visit a museum. Do you think this postcard could have been purchased someplace other than the museum?" he asked handing the postcard to Jewel.

She examined it.

"Maybe. Is that some famous sculpture?" she asked.

"No. I've never seen it before."

"Then, this postcard was probably purchased at the museum," she stated, popping a French fry into her mouth.

"What would you say to a change of plans?" Michael asked with a rare smile.

"What did you have in mind?" Jewel asked cautiously.

"I think we should cancel our tickets to Venice."

"Okay, where do you want to go?"

"New Orleans," he said, setting the postcard on the table and tapping it with his finger.

"I thought you wanted to stay away from the airport," Jewel said. "New Orleans would be quite a drive."

"Well, I think we should risk it. To rent a car, we would need to use a credit card anyway. If we need to use a credit card for that then I would rather fly," he said. "Speaking of staying off of the grid, we probably should turn off our phones," he added.

Jewel stared down at her phone with longing. She looked at Michael. He looked like he was stifling a smile.

"New Orleans, the Big Easy, the birthplace of Jazz . . ." Jewel said, nodding her head.

Michael watched her with expectation.

"That's all I got," Jewel said. "I really don't know much about New Orleans."

"Well, we're about to find out."

Chapter 6
Easter Eggs

Michael made all the arrangements. He booked a red-eye flight to New Orleans. They waited in the airport for three hours then boarded the plane. Jewel slept through most of the two hour flight. Michael shook her awake as the plane touched down.

Her eyes sprang open. She discovered that her head was resting on Michael's shoulder. She sat up straight and wiped away a few strings of drool that had settled on the corner of her mouth. In her embarrassment, she looked around to see if anyone was watching her. She looked at Michael and noticed a quarter-sized wet spot on his shoulder where she had been resting. He wore a smirk until he followed her gaze and discovered the drool stain. She rubbed her eyes and stretched. As she moved to the edge of her seat ready to stand, Michael grabbed her hand.

"Let's wait for the aisle to clear before we go," he said in a low voice.

71

She nodded and sat back. Jewel pulled a compact from her purse and was startled by her reflection. Most of her hair had come loose from its bun. Wiry hairs stuck up in all directions. She pulled the hairpins out and brushed her hair with her fingers. Without a comb, the finished product was not much better than the original mess. She straightened her dress then looked at Michael. He sat with his hands resting on his thighs as he watched the passengers moving down the aisle. She noticed how neat he looked, with the exception of the drool on his shoulder. His clothes were well maintained and his hair still tidy. Only the stubble on his unshaven face gave testimony to his long night.

The last of the passengers were making their way to the exit. Michael and Jewel stood and retrieved their bags from the overhead compartment. As they exited the plane, Michael looked around in assessment of their surroundings. Jewel noticed him turning and looking behind them twice as they made their way through the airport.

"What are you looking for?" Jewel asked.

"Just making sure we aren't being followed."

The New Orleans Airport wasn't as large as the Dulles Airport.

Michael stopped and pulled out a map from his bag, while Jewel studied the large mural on the wall.

"What should we do now?" Jewel asked as she bit a fingernail.

Michael looked at his watch then reached up to his chin and began scratching the stubble.

"Well, it's a little after three in the morning. I figured we would go to the museum about ten o'clock. So, I guess we should get a hotel room," he said, shifting the weight of his duffle bag as he stuffed the map into his pocket. He stood on his tiptoes and looked beyond the sea of people.

"Do you think we can walk it? There are bound to be hotels near the airport."

"No," she said flatly, her voice still hoarse with sleep.

It was a short drive to a nearby hotel.

"I need to find a bathroom," Jewel said, as they entered the lobby. She tried to use water to tame her hair, but her tresses were an entity of their own.

*This is as good as it's going to get, Chica.*

When she reentered the lobby Michael was waiting.

"This way," he said.

Jewel followed behind him.

"We almost didn't get a room. Apparently hotels don't like renting rooms on a cash basis anymore," he said, as he approached a door, unlocked it, and held the door open for Jewel. "Here we go," he said, stepping aside for Jewel to enter. He followed her inside and latched the door. Jewel dropped her duffle bag near one of the beds.

"Only one room?" she asked.

"Well, I thought with our limited finances we would be better off sharing a room. Is that okay?" he asked.

"I guess," Jewel said. "So, how did you talk them into renting you a room with cash?" She walked over to one of the beds, pulled back the spread, and dropped down onto mattress. Her sandals fell on the floor as she kicked them off.

"You know. Charm," he said seriously.

"Charm? You?" she said with a smile.

He stood looking down at her unsmiling.

Michael turned and sat on the other bed. He took off his loafers and socks. Jewel watched as he rolled his socks into a neat ball and put them inside one of his shoes. He stood and set his shoes near his duffle bag. He searched his bag and extracted some clothes. The bathroom door closed with a click.

Jewel was already dozing off when he returned. He wore sweat pants and a white t-shirt. Jewel watched as he folded his dirty clothes into a neat pile and set them atop his shoes. She observed this routine and decided it was well rehearsed. He probably did this every night before he went to bed. As she watched, she could feel guilt about her charm remark creeping into her mind.

"I'm sorry," she said softly.

He turned and looked at her.

"I'm sorry about the charm comment. I guess you could be charming if you really tried. If you relaxed a little, maybe the charm would just come naturally," she continued.

"Thanks. So, are you saying I'm uptight?" he said.

He got into bed and settled beneath the blanket.

"Well, yeah," she said. "Goodnight, Michael."

"Goodnight, Miss Townsend."

"*Miss Townsend?* Really? After all we've been through? I hope that was a joke," she said with a chuckle. "Good one." She stifled a yawn then fell asleep.

∞    ∞    ∞

The taxi dropped them off in front of the New Orleans Museum of Art. They stopped by the reflection pool with the sculpture from Brogan's post card in the center.

"I'm not sure what we're supposed to find here," Jewel said, studying the sculpture.

"I don't know either, but let's go inside and look around and hope we find something."

They climbed the steps and entered the building. Jewel noticed the interior had the cold sterile atmosphere found in most museums. They bought tickets and studied a map of the exhibits.

"Well, now what?" Jewel asked. "This is your area of expertise, Professor."

"There are a few pieces here that I would really love to see, but I don't want to get off track," he said, pointing at the map.

"Yeah, let's not lose sight of our purpose. We have to ask ourselves: what would Brogan be looking at here?" she said.

Michael turned and looked Jewel up and down. He cocked one dark eyebrow.

"What?" she asked as she pulled her light sweater closed.

"He would probably be looking at you."

She rolled her eyes and headed for the stairs. They took the stairs to the second floor, turned left, and strolled through one of the galleries.

"Are you feeling anything?" she asked.

"Like what?"

"I don't know, like some psychic vibe or something?" she said, displaying Jazz hands.

"Well, you said that Brogan was on his way to Germany. I'm just trying to put the pieces together. He was in New Orleans, then Venice, and planned to head to Germany next. I'm not making the connection. Also, he probably visited several other places that we don't know about."

"Maybe we should look at German stuff. Do they have a German department?" Jewel asked.

"A German department? Really?"

"Or maybe a Danish department . . . you know, where they'd keep 'The Dane'. Do they have a database? Like a digital card catalogue?" Jewel asked.

Michael couldn't help but smile at this question.

"No. I doubt it," he said, still smiling.

They walked back into the main hall and studied the map again.

"You're back," a hushed voice said.

Michael and Jewel looked up to see a woman in her late twenties approaching Michael. Her face went through a change and a look of embarrassment replaced her surprise.

"I'm sorry, I thought you were someone else," she said, pulling her red hair behind her ear. She turned to retreat. Her long limbs moved fluidly. She had a beauty and grace that Jewel always wished she had possessed.

*Hussy.*

"Wait, please. I'm fairly certain that you have mistaken me for my brother, Brogan. My name is Michael Walsh," Michael said as he advanced on the woman.

The woman turned to Michael. She drew closer and gave him a dazzling smile.

"Brogan is your brother? That scoundrel said he was going to return in just a couple of weeks, but I haven't seen him," she said with a dimpling smile that exposed perfect white teeth.

*Hussy!*

Jewel noticed the woman's body language and the way she looked at Michael. Jewel sensed that the woman found Michael attractive.

"My brother, Brogan, is . . ."

"Missing," Jewel interjected, cutting Michael off.

She had a gut feeling that introducing murder into this story wouldn't entice the woman to help. The redhead dragged her eyes away from Michael and looked at Jewel for the first time. Although the woman continued to smile, Jewel detected the slightest hint that the woman resented her presence.

"Our brother, Brogan, is missing. He went off on one of his crazy adventures," Jewel said with exaggeration. "But, he told us about his visit here and we wanted to come and see what kind of stuff he was working on. We're just trying to get an idea of where that crazy brother of ours might have run off to," Jewel said, laying her hand on Michael's arm and giving it a small squeeze to urge him to play along.

"Your brother? So, you are Brogan's brother and sister? He did strike me as the adventurous type," she said, with a smile. "I'm Pamela Grant, assistant to the Curator of Decorative Arts," she said, extending a hand out to Michael.

He shook her hand in a very businesslike manner.

"I'm Michael Walsh and this is . . . my sister, Jewel. We were wondering if you could tell us what business my brother had here at the museum," Michael said in his usual formal manner.

The woman's body language was speaking volumes, but Michael appeared completely deaf to this language.

*This hussy wants the cold fish. Perhaps she wants to collect the Walsh brother set. But he's scaring her off.*

"I'm not sure I can help you," she said, growing a little distrustful.

Jewel stepped to a painting behind the woman under the pretense of viewing it. She got Michael's attention. He positioned himself so that looking at Jewel was not so obvious.

"Did Brogan tell you where he was going when he left New Orleans?" he asked slowly, while stealing glances at Jewel.

Jewel was trying to communicate. She made a moony-eyed face and batted her eye lashes, then pointed to Pamela. She then pointed to Michael then back to Pamela. Pamela turned to look at Jewel, obviously curious about what Michael was looking at, but Jewel quickly turned her attention to the painting. Jewel was not sure how, but Michael caught on to the silent message. Jewel watched him make a transformation. His stern face produced a delightful smile, and his body became relaxed in its subtle movements.

"I'm sorry, Mrs. Grant, you're probably very busy. We'll be on our way. I'm so sorry we troubled you," Michael said as he took her hand in both of his. "Wow, you have really soft skin," he said as his thumb stroked the back of her hand. "If you see my brother, please tell him that we're looking for him," he said as he slid closer to the woman.

Jewel watched as Michael's eyes surveyed Pamela Grant from head-to-toe. He suddenly leaned in close to her and sniffed slowly.

"What is that captivating scent?" Michael asked as he backed away slowly, still holding the woman's hand.

Jewel was slack-jawed, watching as Michael displayed a skill that she never imagined he possessed.

Pamela made a sound that could only be described as a squeak. She then cleared her throat.

"No, not at all . . . and it's *Miss* Grant, not Mrs." She corrected, giving him a seductive smile and a wink.

*HUSSY!*

Michael's smile grew a tad larger and he moved a fraction closer to the woman. Jewel stepped further away in the guise of viewing another painting.

"Well, I hope Brogan isn't in any kind of trouble," she said, becoming visibly nervous.

"Oh, no. He does this sort of thing all the time. He runs off on some silly adventure and leaves Jewel and myself to hunt him down," Michael said, his voice deeper than normal.

Jewel watched, covertly. She was impressed by the charm that Michael seeped from every pore. As she watched, she was somewhat envious that he had never been that charming toward her.

"Well, he was only here for a day, but I would be happy to show you where he spent his time," Pamela said, as she tentatively took her hand back from Michael.

*She's hooked.*

"Follow me," she said, as she began walking to the galleries on the other side of the main hall. "He spent his time here, in our Fabergé room," she said.

Jewel rushed to join them as they entered the room. The room was small and held about eight lighted display cases. There was very little overhead lighting. Most of the light came from inside the cases.

"Brogan had questions about some of these pieces, especially the cigarette cases. He also had a lot of questions about the Matilda Geddings Gray collection," she added.

"What's that?" Jewel asked.

Pamela spun around, surprised, as she obviously had forgotten about Jewel's presence.

"Since the late nineteen-eighties the Matilda Geddings Gray collection was housed here. It's an extensive collection of Fabergé art which included three Imperial Easter eggs."

Jewel frowned. "Easter eggs?"

"The Easter eggs are very famous. The Romanov Family, the Russian royal family, used to have these elaborate jeweled Easter eggs. They were made by the House of Fabergé. There were about fifty of them. The Matilda Geddings Gray collection had three of the Royal Easter eggs. However, the collection moved to the Cheekwood Museum in Nashville," Pamela explained.

"I've read about the Matilda Geddings Gray collection," Michael said. "The museum was fortunate to have such a priceless collection housed here."

"That's about all I remember," she said. "This particular exhibit is not where I normally work. But I believe the collection may have been moved again to another museum. So, I'm not exactly sure where the collection is now."

"That is very helpful, Pamela," Michael assured her. "May I call you Pamela?"

Jewel stared at Michael open-mouthed as he leaned closer to Pamela. The woman's breath caught as she responded.

"No, not at all. Please, call me Pamela," she said as a pink color filled her cheeks.

"You don't know where Brogan was before he came here or, maybe where he was heading . . . do you?" he asked.

Pamela beamed at Michael, glanced at Jewel, then back to Michael.

"No . . . I'm sorry. We had lunch together and talked about New Orleans and the hurricanes, but he didn't say where he was headed."

"You have an amazing memory. That was like four months ago," Jewel said.

"No, it was about a month ago and besides, Brogan was very memorable," Pamela stated as the blush on her cheeks darkened.

"Yes, he has that effect on people," Michael said, glancing at Jewel.

"Here," Pamela said, pulling a business card from her pocket and handing it to Michael. "If you have any more questions, feel free to call me. I hate to rush off, but I do have a meeting."

Michael took the business card and slipped it into his pocket.

"Thank you. I will definitely call you if I have any more questions," Michael said with a dashing smile.

Pamela blushed again, excused herself, and left the gallery.

"Well, that was interesting," Jewel said, walking over to a display case.

She couldn't help gazing at an incredible piece. It was a golden snake on a green rock. Jewel marveled at the detail and elegance in the work.

"This stuff is gorgeous," she whispered.

Michael joined her at the display. He moved to another case and Jewel followed. Jewel pointed to a small, golden box.

"What is it?"

"This is one of the cigarette cases. Fabergé made lots of cigarette cases, but they are mostly known for the Imperial Easter eggs that were created for the Russian royal family," he said.

"Well, did the information from Pamela give you any ideas?" Jewel asked.

"The first idea she gave me was that my brother hasn't changed a bit in over six years," Michael said, still looking at the cigarette cases.

"Women were drawn to him."

"He was a womanizer," Michael said, turning to look at Jewel.

"Brogan was fun. He made me laugh."

"I guess you weren't with him long enough, because the laughter always turned to tears."

"Pamela didn't look like she was crying, and neither was I."

Michael shook his head and turned away. He studied the artifacts in each of the display cases in turn.

"I feel like I'm missing something. There's something I should know, but I'm overlooking it," he said.

The collection was small and it didn't take them long to view the priceless art. They moved to the door and headed for the exit.

"By the way," Jewel said, glancing at Michael. "You were really smooth with Pamela. I'm sorry I ever questioned your ability to be charming."

Michael was deep in thought and didn't respond to the compliment.

"You should practice it more often. Not to improve, just to make people . . . respond to you better," she said.

Michael continued to descend the stairs without comment. Jewel realized that he wasn't listening.

"Yeah, people might think you're a robot, a corpse, or just some uptight guy that behaves like he has a stick up his butt," she added.

"What?" Michael asked, as he pushed the exit door open and let Jewel pass.

"Nothing," she said.

They walked down the steps to the sculpture in the reflection pool.

Michael began patting his pockets in search of something, and then grimaced.

"I almost forgot; no cell phones. I put mine in my duffle bag so I wouldn't use it. We need a cab. I'll go see if they'll call a cab for us," Michael said, turning and trotting up the stairs.

He disappeared back into the museum. Jewel looked around. The driveway leading to the museum was long but made a circle round the building. It was very hot. She peeled off her sweater and draped it over her arm. Jewel crossed the circular drive and walked slowly along the driveway. A man jogged by going in the opposite direction. He smiled and waved hello. Jewel stopped walking. She tilted her head up and let the sun bathe her face. She took in a deep breath and slowly released the air trying to let some peace flow into her body.

"Pardon me, Ma'am," a voice said.

Jewel turned to the sound of the voice. A black sedan had pulled to the curb. A man was standing beside the passenger door. He was in his mid-fifties and the buttons of his pale gray suit strained against his round belly. He wore a straw Panama hat and held something white in his hand, which Jewel took for a map.

"I was wondering if I could have a word with you," the man said.

She gave the man a smile.

"I'm not from around here, so I don't think I'll be of any help," she said, walking toward him.

"Ma'am, my employer would like to have a word with you," he said, stepping closer to Jewel.

The smile fell from her face as she froze with panic. Her heart instantly began pounding with fear.

The man reached down and opened the back door of the car.

"He just wants a word with you, Miss Townsend."

Jewel couldn't believe what she was hearing. She glanced to the side. The jogger was already about thirty yards away and there was no one else close by. She spun around to run toward the jogger, but she was pulled backward as something covered her mouth. She tried to scream, but the towel on her mouth muffled the sound. A white pillow case was put over her head and her arms were held tightly to her body. She was kicking, but never made contact with anything fleshy. She felt a burning sensation in her arm and realized she had been stuck with a needle. Within a count of twenty she was feeling weak and groggy. She continued to kick and flail right up until she lost consciousness.

Chapter 7
It's a Date

Jewel was being bounced. She wondered in her foggy mind if she were bungee jumping. The continued bouncing stirred her into consciousness. She opened her eyes to discover she was being carried over someone's shoulder. She found it difficult to breathe, being upside down. The person carrying her stopped, leaned over, and dropped her onto a leather couch. She blinked her eyes and tried to focus. She felt hands shake her lightly.

"Jewel," a voice said. "Jewel, are you okay?"

She strained to focus her vision. Michael was sitting on the couch beside her. He shook her again, but she brushed his hand away.

"Get off of me," she grumbled. She pulled up her sleeve and peered at the site where the needle had plunged into the small cluster of veins inside her elbow. A small red dot was the only evidence of this violation.

"Are you all right?" Michael asked.

"Get her a glass of water," a voice said.

Jewel opened her eyes wide and took in her surroundings. She looked in the direction of the unfamiliar voice. A man in a gray suit was standing a few feet away. She recognized him as the man from outside the museum.

*Kidnapped! I've been kidnapped?*

Another man entered the room. He was carrying a glass of water. He was tall and built like a gorilla. He wore a chauffeur's uniform. He leaned down, holding the glass out to Jewel. She glared at him and did not accept the water. The gorilla gave up on Jewel accepting the water, and set it on an end table beside the couch. She looked from him, to the man in the gray suit, and to Michael.

Michael did not display his usual emotionless expression. His lips were tight and his brow furrowed in concern as he studied Jewel.

"Are you all right?" he asked softly. "When I came out of the museum they were putting you in the car. They told me to come, so I did."

"What in the hell is going on?" she asked, as she repositioned herself on the couch.

"Everything will be revealed," the man in the gray suit said, taking off his hat to reveal his bald head. There was something familiar about him, but Jewel could not place him with her foggy brain. "In due time," the man added.

They were in a large room with marble floors. Jewel was in awe of the huge ornate desk that was the centerpiece of the room.

*It looks like someone is compensating for something.*

Under the desk was a beautiful Persian rug. There were two sets of double doors opposite each other in the room. The furnishings were all dark and masculine. The room, however, felt cold and restrained.

She turned again and looked at Michael. He appeared to have composed himself. He wore his usual stern expression.

"What is going on?" Jewel asked Michael. "Who are these people?"

Michael was about to answer, but the sound of footsteps drew everyone's attention to the double doors behind the desk. The doors burst open and a man entered. He was in his early sixties. His hair was slate gray and matched his neatly groomed moustache. He walked with purpose to the couch. He stood looking down at Jewel and Michael.

"I asked Mr. Gruber to extend a warm invitation to you so we could have a little sit-down, as I like to call it," the man said, as he laced his fingers.

He had an accent that sounded like he came from Boston, but not quite.

"A warm welcome? Are you insane? You've kidnapped us! And I will not allow you to get away with this," Jewel said, unsteadily getting to her feet.

"Sit," the mustached man commanded. Jewel did not obey.

*I'm not a dog. I don't obey commands.*

The man subtly flicked his head to the side. The chauffeur approached Jewel, placed massive hands on her shoulders and pushed her down on the couch with ease. She fell back with a thud. Michael sprang to his feet. His chest was heaving with furious breath.

"Don't touch her," he said through clenched teeth.

"Gentlemen, gentlemen . . . Let's play nice," the mustached man said.

The chauffeur was face-to-face with Michael. Upon the mustached man's words, the chauffeur stepped back.

"Please, let's sit," the mustached man said. At these words the chauffeur grabbed a chair and set it behind the man.

"I suppose you know who I am," the man said, as he sat down in front of the couch.

"You're Simon Chauvin," Michael said.

"Simon Chauvin?" Jewel asked. "Simon Chauvin the entrepreneur?"

"And a whole lot more," Chauvin said. "Landry, coffee."

The chauffeur hurried out of the room.

"So. I'm sure you know why we brought you here."

"No," Jewel answered.

Chauvin raised his eyebrows.

"Playing dumb won't make things easier for any of us," Chauvin said.

Michael and Jewel looked at each other then back to Chauvin. Silence dominated the room.

"Okay, I'll tell you a little story," Chauvin said. "Brogan Walsh was employed by me to acquire something. He did acquire it and I was most grateful. However, while still in my employ he also discovered the whereabouts of another object. I want that other object as well," Chauvin said. He paused to watch the captive pair closely. "Brogan Walsh, yes sir, he was good at what he did. He was a master at finding lost treasures. He will be sorely missed."

Jewel heard Michael grunt beside her. She thought perhaps the talk of Brogan was painful. She glanced at Michael. He was staring down at the floor with a look of concentration.

Landry returned and handed Chauvin a cup of coffee on a saucer. Chauvin grabbed the cup and took a sip while Landry continued to stand with the saucer thrust forward like a human coffee table.

"Well, this object is important to me, and Brogan was keeping it from me. I sent Gruber," he said, pointing a thumb at the man in the gray suit, "to talk to Mr. Walsh, but Brogan Walsh didn't want to cooperate."

Jewel sensed Michael's tension at Chauvin's last statement.

"So, the question is . . . are *you* going to cooperate?" Chauvin added.

Jewel took the question for the only thing it could be: a threat.

"You know you'll never get away with this," Jewel said. "I'll see to it that you fry for this. This is kidnapping," she said with her chin tilted up in defiance.

"Miss Townsend, you were never here," Chauvin said with a light chuckle. "Who is going to believe that I kidnapped a librarian? From what it looks like, you are a woman who is obviously having some kind of nervous breakdown. First, you're the last person seen with a murdered man. Then you call the police with a crazy accusation that someone ransacked your house when nothing was taken. And then you call the police about a man attacking you which has been filed as a domestic dispute."

"I . . . you . . ." Jewel sputtered.

Chauvin laughed.

"You know if the right kind of evidence was brought to the Italian police, you could be a prime suspect for the murder of Brogan Walsh," Chauvin added.

Jewel had a hopeless feeling. She considered running out into the street and crying for help, but could she make it to the street? She looked at the man called Landry. He was solid; someone she knew could easily handle her one hundred-four pounds. As she studied him, the character "Lurch" from the Addams Family came to mind.

"Mr. Walsh," Chauvin said to Michael. "Professor, I love to be in the presence of another art aficionado. I take great pride in my collection. You could say it is my passion," he said, getting to his feet. "I would love to share my passion with you. This way, please."

*That sounded totally inappropriate.*

Michael stood and pulled Jewel to stand beside him. Landry stepped forward to stop Jewel.

"She can come, too," Chauvin said.

They all followed Chauvin through the double doors behind the desk. The room was dimly lit. Jewel noticed that the lighting came from within display cases, just like in the New Orleans art museum. One case had a collection of small pieces all containing swastikas. Jewel's flesh crawled and she rubbed her arms trying to drive away the goose pimples that had formed.

The group continued walking through the room until they approached a long display case that was the highlight of the collection. Jewel looked in awe with Michael by her side. Inside the case were three jeweled eggs. One was pink with an ornate gold grid-like pattern. The next egg was green and decorated with gold emblems. Jewel leaned in and looked closely to discern a double-headed bird. Standing in front of both of these eggs were two sets of little paintings joined together with hinges. The last egg was ruby red and had little doors open on four sides. Inside the doors there were tiny paintings of buildings. This egg was decorated in pearls and diamonds. There was a number on each door. While looking at this egg Michael muttered, "Eighteen-ninety-three. It's a date." He stood up quickly with a strained expression before his face cleared and a smile flashed, briefly showing his teeth.

"So, Professor Walsh, these are the crown jewels of my collection," Chauvin said, staring down at the beautiful decorative eggs. "What do you think?"

Michael's brow furrowed.

"Surely these are copies. I recognize that one as The Napoleonic Egg and I happen to know that it is part of the Matilda Geddings Gray Collection," Michael said.

Chauvin wore a smile of pride. "No, yes, and no. These are not copies, and yes they did belong to the Matilda Geddings Gray collection."

Michael stared at Chauvin in disbelief. "Are you saying that you stole the Matilda Geddings Gray collection of Imperial eggs?"

"Professor Walsh, 'stole' is such a common word. Let's just say I acquired them," Chauvin replied.

"You're delusional."

Chauvin's smile vanished and was replaced with a look that caused Jewel's throat to tighten in fear.

"Professor Walsh, I can assure you these are the original Imperial eggs. The eggs that moved to the Cheekwood Museum in Nashville are fakes. They are expensive and exquisite copies, thanks to small miracles and really big hurricanes. My artisans did an extraordinary job creating perfect copies of the eggs."

"So, you're an art thief *and* a kidnapper," Jewel spat.

"Are you a religious man, Professor Walsh?" Chauvin asked, ignoring Jewel's comment.

The group was silent as they glanced at each other in confusion.

"Finally acquiring something that you have coveted for so many years has a euphoria that is akin only to a religious experience; not that I invest much in piety," Chauvin said. "I tried to negotiate the purchase of these eggs with the Matilda Geddings Gray Foundation, but they were not receptive to my offers."

"How did you do it?" Michael asked, still calm.

"Oh, I won't bore you with the details. Let's just say, with Hurricane Katrina and then the collection's relocation to Nashville, I had my opportunity," he said, and ushered them to another display case.

As Jewel examined the items in the new display case, she started recognizing the craftsmanship. These pieces were also Fabergé.

"There are several pieces in my collection that were procured by your brother," Chauvin said. He walked to a small sitting area in the corner and sank down onto a chair.

Jewel was feeling like the entire experience since she woke up on the black leather couch was a dream. She reached over and pinched Michael, not wanting to pinch herself. He jumped and looked at her, but didn't say anything.

"This is all a joke, right?" Jewel asked. She felt as if she were in emotional shock. She had too many feelings pulsing through her that she didn't know which to acknowledge first. She looked at Michael. He wore his characteristic Moai stone-faced expression.

"Please take a seat and we'll have our little chat about my art acquisitions, as your brother used to call them," Chauvin said. "I will miss Brogan's services. He was a very talented treasure hunter."

"Is that why you killed him?" Michael asked, free of any emotion.

Chauvin mirrored Michael's stony expression.

"Brogan's death was a terrible loss. And an accident."

"Accident? He was torched."

*Atta boy, Michael. You let him have it.*

"That did not work out the way it was supposed to. I'm looking for the man responsible, but he appears to be missing. Brogan had ample opportunity to cooperate. I even sent Gruber to make him a very attractive offer," Chauvin said, nodding toward the chubby man.

Jewel looked at Gruber and a puzzle piece fell into place.

"You were the man in Venice. You were the man that approached Brogan when we were at dinner. You were also at the sports bar in D.C. You have been following us!"

Gruber gave Jewel a quick glance, but didn't respond.

"You were supposed to be covert, Gruber," Chauvin said. His eyes narrowed as he looked at the round man. He turned back to Michael.

"So, where is it?" Chauvin said, his expression menacing.

It occurred to Jewel that until now Chauvin had been fairly light-hearted in his tone and manner. The things he was saying were horrific, but he spoke them as though he were chatting about the weather. Jewel detected a distinct change in the atmosphere. She also sensed the nearness of Landry, or Lurch, as she now thought of him. She glanced behind her as the man moved closer. Michael also noticed the movement.

"How important is Miss Townsend?" Chauvin asked Michael.

Jewel's eyes grew at the question.

*Very damned important.*

"I assumed Brogan gave her the item, or was he just using her to throw us off the path?" Chauvin asked.

"She has nothing to do with this," Michael replied, still devoid of emotion. "She knows nothing. If you let her go, I will cooperate. I thought she might know something. I thought my brother might have given it to her, but she has nothing and she knows nothing," Michael said maintaining eye contact with Chauvin.

Chauvin studied Michael. He glanced at Jewel, then back to Michael.

"Then why did you bring her along?"

The room was silent. Michael slowly turned and looked at Jewel. His face had changed. It was a look that Jewel had never seen on him before. She was surprised as his mouth widened into a wry smile—almost evil. He shrugged his shoulders.

"Well, you know," he replied, turning again to face Chauvin. "A distraction."

Chauvin appraised Jewel up and down before a chuckle rolled up from deep in his throat. He looked at Michael, while shaking his head.

"You're just like your brother. You think with the wrong head. But frankly I wouldn't have bothered."

Jewel felt as if she were watching a movie—a horror movie. She couldn't believe what she was hearing.

"Put her on a plane back home and we'll go find your prize," Michael said.

Chauvin nodded, and then rubbed his chin in thought.

"Do you have it?" Chauvin asked.

"No, but I can find it."

Chauvin studied Michael with a look of distrust.

"I don't believe you. In fact I don't think you know what the item is."

"Of course I do. My brother and I worked together on several of his finds," Michael said coolly.

Jewel gaped.

*He was leading me on this whole time. Everything he said to me was lies. It was all lies.*

Michael looked at Jewel then back to Chauvin. The room was silent for several moments.

"You want the Danish Jubilee," Michael announced.

The room continued in silence. Chauvin sat staring at Michael. Jewel stepped forward, but Landry immediately grabbed her arms to stop her advance.

*What the hell is the Danish Jubilee? Is that 'The Dane'?*

"You son of a bitch. I trusted you. You've been lying to me the entire time," she shouted, as she strained against the man that held her back.

She realized that her arms were useless as they were pinned in the gorilla's grip, so she began kicking her legs trying to reach Michael. He looked at her and gave a laugh. Chauvin joined in the laughter. After several unsuccessful kicks, Jewel gave up. Her legs hung a foot off the floor as the gorilla held her. She looked daggers at Michael. Her breath was uneven. She blinked several times trying to stave off the tears, not wanting Michael to have the satisfaction of seeing her cry. Landry slowly set her back on her feet.

"So, he told you about the Danish Jubilee? Can you believe it? What a find. It has been lost for decades. So, where is it?"

"Well, I'm not sure, but I have some ideas," Michael responded.

"Is it in Venice? You scheduled a flight to Venice," Chauvin said, vibrating with excitement.

Michael looked around the room. His eyes passed, briefly, over Jewel.

"Let her go, and I'll go to Venice to find it. I'm done with her. She is of no use. Frankly, she will just be in the way," Michael said, coldly.

Chauvin laughed lightly.

Jewel lunged toward Michael. Landry grabbed her in a bear hug. She struggled against him while yelling obscenities. Chauvin made a sign to Gruber.

Gruber stepped forward with a bottle and a syringe. She was helpless in the grasp of the gorilla, and could do nothing but watch as the needle plunged into her flesh. She kicked, protested, and then succumbed.

"She is positively feral," Chauvin said.

*You have no idea.*

Chapter 8
I Hate You


Jewel struggled to consciousness. She cracked her eyes open, but sensitivity to the light caused her to snap them shut again. She heard voices, but couldn't make out the words. They were being masked by a humming sound.

*My head is killing me. What is that annoying sound?*

When Jewel noticed the pressure in her head and ears, she became aware of where she was: on an aircraft. Her eyes flew open. She was lying on her back. She could see the rounded ceiling of the jet cabin. She tilted her head and stared at the blue and white striped upholstery for a moment. She slowly turned her head to see the oval windows to the right. She swung her legs off the couch and sat up. The cabin was about fifty feet long.

"Welcome back, sleeping beauty," Chauvin said.

Jewel looked in his direction to see him sitting on an overstuffed blue seat.

"Where am I?" she demanded, her voice hoarse.

"You're aboard a Gulfstream G650ER, my private jet. Isn't she beautiful?" Chauvin said as he rubbed the arm of his chair.

Jewel was still groggy. She reached up and wiped her face. Her body was stiff and aching. She noticed a small adhesive bandage on her right arm. She reached down and tore the bandage off to expose several small dots.

"You drugged me? Again?" Jewel asked, her blood boiling.

Michael stood. Jewel had not seen him at first, as his seat was turned away from her, facing Chauvin. Michael walked over to Jewel and squatted down in front of her.

"Are you feeling all right?" he asked, with his soft Irish lilt.

"Get away from me," Jewel demanded, her eyes narrowed in rage.

"Now, you be a good girl, and we won't have to do that again," Chauvin said, as if he was scolding a child.

Jewel thought of how calm he was and wondered how many people he had drugged and abducted. Jewel looked around the cabin. Gruber sat at a table reading a book, while the chauffeur was reclined in another overstuffed seat. His eyes were closed and he appeared to be asleep. Besides the four men, Jewel saw no one. She knew there must be someone flying the jet and wondered if she could appeal to them for assistance. Her gaze returned to Michael. He was watching her closely. She expected to see his usual expressionless face, but this time she noticed a look of concern and pity in his eyes.

"You're a real bastard, you know that?" Jewel said to Michael. "I trusted you and all along you were using me. You knew what 'The Dane' was, you lied about . . ."

Jewel was cut off as Michael grabbed her and covered her mouth with his. She pushed him away and stared in disbelief.

"You son of a bitch!" she said, as she slapped him. Michael released her, but stayed squatting in front of her. A look of agony marred his face.

"Oh, a lover's quarrel," Chauvin said with amusement. "Someone bring me popcorn because I'm enjoying the show."

"You have been playing me the entire time," she said, biting her lip to hold back her emotions. "You knew all about this Danish Jubilee thing."

"Danish Jubilee *thing*?" Chauvin echoed with shock. "Dear girl, don't you understand how precious it is? I believe the Professor needs to give you an art history lecture on this treasure."

Michael looked at Chauvin, then back to Jewel.

"Go on, Professor," Chauvin said. "We've got the time."

Michael gritted his teeth. Jewel watched the muscle in his jaw. He closed his eyes briefly and swallowed.

"The Danish Jubilee, also known as the Royal Danish Egg, was the Imperial Easter Egg for the year nineteen-hundred-three," Michael said slowly, emphasizing the date. "Tsar Nicholas II, the last Tsar of Russia, had it commissioned for his mother, the Dowager Empress. It was a tradition in the Romanov family to commission Fabergé to create these Easter eggs. In the year nineteen-hundred-seventeen the Bolsheviks overthrew the Russian royal family. The treasures of the Romanov family were divided up; some were stored, and some went missing. As the years passed some of the treasures that were stored and catalogued also disappeared. There are six Fabergé Imperial Easter eggs missing. They are lost treasures . . . and the Danish Jubilee is one of the six."

"Good job, Professor," Chauvin said.

"I wrote my Master's thesis on the House of Fabergé and the Imperial Easter eggs. I guess you could say it is one of my *specialties*," he said, stressing his last word and giving Jewel a brief smile.

Jewel was having trouble staying still. She wanted to strike out. She kept looking from Chauvin to Michael and back. She wasn't sure which one she wanted to pummel first.

"Do you need anything?" Michael asked. "Something to drink?"

"Landry, get the lady some water," Chauvin commanded.

Landry shot up. He looked as if an alarm had gone off. His bulky figure stumbled as he got to his feet and walked down the center of the cabin. He returned and handed Jewel a bottle of water. She wanted to throw it at someone, but suddenly realized she was incredibly thirsty. She drank half the bottle before she stopped for air.

She looked to her right and left, then formulated a plan.

"I need to go to the restroom," she said.

Michael stood and offered his hand to her. She ignored his hand and got to her feet. Michael started to walk down the aisle to lead her.

"No. You stay here with me, Professor," Chauvin said. "Landry, take the lady to the restroom."

Landry walked up behind Jewel and gave her a shove forward. She tripped, but kept her feet.

"Mr. Landry, be polite to our guest, at least while she's behaving herself," Chauvin said.

Jewel was shuttled along to the back of the cabin where she found the restroom. She made use of the facilities then washed her faced and studied her reflection. The bruise on her left cheek had turned a sickly yellow. She straightened her clothes and hair before opening the door.

Landry was standing in the walkway. He stepped aside as Jewel exited the washroom.

She slowly walked in the direction of her seat, and then bolted for the front of the jet. She zoomed past Gruber then Michael and finally past Chauvin.

"What the hell is she doing now?" Chauvin said as she sprinted by.

She heard footsteps behind her as she ran through a galley and to the cockpit door. She pulled the door open. The two men inside spun around and looked at Jewel in surprise.

"Please, help me! These men are holding me against my will. Please, I need your help," she pleaded.

She was grabbed from behind and lifted off her feet. Landry pinned her arms to her side. He pulled her backward while she struggled for freedom. Gruber and Chauvin loomed up in front of her. Gruber was holding a syringe tipped with a needle. Chauvin grabbed her arm and held it out for Gruber. As soon as the needle plunged into Jewel's skin, she stopped fighting. She felt defeated and knew that it was only a matter of moments before she would be unconscious. She gazed at the pilots pleadingly, but they appeared unconcerned.

"My niece. As I told you before, she's mentally unstable. I just hope the doctors in Italy can help her," Chauvin said as he stroked Jewel's cheek. His hand stroked the side of her face that was turned away from the pilots. Chauvin stroked it softly once more then closed his fingers. He pinched her cheek hard—so hard that involuntary tears filled her eyes and spilled down her cheeks.

The faces and voices were fading in and out for Jewel. She tried to speak, but it only came out as a moan.

"I'm sorry, gentlemen," she heard Chauvin say as he shut the cockpit door.

Landry dragged Jewel back to the couch and dropped her onto the cushioned seat. She fell with a thud. Michael hurried over and laid her back. He pulled her legs up and arranged her in a more comfortable position. His face was close to hers. She saw his mouth moving. He was saying that he was sorry. He rubbed her cheek that now had a red splotch from the pinch to match the yellowing bruise on the other side. At this point Jewel wasn't sure if she was dreaming or not. Michael leaned down and gently kissed her cheek, with a pained look in his eyes.

*I hate you.*

She wished she could protest him touching her, but within a moment she lost consciousness.

Chapter 9
I Hope Street Urchin is the New Style


*I have to pee so badly!*

Jewel sprang up into a sitting position. She was on the bed of an exquisitely decorated room. The shock of her surroundings almost made her forget the urgent message her body was screaming—that she was about to wet the bed. A door stood ajar and she could see the tile floor which was a good indication that it was a bathroom. She started for the bathroom, but when her feet hit the floor her knees buckled and she fell. She hit the beautiful white Berber carpet with a thud.

*Am I drunk?*

With great effort, she got to her feet and darted for the toilet. She made it just in time. While she sat, having what she thought had to be the longest pee in history, disjointed images flashed through her brain. The images didn't make any sense. It was flashes of faces and places. The last lucid thing she remembered was Michael's face. A pang of rage passed through her.

She looked around the bathroom. There were tiny shampoo bottles and wrapped bars of soap on the beautiful marble counter top.

*This is a very expensive hotel.*

She washed her hands while she studied her reflection. The bruise on one check was fading, but the other one was a red purple color. Her hair poked up at all angles. She ran damp hands over her locks and tried to tame the beast. She reconciled herself with defeat and accepted her image.

"I hope street urchin is the new style this season," she said to her reflection.

She grabbed a glass from the counter and was greedily drinking water when she heard a scratching sound. She turned and quickly lost her balance. She grabbed the counter to steady herself. It felt as if the floor wouldn't stay still beneath her feet.

She slowly returned to the bedroom and listened. The room was beautiful with no expenses spared in the decorating. She noticed the light filtering through a curtain above the bed. She pulled back the curtain to expose a window. Through the glass she saw a sight that caused her to squeeze her eyes shut and reopen them. She was on a boat and outside the window she could see land in the distance.

*Well, this is new.*

Jewel turned and looked around the room. She walked to a set of double doors and opened them. She was staring into the interior of an empty closet. She closed the closet door, turned, and walked to the other door. She turned the handle, but the door would not open.

She heard the scratching again. Jewel listened closely and looked around the room, trying to locate the sound. The image of ship rats popped into her mind as she searched for the beasts. The sound was coming from the closet. She opened the double doors again and jumped back. The closet was empty, but the scratching was coming from inside the closet wall.

She gave the wall a hard swat to scare the rodents away. The scratching stopped.

"Jewel," a voice whispered.

Jewel was startled. She wondered if she were hallucinating. She rubbed her head, and then looked down at her arm. She discovered another adhesive bandage. She ripped it off and detected small red dots where the bandage had been.

*Those jerks are giving me brain damage. Now I'm hearing ship rats call my name.*

"Jewel," the voice whispered again.

*What kind of drug gives you auditory hallucinations?*

"Jewel, answer me," the voice demanded.

Jewel moved closer to the closet and knelt down.

"Please answer me," the voice pleaded.

Jewel recognized Michael's voice.

"What the hell do you want?"

"Shh, keep it down," he demanded. "Can you hear me all right?"

His voice was muffled and low, but audible. Jewel didn't want to talk to Michael. She folded her arms, deciding whether or not she was going to answer him. She heard a cracking sound as the thin paneling inside the closet buckled slightly and then broke apart. Something pointy pushed through the splintered wood. She moved away from the destruction. She identified the object as a metal statue of a woman. The statue's upstretched arm was the point that pushed through the paneling. The statue disappeared and was replaced by fingers. Michael pulled at the splintering wood until he formed a hole large enough to accommodate his hand.

Jewel had an urge to bite his fingers. She got on her knees and was actually leaning down to do so, when the fingers disappeared. "Jewel?" he said.

Staying about six inches away, she looked in to the hole. She could see light, then a vivid green eye.

"Are you all right?" he asked.

"Why the hell do you care, you son of a bitch?"

She heard a deep sigh.

"Please just tell me you're okay."

"Yes, no thanks to you," she said. "Why are you busting a hole in the wall?"

"So I can talk to you."

"There's nothing for you to say. I don't want to hear any more of your lies, Michael," she said as she started to get up from the floor.

"Jewel, I'm so sorry. It was killing me to watch them treat you like that, but it was the only thing I could do to save you."

Jewel wondered where this explanation was going to lead. She wanted to hear what he had to say, but she was so angry.

"Jewel, I haven't been lying to you. Everything I told you is the truth. I only figured out what 'The Dane' was when we were looking at the Imperial eggs in Chauvin's office. It was the date. The egg had a date. Eighteen-ninety-three, remember? I was thinking about the postcard from Brogan. I was trying to put all the clues together. When I saw the date on that egg, it all made sense. The postcard had two clues. The first clue was 'The Dane' and the second was the date. Brogan didn't write that card on

March nineteenth. The date was a clue. Nineteen-hundred-three, get it?" Michael said.

"No," she replied.

"The Danish Jubilee Egg was one of the 1903 eggs. I only knew that because of my thesis research. Brogan knew that I did a ton of research on the missing eggs, so that's why he needed my help," Michael continued. "You were right. You speculated on what he would need my help with. The missing eggs are a specialty of mine. He would ask me for help with that."

"Well, I'm so happy that you figured it out in time to make a business deal," Jewel said.

"No. Jewel, are you daft? I'm not working for Chauvin. I'm a prisoner just like you. I'm just cooperating. That's why they aren't sedating me, besides, they need my help. But now I need your help," he said.

"I don't believe you and I'm not helping you," Jewel said, as she got to her feet.

"Jewel? Jewel!"

She refused to answer. She could hear Michael's persistent whisper calling her, but she also heard something else—a motor. She walked to the window and pulled back the curtain. A boat pulled away from the yacht. She recognized Chauvin by his gray hair. She also saw the black clad figure of the chauffeur, but she didn't recognize the man driving the boat. She returned to the closet and sat down.

"Your buddies are leaving," she stated with disdain.

"Jewel, you have to believe me. I have nothing to do with them. Deep inside, you know I'm telling the truth. How can I prove it to you?"

Jewel thought about this for a moment. This was the first time that she felt like she had the upper hand over Michael. It gave her a feeling of strength. She tapped her fingers on her leg in thought. She felt certain there was nothing he could say that would convince her of his loyalty. She considered using this opportunity to humiliate him and then tell him that nothing had changed. A devilish smile spread across her face.

"You told me that you and Brogan hadn't spoken in six years. Why?"

After a long pause Michael answered.

"You go right for the jugular, don't you?" he mumbled, his Irish brogue strong.

"Spill, or no deal," she said as she positioned herself on her stomach looking through the hole.

"Elizabeth . . . you were correct when you assumed that it was a woman that Brogan and I quarreled about," Michael said after another long pause. "She and I were to be married."

"So, what happened?" she prodded. Any instincts to be gentle when someone was speaking of painful things were gone. At this point, she didn't care about his feelings.

"What? You want the details?" Michael asked.

"Yes, indeed I do."

There were several more moments of silence. Jewel waited and wondered if he would answer at all. She was moving to stand when he began speaking.

"Elizabeth and I were engaged to be married. Brogan kept trying to convince me that Elizabeth was unfaithful. I didn't believe him. He tried different methods of convincing me, but I didn't listen. I was in love. Well, he devised a scheme to convince me. He arranged it so that I would walk in on Elizabeth with another man."

Jewel was so interested in the tale that she moved closer to the hole to ensure she didn't miss a word. Michael paused in his story.

"The problem was . . . he was the other man."

*Whoa.*

She blinked several times, processing the story.

"What did you do?" she asked.

"Something I'm not proud of . . . I attacked him. I beat him relentlessly. I broke his nose. God, he was a bloody mess," he said, his voice strained by the painful memory.

Jewel thought back to the image she held in her mind of Brogan. His nose was one of the first things she had noticed. Brogan's crooked nose was an imperfection that only enhanced his good looks.

"Well, he kind of deserved it."

"That's the thing. He could have beaten me. He was always stronger. He could have beaten me or least stopped me, but he didn't. He didn't raise a hand, even to deflect my blows. I beat him senseless. I remember how he looked. He was on the ground and I couldn't stop beating him. It's a wonder I didn't kill him. At the time I wanted to," Michael said.

"What did he say about it?" Jewel asked.

"That he wasn't sorry. He said that it was the only way he could stop me from making the biggest mistake of my life," Michael said.

Jewel peeked through the hole. She could see Michael's profile. He was looking down.

"The thing is after I called the engagement off several friends of mine came forward. They all knew about Elizabeth's infidelities, but they never tried to save me from the marriage. Brogan was the only one that risked my wrath by telling me that my future wife was a whore, but I couldn't forgive him," Michael said.

Jewel pushed her finger through the hole, trying to widen it for better vision. She felt the warmth of Michael's touch on her finger and withdrew it.

Jewel rested her head on her folded arms and thought about the tale she had just heard.

"Do you forgive him now?" she asked.

There was no response. Jewel could see Michael's face contorted with emotion.

"It's pointless to think about it now. I can never tell him that I forgive him, or thank him for saving me from the heartbreak of a painful marriage."

Jewel rested her head on her arm, once more, reviewing all she had heard.

"So, are you ready to believe me?" he said, sounding like his annoying self once again.

Jewel noticed how strong his Irish brogue was during the emotional telling of his past. While she was not quite ready to believe him, she still could feel herself unwillingly warming to him. She was no stranger to a broken heart. When she was left standing at the altar she hadn't wanted to talk to anyone about it. In the two years since the event she had only discussed it with two people besides her therapist: Mary, her co-worker; and Jane, her sister.

"Michael? How many people have you told this story to?"

Michael was silent for several moments.

"One."

Jewel tried to picture who he would tell; a girlfriend, cousin, co-worker?

"Who?" she asked.

"You."

Jewel didn't know what to say. She sat twirling a loose string from the Berber carpet between her fingers.

*Crap! He's tugging at my heart. Am I being played again?*

"Michael, what are they going to do with me?" Jewel asked.

"I don't know. If I can find the Danish Jubilee, then they won't have any use for us and God knows what will happen then. We may be killed and disposed of. Our only hope is to drag this crazy treasure hunt out until we find an opportunity to escape. But even if we escape, a man as powerful as Chauvin will probably find us. I'm not sure there's a limit to what he can accomplish. The man is filthy rich and very well connected. I believe he can get away with murder. He probably already has," Michael said.

"Do you think he'll frame me for Brogan's murder?" she asked.

"I'm not sure . . . probably."

This chat wasn't boosting Jewel's spirits. She thought about Brogan again. He was a cad, but in a good way. Once again she made the comparison that she had made so many times in the past few days— Michael and Brogan. Then she realized that the Michael she was talking to right now wasn't the frozen fish stick that she was used to. He had changed or she had changed or they just opened up a bit.

"Michael, you never answered me. Why are you talking to me through a wall?"

"I told you, I'm a prisoner, too. I'm locked in this room. Chauvin doesn't trust me. The only reason he wasn't drugging me was because I wasn't causing trouble, like you. Besides, I think he really hates you," he said, his voice displaying amusement.

Jewel looked through the hole to find Michael smiling. She thought of the encounter on the airplane when Chauvin pinched her cheek. Then another thought occurred to her.

"Michael, why did you kiss me?"

She watched Michael's smile grow.

"To shut you up. You were about to say something about the postcard. I didn't want them to know about it. They looked through my bag, but they just breezed right over the cards."

"They have your bag?" she asked.

"No. I have it right here. I have yours too. They forced me to check out of the hotel and get our bags. As far as anyone knows, you and I are just traveling together. No one suspects that we've been abducted."

"When did you check out of the hotel? When did you have time?"

"Jewel, it's Tuesday. You've been unconscious for quite a while," he said, tilting his head to peer through the hole.

*A day and a half. Crap! That's why I'm so hungry.*

"My job," Jewel interjected.

"It's okay. You sent your coworker, Mary, a text explaining that you needed some time off for personal reasons," Michael said.

"How?" Jewel asked. She wondered if there was some drug that made her do things without remembering.

"I sent the text. Your coworker didn't sound surprised. She did keep insisting on your 'getting back out there'," Michael said.

"She wasn't suspicious about the text?" Jewel asked.

"I don't believe so. She must be a very understanding employer," Michael said with a contemplative tone. "Although it would probably be best if you called her and just told her that you are well."

"Where are we?" she asked.

"Venetian Coast."

"What? Venice, Italy? No way."

She jumped up and ran to the window. She could make out a couple of tall structures on land, but they didn't resemble the skyscrapers found in other cities. She thought of her sister Jane.

*I'm glad Jane isn't here. I would be tempted to go to her, and that would put her in danger.*

She paced the room as she thought. She went to the door and pulled. She could hear a slight rattle.

"Michael," she said dropping to her knees once more. "How are the doors locked?"

"Padlocks. Landry put them on especially for us. I was hoping we would be locked in together."

*Crap!*

Now do you believe me that I haven't been lying to you?" Michael said as his eye flashed through the hole.

She still wasn't sure if she believed him. She paced the floor again.

"Chauvin and Landry left in a boat with some guy I didn't recognize. So, who is left here on the yacht?"

"Probably Gruber. And the boat crew. Why?"

She paced and looked around the room. She was feeling desperate.

"I have a plan," she said, as she dropped down on her knees. "Can you make this hole bigger?" she asked as she proceeded to tell him of her idea.

Chapter 10
Never Trust a Man

Jewel was prepared. She tested the statue that was on the chest of drawers. It was small, but heavy. It was a bronze statue of Aphrodite on her clam shell. Jewel closed the closet and went to the other door.

"Help! Someone, help me!" She started screaming and kicking the door. She really did try to kick the door open only to discover that it was more solid than it looked. "Let me out of here, now!"

She continued her squawking until finally she heard movement outside her door. There was a jingle of keys and the rattle of the lock. The door opened slowly. Gruber's red round face peered at her.

"You have to let me out of here. There's something in the closet, I swear," she said with excitement.

Gruber looked at her incredulously as he slid the barrel of a gun in the room.

"Please, just help me," Jewel pleaded. "Just put me in another room."

Gruber opened the door further and looked around the room. Jewel saw the syringe in his other hand. Gruber jumped back as he heard movement in the closet. Jewel inched closer to Gruber and gently touched his arm, while staring wide-eyed at the closet.

The movement in the closet was so strong that the door shuddered.

"Don't leave me alone with it, please," Jewel begged.

Gruber turned to her, with gun pointed, and she stepped back.

The violent movements made the door shudder again.

Jewel let out a yelp and moved closer to Gruber. This time he was focused on the closet.

His round face held a look of confusion.

He had the gun pointed at the closet and turned to Jewel again. Jewel held her breath. Another shudder of the doors had Gruber pointing the gun at the closet.

Jewel moved closer to Gruber until they were almost shoulder to shoulder. As they approached the closet, Jewel dropped back just a touch. Gruber watched the closet so intently that he didn't notice. He approached the closet with his gun in hand and then yanked the door open. He had only a moment of surprise when he saw a hand holding a garment hanger near the floor moving about before he received a blow to the back of the head. He grabbed his head and cried out. Jewel lunged for the gun and tossed it across the room. She sat on top of Gruber as he writhed in pain. She grabbed the filled syringe, uncapped the needle and plunged it into his leg. She stayed on top of him while he bucked. He was weak from the blow to the head, but he continued to fight while the drug took effect. She felt like she was on a mechanical bull ride until the movement slowed, his eyes fluttered and then closed. While still lying on top of him, she searched the fat folds on Gruber's neck until she found a pulse. She hated the man, but she didn't want to be responsible for his death.

She looked up to see Michael peering at her through the hole.

"Jewel?" he said, his voice frantic.

"I'm okay!"

She searched Gruber's pockets for the ring of keys. She locked Gruber in the room and went down the hall. She stood in front of Michael's door. As she searched through the keys, she stopped and wondered if it was wise to release him.

*Can I trust him? No, not really.*

She started to walk away, but turned around and returned to the door when she thought about what Chauvin would do to Michael when he realized that Michael helped her escape.

She slid the key into the lock. With a click she opened the lock and swung open the door. Michael looked at Jewel with an unguarded smile.

"You did it," he said, as he stepped forward, but stopped uncomfortably, after noticing the look in her eyes. He reached down and grabbed the two duffle bags. "Let's go."

They slowly moved down the hall and out onto the deck. The smell of the Gulf overtook her senses. She shielded her eyes from the harsh sun.

"Stay here," Michael said. He stepped around the corner, and returned after a few seconds. He went in the other direction, and returned again. "Well, apparently, the boat Chauvin left in was the only life boat."

"So, now what?" Jewel asked.

"We swim."

"Swim?" she said, looking out toward the land. She could see two strips of land and wondered which one Michael intended to swim to. "That has to be like three or four hundred yards. You don't even know where we are," she said.

"The Gulf of Venice," he replied, as he disappeared around a corner again. He returned holding a life preserver. The donut-shaped flotation device had the name, *Gloria,* printed on it, which Jewel assumed was the name of the yacht. Michael disappeared once more and returned with two orange life vests. He handed one to Jewel, then slid one on his body and buckled it. He slipped off his loafers and shoved them into his duffle bag. He deftly tied the bags atop the life preserver and walked to the side of the boat. He was ever watchful as he stepped down the ladder and into the water.

"Pass down the ring with the bags," he whispered.

She passed the ring down. He set it on the water where it bounced up and down with the waves.

"Come on," he said, reaching a hand up to Jewel.

"I don't want to do this," Jewel said, pulling on the life vest. "What if there are sharks?"

"I would rather take my chances with the sharks than with Chauvin," Michael told her. "You didn't see how he beat the crap out of Landry because he didn't stop you from running to the cockpit on the jet. The guy is a monster."

Her brain instantly went to old Noir gangster films.

"Either way we're swimming with the fishes," she said as she stared down into the water.

"Jewel," Michael said, as he looked at her with pleading green eyes. "Please get in the water."

Jewel turned around and slowly backed down the ladder. The skirt of her dress was in the way and she could see a real problem.

"This isn't going to work," she said.

"Can you pull it up and tie it or something?"

Jewel started to pull the dress up then looked at Michael. "Turn around," she commanded.

He rolled his eyes, but turned to face the shore.

Jewel pulled the skirt of her dress up and threaded it through her life vest causing it to look like a billowy halter top. She stepped quickly down into the water. Michael held the ladder until she joined him. He put his arm around her and pulled her to the life ring.

"We'll both hold onto this and kick," he said, indicating the life ring with the duffle bags.

Jewel held on and they began kicking.

"I just hope no one from the ship sees us," Michael said.

Jewel looked past the duffle bags and concentrated on the land. She kicked with all her might at first, but she was tiring easily, so she paced herself. Michael kicked at a steady pace. Jewel tried to look back at the yacht, but her life vest constricted her head movements, so she couldn't see it.

"Are you doing all right?" Michael asked.

Jewel didn't speak. She nodded in response.

From the yacht she had noticed a few boats travelling between them and the shore, but none of the boats were nearing their path.

*This is crazy. I wonder if we can go to the police. Would they even believe us?*

Michael saw it at the same time as Jewel—a boat was cruising toward them. Jewel started breathing harder in fear. Michael increased the pace of his kicks. At about fifty yards away, the boat veered slightly, changing its course. Jewel wasn't sure if the boat's driver saw them or not. She hadn't realized that her quick shallow breathing continued even after the boat had passed, but Michael noticed.

"You should take a rest," he said. "Let go of the life ring and hold on to my vest. I'll pull you along for a while," he said.

"No," she insisted.

She didn't think it would be fair for Michael to exhaust himself. It brought a question to mind. She turned and examined his face.

"When was the last time you've slept?" she asked, noticing the dark smudges beneath his eyes.

"I slept a bit on the plane," he replied, avoiding eye contact.

"Maybe you should take a rest," she said.

He turned to look at her. Their faces were about eight inches apart. She marveled at his green eyes for a moment, but quickly turned away.

"No, I'm fine," he said.

Jewel was certain he was smiling. She could hear it in his voice.

As they drew closer to the shore, Jewel saw that it was a beach teeming with tourists in bathing suits. She was thrilled to see other people. She craved the comfort and safety of a crowd. She pondered for a moment how she had always avoided crowds because they made her feel anxious and closed in, but right now she wanted a crowd—a big one.

They were getting much closer to the shore. Jewel was feeling somewhat giddy from the experience.

"Let's rest a minute," Jewel said, laying her head on her arms that stretched out in front of her. She closed her eyes and took deep calming breaths. She opened her eyes to find Michael in the same position as she. He had droplets of water on his face that caught the sun and sparkled.

Jewel closed her eyes again. She took another deep breath then lifted her head and started kicking.

They were very close now.

"We may be in luck," Michael said. "I think this is Lido. I have a friend on Lido. At least I did. I hope he still works here."

"What is Lido?" Jewel asked.

"An island and beach resort near Venice."

Jewel could make out structures. The beaches were crowded. She saw the chairs and umbrellas lining the sandy shore.

She started thinking about Chauvin and what action he might take when he discovered their escape. Her stomach tightened into a knot. She tried to turn around to look at the yacht, but found herself suddenly fighting against the life vest. Her hands slipped off the life ring and her face went into the water. She sputtered and flailed. Michael caught her around her waist and pulled her back to the ring. She grabbed it with both hands.

"What was that all about?" Michael asked.

"I was trying to see the yacht," she said.

Michael released one hand from the life ring and swam on his side allowing him to look toward the yacht.

"Chauvin is back," he said without alarm. He increased his kicks.

Jewel started to panic. She was kicking as fast as humanly possible.

"It won't take him long to realize we're gone," she said. She guessed they were about thirty yards from the seawall.

"Michael, what are we going to do?"

"Just kick."

Twenty more yards.

The distance was closing fast, but not fast enough for Jewel. She released the ring with one hand and tried to turn around like Michael had.

"No," Michael said. "Focus on the shore. Don't look back."

Jewel obeyed.

Ten more yards.

Jewel felt like her heart was going to explode. She was waning. Michael put his arm around Jewel's waist. She could feel his powerful kicks propelling them through the water.

"Come on, you can make it," he urged.

Jewel made a kick that impacted with something, only to discover it was the sandy bottom. Michael was already getting to his feet. He pulled Jewel as he went. She got to her feet and pulled at her dress trying to release it from the vest. Finally it fell around her body and clung to her legs like sticky octopus tentacles. Michael was struggling to pull the duffle bags and remove his life vest at the same time. Jewel grabbed the life ring and bags so that Michael could remove his vest. The vest fell into the water and floated on the waves. He then grabbed the bags and ring. Jewel removed her vest and dropped it. As they moved closer to the shore they drew the attention of the beach crowds.

Fully clothed and dripping wet, they finally emerged from the Gulf. People stared and pointed as they darted away from the water.

"We're drawing too much attention," Jewel said.

"I don't think they can come any closer to the beach with the yacht. I think it may be against the law," Michael said.

"Well, the law hasn't stopped them yet," Jewel responded.

Michael dropped the ring and bags. He was pulling at the knots. They had swelled and tightened with the water. Finally the bags came free. Jewel grabbed the strap of her bag, but Michael snatched it from her hand

and hoisted both bag straps onto his shoulder. He grabbed Jewel's hand and they were off again.

"Where are we going?" Jewel gasped.

"Away."

The sand made it difficult to run, especially with legs already exhausted from the long swim. Jewel turned as she looked for the boat. Laws be damned, the small boat that Chauvin was in earlier pulled close enough to drop off Landry. The man looked as strange on the beach in his chauffeur uniform as Jewel and Michael had.

Jewel wasn't sure where Michael was taking her, but she let him lead the way. The crowds were thinner between the rows of bathers and the hotels. That is the path Michael searched. People pointed and gaped as they ran by.

"We're drawing too much attention," Jewel repeated.

She looked back. Landry was on the beach, searching. He looked up, spotted his prey, and burst into a run. Michael and Jewel increased their speed in response. They ran through a breezeway and into the lobby of a hotel. They were confronted with disapproving looks. Jewel was dripping water from the folds of her dress and Michael was wearing sand-covered socks. They were a spectacle and people were gawking.

They continued through the lobby and exited out the front door. They ran to another hotel. Jewel kept glancing behind, but saw no sign of Landry. As they entered the hotel, Michael slowed his pace; Jewel pulled her hand away from his. She grabbed her side trying to alleviate the stitch that had formed there. She couldn't catch her breath.

"We have to keep moving," Michael said to her bent form.

She shook her head. She looked up and noticed the door with the letters W.C. posted above. She grabbed Michael's hand and pulled him inside the restroom. She grabbed her duffle bag, unzipped it, and began rummaging through the contents.

"Turn around," she told Michael breathlessly.

"What are you doing?"

"Do you have a swimsuit in your bag?"

"No," he replied.

"Well, go out to the desk and ask for scissors," she demanded.

Michael understood her plan and left the room. Jewel was not sure how long it would take for Michael to return, so she changed as quickly as possible. As she was dropping her wet dress and underwear into the trash bin, the door swung open. Jewel spun around with a start. A man was standing in the threshold. He said something in a foreign language.

"I will be out in a moment," she said, while using her hands as a signal to back him out the restroom.

Michael returned holding a scissors. Jewel took the scissors, dropped to her knees and began cutting the legs of Michael's pants. Michael started taking off his shirt. Jewel pulled his pant legs and socks off and tossed them into the trash bin atop her dress.

"Let's go," she said, grabbing her duffle bag and pulling it onto her shoulder.

Michael followed. They exited the restroom and after dropping the scissors on the front desk, exited the building.

"They kept asking me if I'm a hotel guest," Michael warned. "These beaches must be private and belong to the hotels. We might run into trouble."

"We're already in trouble!"

They joined the crowded line of people along the shore. Jewel picked a spot and sat down. She was still breathing heavily.

"I just need to rest for a little bit, please Michael," she said as she dug in her bag. She pulled out a scarf, folded it, and formed a head covering to cover her hair. She pulled out some sunglasses and handed them to Michael. He put the glasses on and looked down at her. He reached out, took her hand, and gave it a little squeeze. Jewel looked to the water searching for Chauvin's boat, but saw nothing.

"Where do you think they are?" she asked, still breathing rapidly.

"Probably docking somewhere so they can search the beach."

Jewel looked up at him with fear in her eyes. He squeezed her hand again to reassure her. She studied him. His cut pants would have been more convincing had they not been made of sturdy twill. Although his attire was casual, Michael had his usual stiff posture, which reminded Jewel of a Military line-up. Her eyes moved over his body. His chest was smooth with a small patch of dark hair in the middle. He turned to check for signs of Landry, and she surveyed his shoulders and back. She was surprised by what she found behind his left shoulder. She leaned back slightly for a better look. He had a tattoo of an elaborate Celtic knot that was very similar to the one she had seen on his wallet. She thought back to the night in the restaurant and realized it was only a few days ago, but it felt like weeks.

"I think we should get moving," he said.

"Where?"

"I'm not positive, but I have an idea."

He reached down and pulled Jewel to her feet. He took her bag as they walked with the crowds down the beach.

"I'll be right back," he said, walking toward a man. Jewel watched. The man was wearing shorts and a shirt. Jewel noticed the shirt sported a logo, but she didn't recognize it. From her distance she couldn't understand what was being said, but then realized that distance was not the problem; they weren't speaking English. Michael returned to Jewel.

"This way," Michael said, taking her hand.

"Do you speak Italian?" Jewel asked.

"Yes, why?"

Jewel shook her head in response. She felt safer being with someone who spoke the native language.

They continued down the beach, looking carefully around for their pursuers. Jewel was exhausted and when Michael turned toward a hotel, she didn't even question him. The hotel looked expensive. They walked into the lobby, Michael approached the desk, and conversed with the clerk in Italian. The clerk picked up the telephone, made a call, then spoke to Michael again.

"Let's wait here," Michael said, pulling Jewel to the side and leaning against a wall. Jewel leaned beside him and closed her eyes. She realized that they were still holding hands. She dropped his hand and took a deep breath. A man in his late thirties approached. He had dark curly hair with thick eyebrows. He walked very quickly to Michael with open arms. He kissed Michael on each cheek and began chattering in Italian. Michael added a few words. Jewel watched as the tone of the conversation turned serious. The curly-haired man was nodding his head as he listened to Michael. He looked at Jewel and the corners of his mouth curled up. Michael continued to speak, but the man didn't appear to be listening. The man stepped closer to Jewel and smiled. He reached up and twirled one of his thick eyebrows in a sinister way.

"I am Phillip Costa, but you can call me Pepo," the man said, reaching out and grabbing Jewel's hand. He gave her a sly smile exposing yellow teeth. He lifted her hand and kissed it softly. Michael said something in Italian. Pepo took on a look of surprise. He glanced from Michael then back to Jewel. A laugh came deep from his gut. He grabbed Jewel by the shoulders and kissed her on both cheeks.

"Okay, we do it," he said, releasing Jewel and walking behind the hotel desk.

"What's going on?" Jewel asked.

"We're getting a hotel room. Pepo and I go way back. Of all the places in Italy, it is a miracle that we ended up in Lido," Michael said, as he made a quick gesture of touching his forehead, chest, and then both his shoulders.

Pepo returned and made a sign with his head for them to follow. They climbed one flight of stairs. Pepo unlocked and opened the door to a room. Jewel and Michael stepped inside.

"I can't stay, but let me know if you need anything else," Pepo said with a strong Italian accent, then handed Michael the room key. The two men had a few words in Italian. The conversation must have led to something comical by the tone. Pepo had a large smile as he made his way to the door. Michael was about to shut the door when Pepo popped his head back in. "*Signorina*, if you need anything then you call Pepo," he said before Michael pushed the man out of the room.

The room was small, but lovely. Jewel went to the window and looked out. The beach lay below with its crowds. She searched, but didn't see any sign of Chauvin or Landry. Michael dropped the bags and startled Jewel out of her thoughts.

He opened his duffle and started pulling things out.

"Here is another miracle," Michael said, holding something up. Jewel recognized the blue exterior of a United States passport.

"Is that mine?"

"No, mine. It's a miracle that they didn't take it," Michael said.

She stepped forward and looked at the cover.

"You're a U.S. citizen?" she asked.

"Yes, my father was American. I thought Brogan would have told you that," he said.

"I wonder if I still have my passport."

She went to her bag and emptied it of its contents. Much to her dismay her clothes were wet. Not dripping like her dress was, but damp. She found her passport in her makeup bag, where she had stored it. She removed clothes from the bag and began laying them out to dry.

"Damn, my phone is gone," Jewel stated. She pulled the small book that she used as her journal. The pages were wet. She tried to fan them out to dry.

"My phone is gone too," he said as he looked up at her. "I don't think that book is going to survive," he said as he watched Jewel.

She tossed the journal aside and began biting her right thumb nail.

"Michael, do you think we'll be safe here?"

"Yes. Pepo is doing us a great favor. He is giving us this room and he isn't taking our passports during our stay. He has us registered as Mr. and Mrs. Daniel LaRusso."

"Daniel LaRusso? As in the *The Karate Kid*?" Jewel chuckled as she continued emptying her bag until something occurred to her that stopped her progress. "Umm, there's only one bed."

"That's the best we could do. We're lucky to get a room at all especially one with a private bath."

Jewel had not slept beside a man in over two years. She wondered if the inconvenience of one bed was a ploy. She narrowed her eyes as she looked at Michael. He was busy with his bag and didn't notice. He seemed harmless, but she spent so much energy hating him. She wondered in that moment if she would ever be able to trust a man. She had been chanting her mantra of "never trust a man" for two years. She wondered if she had poisoned herself against ever finding a relationship again. Michael felt eyes upon him and looked up. Jewel was still looking at him with suspicion.

"What? What have I done now?" Michael asked.

"Nothing . . . You trust this Pepo person?"

"Yes. I would trust Pepo with my life as well as yours," Michael stated.

"Don't bargain my life so easily. How do you know him?"

"We used to spend holidays here in Lido when I was a boy. My aunt owned a small villa nearby. That's how I learned Italian and how I met Pepo. You could say we grew up together. His family owned this hotel when I was young, but a corporate chain bought out his family. He still works here as an assistant manager. He is a very good man and we can trust him," Michael said with conviction.

Jewel was running low on trust, but she was also running low on options.

"May I have the first shower?" she asked.

Michael gestured to the bathroom without looking up.

Jewel showered. She was grateful that they had a private bathroom, as she crept out in only a towel. Michael was standing by the window when she entered. He turned around and stared. He kept his stony face, but Jewel detected the humor in his eyes.

Jewel pulled the cover off the bed and wrapped it around her body like a toga. She lay on the bed trying to decide if she were more hungry than tired while Michael showered. Tired was winning the debate when

Michael exited the bathroom wearing a towel around his waist. He stood beside the bed looking at Jewel.

"Do you mind if I join you?" he asked.

Jewel's eyes grew large at the question, but she remained silent.

"I would rather not sleep on the floor," he added.

Jewel felt silly for a moment.

*Of course Michael wasn't suggesting anything romantic or sexual. The guy probably never thinks about sex. Wait, he's a man, Jewel. "Never trust a man."*

She moved over and Michael lay back upon the bed. She wondered what Brogan would do if he had been here with her, rather than Michael. The thought brought a smile to her face, as she knew exactly what Brogan would do.

"What are you thinking about?" Michael asked.

Jewel looked over to find him watching her with the smallest smile upon his lips.

"I was just thinking about Brogan," she answered truthfully.

His smile vanished. He rolled over to face the wall. Jewel stared at his back.

"So, tell me about the tattoo."

"It's just something I got when I was young and foolish."

"It's pretty."

"Men don't like to hear that their tattoos are pretty . . . it's somewhat emasculating." Something in his tone alerted Jewel.

"Are you angry with me?"

"No," he replied.

Michael pulled the sheet up above his waist and rolled over onto his back. Jewel felt the bed move as he turned.

She continued to stare at the ceiling. She was reviewing the events that had led them to this point. She thought that there was nothing stopping her from going to the police. She could tell them that she was abducted and tell them all about Chauvin and his stolen eggs. Once she reviewed her options, she realized that Chauvin was more powerful than she knew. He probably has a cop or two in his employ.

*He could make my life miserable . . . that is if he didn't just kill me.*

She was feeling the fear and exhaustion of the past days washing over her. It felt as if a large weight had finally crushed her and she was having trouble breathing. To her surprise, she felt warm salty tears well up in her eyes and roll down her cheeks.

Michael reached over and wiped a tear away. She quickly turned her head to look at him. Sympathy dwelled in his green eyes.

"Shh," he comforted.

His kind gesture opened a floodgate inside of Jewel. More tears followed, but she didn't know where they were coming from. She didn't cry very often. She chalked it up to emotional exhaustion and perhaps side effects of the sedatives she had been given. When the tears flowed freely Michael moved closer, put his arms around Jewel, and pulled her head onto his chest. She was startled at first, but liked the feeling. She hadn't been held in years. Michael cooed in his Irish tongue as he stroked her head. He held her in his arms. She could feel the rise and fall of his chest. She could hear whimpering and realized with alarm that the sound was coming from her own mouth. She suddenly felt ashamed and buried her face into his side. He gently stroked her head and whispered calming words in the odd language. The whimpering stopped and she took comfort in his touch. At first she wanted to object. She wanted to protest. She wanted to scream that he was an ass, a fool, and he had no right to touch her. However, she loved the smell of him. She loved his touch. It had been so long since someone had touched her like this. Yes, Brogan had touched her. He kissed her. He made parts of her that had been asleep wake up and say, "Hey, remember me?" This touch was different. This touch spoke words of comfort. Michael's touch said things like: "I'm here for you, I won't let anything hurt you, I will comfort you, let me heal your pain."

Jewel became overwhelming self-conscious.

*He must think I'm insane. Hell, I might be, but I don't like him to see me like this.*

"This is because of the drugs," she told him. "That's why I'm crying, okay, so don't get any ideas. This is just because of the drugs," she sobbed.

Michael didn't respond to her explanation, but continued to comfort her. Jewel didn't want to move. She stayed perfectly still. Only her breath stirred a few loose strands of her hair. It didn't take long for exhaustion to overcome them. They both fell asleep within a few moments.

Chapter 11
The Stupidest Trusting Fool on the Planet

Gentle light filled the room.

*Have I been asleep for hours or days?*

Jewel stretched her arms over her head, but grabbed at the blanket when she remembered that she wasn't wearing any clothes. She thought about Michael comforting her last night, and how wonderful it had felt to be held. But this morning the memory made her uncomfortable. She looked beside her to confirm her suspicions. The space was empty.

"Michael," she called.

No answer.

She got out of bed with the cover still wrapped around her naked body. She poked her head in to the bathroom, but it was empty. She looked around the room for a note or a sign of where he had gone, but saw nothing.

Michael's clothes were gone. Jewel realized that her clothes were gone, too. All the clothes that she had laid out to dry were gone along with her duffle bag. Only her sandals and tennis shoes remained on the floor where her bag once sat. She walked into the bathroom. At least her makeup bag was still there, along with her passport. She returned to the bed and sat down.

*Crap! Did he really steal my clothes? I must be the stupidest trusting fool on the planet.*

She wondered how long she would be able to sit in the hotel room naked before they would kick her out. She was reflecting on how she could get some clothes when the sound of the doorknob turning brought her to attention.

*Oh, no. Chauvin!*

She wildly wondered if Michael, after stealing her clothes, had ratted her out to Chauvin. She scurried to her feet and pressed her body against the wall. She thought she could perhaps take the person by surprise and therefore escape. She held her breath as the door opened, and then closed gently as if the person was trying to be very quiet. As the figure stepped past, Jewel lunged forward to get to the door, but the folds of the blanket wrapped around her body caused her to fall with a thud. She quickly looked up to find Michael blinking down at her.

"What are you doing down there?" he said with his Irish brogue.

Jewel struggled to her feet.

"You stole my clothes!"

"No, I didn't. I dried them," he said as he dropped her duffle bag on the floor beside her.

She noticed he carried his own duffle bag along with a few other bags.

"The clothes were still wet when I awoke, so I took them downstairs to the laundry facility. They're a little stiff from the saltwater, but there was no time to wash them. I just threw them into the dryer," he said, as he walked to the small table near the window and set down the bags. "I got you some tea," he said, opening a brown paper bag and carefully removing two paper cups with lids. "I also brought you a couple of croissants for breakfast," he said.

Jewel was touched by the kindness. She felt silly for her anger and suspicion. She closed the space between them and took the tea he now held out to her. She looked up into his eyes and smiled. To her surprise he returned the smile.

"I thought the worst," she said honestly.

Michael tilted his head in confusion.

"I thought you stole my clothes and ran off," she added.

"What would I do with your wee dresses? They're not my style," he said with unusual humor.

Michael was smiling. She stared at his bright face and stored the memory. She hoped she would see the smile again, but she wasn't going to hold her breath.

"I also bought these," he said, holding up a large bag. He dumped the contents onto the bed. Two backpacks fell out. "I think these will serve us better. Which would you like, the green or the blue?"

Jewel shrugged. She was still marveling at the change in Michael. She sat down at the small table and sipped her tea, while watching him emptying the duffle bags onto the bed. She picked up a croissant and was about to take a bite when Michael began humming. Jewel froze in mid-bite. This was too much. She watched him carefully as he went about his task humming a jolly tune.

"What's going on?" she asked, setting down the croissant.

"What do you mean?" he said, glancing at her.

"You're different. You're smiling and . . . humming."

A smile spread on his face.

"I am, aren't I?"

Jewel ate in silence, contemplating her companion.

"I have assessed things. We are incredibly lucky that Chauvin didn't take our passports or money. A mistake due to his arrogance, I'm sure. So, we will pack our things into the backpacks, get dressed, and set out to find the Danish Jubilee," Michael said, returning to his no nonsense manner. But there was still something different. He had a spring in his step. He made it sound like a solid plan and he spoke it with confidence.

"Michael, why not go to the police?"

"Well, if I'm not mistaken, Chauvin has probably already drawn suspicion to you for Brogan's murder. And re-located his collection of stolen eggs. With unlimited power and money, he has the upper hand. The way I see it, all we can do is find the Danish Jubilee before he does, and hope to trade it for our safety and for your exoneration. We were intending to come here and look for clues before the visit to New Orleans, so we will continue on that course. Where did Brogan stay when he was in Venice?" Michael asked.

"Just a minute. You're saying that if we find it, you'd be willing to give up the Danish Jubilee?" she asked, her eyes studying him for any sign of dishonesty.

He sighed heavily and shook his head.

"It's an amazing treasure. It is a treasure that the world should be able to enjoy, but we're up against a man that is powerful, rich, and

135

obviously lacking a conscience. He's dangerous. Yes . . . I'm willing to give up the Danish Jubilee if it means we can walk away from this safely."

"What makes you think Chauvin would allow us to walk away?"

"Well, I can't be sure he will, but I think the egg is the only leverage we have."

She finished her croissants and tea, grabbed a change of clothes, and went into the bathroom. She felt relieved to be out of her bedspread toga. She combed her hair, but was disappointed to find that all of her hair pins were gone. Her hair hung just below her shoulders. The frizzy curls sprung up and framed her face. She repacked her toiletries and exited the bathroom. She walked to her new backpack and tossed her makeup bag inside.

"Are we going to bring all our stuff, or will we come back to this room?" she asked.

"We will probably spend another night here, but bring your stuff. We never know what will happen," he said as he looked up at her from the floor. "Jewel, do you have anything to wear that is more suited to, er, sports?" Michael said, looking at Jewel's long gauzy skirt and blouse.

Jewel looked down at her clothes.

"Well, I plan on wearing my tennis shoes," she replied.

"I mean, do you have any trousers?"

"No," she said. "I almost never wear trousers . . . pants."

"Why is that?"

"The Wish Book," Jewel stated as her lips tightened into a frown.

"The what?"

"I don't want to talk about it right now."

"So you don't have anything else to wear?"

Her temper was rising. She knew it was silly to be angered by his questions, but she could feel the blood filling her cheeks. She waited for him to say something rude or "Michael-like" but, she realized that he hadn't been rude for a while. She swallowed back the anger that had quickly risen and gave him a smile.

"Nope, this is all I've got," she said, spreading her arms and turning a circle. She noticed him look her up and down. The corners of his mouth turned up slightly.

"You look nice," he said.

The compliment made her uncomfortable. She was never good at receiving compliments. She smoothed out her skirt and folded her arms.

"Thanks," she said. She looked Michael over. He was wearing Khaki pants again with a pale blue shirt. His thick dark hair was perfectly in place and he was freshly shaven. "You look nice, too."

*I can't believe we're standing here exchanging pleasantries. This man has been rude, and cold, and he kissed me . . . yeah, he kissed me. I really don't like him. Why did he kiss me again? Oh, yeah, to shut me up. I really don't like him.*

"Are we ready?"

"One more thing. I got you this," Michael said, handing her a small pouch with a long strap.

"A fanny pack?"

Michael made a sound like he was trying to stop himself from laughing.

"That's not a good word," he said.

"What? Fanny pack?"

"Yes. Where I'm from, the word 'fanny' is what we call the female . . . er," he stuttered, waving he hands indicating the space below his belt. "The female parts."

137

Jewel's mouth opened wide in shock.

"Are you okay?" Michael asked after several seconds passed and Jewel had not moved.

"Yeah, I'm just thinking about the Bee Gees song 'Fanny' and it has a whole new meaning for me."

Michael turned his head away from Jewel and she could see his shoulders moving with laughter.

"This is not a *fanny pack*. It's a money belt. Please put your money and passport in it. I've got one too," he said. He began unbuttoning his shirt.

"You have a fanny pack too? Cool."

After donning her money belt under her blouse she was ready. She stood by the door with her backpack.

"You still haven't told me where Brogan stayed when he was here," he said.

"Hotel Alexa."

She had not stayed at the hotel with Brogan, and had only stepped into the lobby so he could change his shoes. But she felt that it wasn't necessary to mention such details at this time.

Chapter 12
Basilica dei Frari


The sun was bright. It was past noon when the water taxi carried them to Venice. They disembarked near Piazza San Marco. As soon as Jewel stepped off the boat, Michael caught her hand.

"We need to stay away from the touristy places," he said. He pulled her away from the stream of people. "Do you remember where Hotel Alexa is?"

"Well, no, not really. It was near a big church. Brogan told me it was a famous church. I don't remember the name, but it was kind of like Ferrari," Jewel said, sheepishly.

"Frari?" Michael asked.

"Yeah, do you know where it is?"

"If you are referring to the Basilica di Santa Maria Gloriosa dei Frari, then I have a general idea of where it is. Stay here," he said, then walked to a gondolier and chatted with him. He handed the gondolier some money, then returned. "He said it is in San Polo which is this way," he said, taking Jewel's hand and walking through the crowds.

They purchased tickets for the *vaporetto* or water bus and boarded. Michael had been holding her hand through the crowds. When they sat down on the *vaporetto*, Jewel noticed that he still held her hand. She wasn't sure what to make of this development.

*Why is he being so nice to me? Perhaps he needs me for something and after he's used me, he'll run off. Maybe he'll take the egg with him and leave me to answer to Chauvin.*

She pulled her hand away and set it on her leg. Despite their circumstances, she loved being back in Venice. She looked down into the green canal. She thought of Brogan joking that the water was that color because it was so polluted that the fish kept puking. Of course it was just a joke. She unknowingly smiled.

"What's so funny?" Michael asked, as he reached over and casually took her hand.

"I was just thinking of something Brogan told me."

Michael became sullen and quiet.

*Just the mention of his brother's name turns him cold. He must really be torn up about his death, or he hated him that much. Okay, Jewel, you need to be more sensitive. This guy just lost his brother.*

When they reached their stop, Michael exited and Jewel rushed to follow. He walked at a quick pace and Jewel struggled to keep up. His long legs gave him an advantage. She followed behind him through a few turns then was surprised when they stepped out in front of the church she had visited the week before.

Michael approached a vendor and spoke to him in Italian. Jewel waited. The man shook his head. Michael approached another man and spoke. They were too far away for Jewel to hear their words. The man was pointing and talking, while Michael was nodding his head.

Michael began walking in the direction the man indicated. Jewel had to jog to catch up.

"Hold on," she said, grabbing Michael's arm. "Are you trying to lose me?"

"No," he snapped. "Perhaps you should just go somewhere and hide out until this is all over. I will find the egg and bargain with Chauvin for your safety as well as mine."

"Get real. Like I'm going to trust you," Jewel said.

Michael's face contorted. "What do I have to do for you to trust me? I have cuts and lumps on my head right now from trying to protect you. What is it about me that you don't trust?" he said as he stared into her eyes. "Or is it just men in general . . . how is it you could trust Brogan and not trust me? You trusted him, a thief, a liar, but you cannot trust me," he stated with anger.

Jewel didn't know why. But now that she thought about it there was no need to trust Brogan. They had only spent the day together. An issue of real trust never came up. She wondered if it was time to come clean about her relationship with Brogan. But she wasn't ready to come clean. She realized at that moment that the reason she didn't tell Michael the truth was because she liked the lie. She liked the thought of someone, anyone, believing that she had a relationship. She wanted someone to believe that a man would like her enough to have romantic feelings for her. The realization was painful. She stared down at the ground and didn't respond.

"Let's just go," Michael said, turning and walking away.

When they first noticed the sign for Hotel Alexa, Michael stopped. He looked around.

"Keep alert," he told Jewel.

They entered the small hotel. A slender woman who looked to be in her seventies was standing behind a desk. She looked up at the pair, as they entered the tiny lobby. The woman's dark eyes grew to an enormous size as she watched them. She mouthed something while she touched her forehead, the center of her chest, then her left and right shoulders.

Jewel recognized the Catholic sign of the cross and realized that Michael had done the same thing the day before. This woman looked terrified. She was mumbling something in Italian. As the couple drew nearer, the woman took off at a quick pace into another room.

"*Mi scusi*," Michael called to the woman.

"Well, that was weird," Jewel said.

Michael started to walk toward the door where the woman disappeared, but before he could reach it a man stepped out. The man also wore a look of shock like he had seen a ghost. Jewel suddenly realized what was going on.

"The hotel is closed," he said, wiping his hands on a towel.

He was looking at Michael from the time he walked in, but now his gaze turned to Jewel. He blinked several times and shook his head.

"My name is Michael Walsh. Brogan Walsh was my brother."

The man tapped his own head as if he just remembered something. He reached out and shook Michael's hand.

"I am Mario. My mother ran into the kitchen and told me you were a ghost. But, when I see the lady, I remember her and know that she did not die here. Forgive me. I am very sorry for your brother's death," he said. "We liked your brother very much. He would stay here every time he came to Venice."

"Did he come to Venice often?" Michael asked.

"About once per year. A couple of years ago, he stayed for about two months," Mario said.

"Did he leave anything behind?"

"No, I gave everything to the police. You would have to see them for his things."

"Could we see the room?" Michael asked.

"I'm sorry. The hotel is closed since the fire," Mario said.

"Please," Michael pleaded.

Mario studied Michael for a moment.

"Okay, I understand. I have a brother, too. But please be careful," Mario said.

They followed Mario up the stairs. Jewel touched the wall on the way up, but when she looked at her hand it was covered in black soot.

"We are going to have to clean all the walls and ceilings," Mario said when he saw Jewel looking at her hand. "Everything will need to be wiped down. This room will have to be completely fixed. It was one of our best rooms. It has a private bath," he said as he opened a door.

The smell was horrible. Jewel had never smelled anything like it before. The bed was gone, but the rest of the blackened furniture remained.

"We were lucky that the fire was discovered shortly after it started. I'm sorry that Mr. Walsh was not so lucky," Mario said, handing Jewel the towel he held so she could wipe her hands.

Jewel looked at the rectangular shape on the floor where the bed had once stood. It was the only spot that was not covered with black. She turned away from the horrific sight and walked to a window. The window was positioned on the side of the building and was about three feet from a balcony. If she stepped to the side she could see a small café on the street.

"And you saw no one that was not a guest come upstairs?" Michael asked.

Jewel turned to look at Mario.

"No, like I told the police. I saw no one."

A woman's voice softly called from downstairs.

"Ah, I better let my mother know you're not a ghost. Please take your time," he said, turning and leaving.

Jewel stared at the clean area on the floor again.

*This is where Brogan died.*

She and Michael looked at each other. Both their eyes shone with moisture. She was shocked to see Michael, the stone-faced man, with eyes sparkling with tears. She set down the towel that Mario had given her and wrung her hands for a moment. Michael walked around the room looking under furniture. As he passed by Jewel, she touched his arm. He stopped and looked at her. She stepped in front of him, reached up and put her arms around him. She wanted to comfort him. She felt he needed it, but she also needed to be comforted.

*He may be a liar, but he's also grieving.*

They stood holding each other in the charred remains of Brogan's room.

"Let me look around a bit more and then we'll go, okay?" Michael said in a soft voice.

Jewel stood in the middle of the room, sniffling, as Michael moved to the bathroom to continue his search.

She looked at the black ceiling and wondered how the room was still intact with so much damage.

Jewel stepped to the window and looked down at the street once again. Something caught her eye that caused her to jump away from the window.

"Michael, we have company," Jewel called out.

Michael rushed to Jewel's side. Seated at a table at the café across from the hotel was Gruber. Jewel noticed a white bandage on the back of his bald head, which gave her a vague sense of satisfaction that the blow she gave him had had a lasting effect. Michael mumbled something in Irish.

"Did he see us come in?"

"I'm not sure. He's not paying very close attention to the door. Let's get out of here," he said, taking Jewel by the hand and heading down the stairs.

"Did you see that balcony? There was a balcony almost touching the window to Brogan's room. Maybe that's how the murderer got in," she said as Michael was pulling her down the stairs.

After talking to Mario, they exited through a back door that led to an alleyway used for garbage pickup. With this route they were able to access the street from two buildings down, therefore avoiding Gruber. They ducked into a small bakery. Michael stepped to the window and watched the street while Jewel looked around the shop.

"So, now what?" Jewel asked.

"I don't know," Michael said as he ran his fingers through his hair. Jewel noticed that his hair was different than when she first met him. When he walked into her house a few days ago Jewel found him to be so stiff. His hair was straight and well groomed. Now his hair had waves like it was fighting its instinct to curl. It reminded her of Brogan's hair.

A brief smile touched her lips as she watched Michael. He froze in his movements and his face made a transformation as a smile formed. Jewel followed his gaze out the window to understand his change, but saw nothing.

"A map. I need a map of Venice," he said. He turned to the bakery worker at the counter and spoke in Italian. The conversation was brief. Michael looked disappointed, but then he nodded his head with a smile, grabbed Jewel's hand, and pulled her out to the street.

"Where are we going?"

"Basilica dei Frari," he responded. He pulled her along through the crowd until they were standing in front of the huge church.

"Why are we here?" Jewel asked.

Michael didn't respond, but pulled Jewel into the church. Jewel's eyes adjusted to the dim interior. She tilted her head to look up at the high ceiling.

"Wow," Jewel said in a hushed voice. The interior was amazing. She turned to Michael, but he wasn't where he was supposed to be. He was down on one knee.

*Oh crap. He fell.*

He made the Catholic sign of the cross; touching his forehead, center of his chest, left shoulder, and then the right shoulder. His eyes were fixed on the front of the church. As he stood he looked around the ornate house of worship. Jewel was a little uncomfortable and wondered if she too should get on one knee and make the sign of the cross.

"Are you Catholic?" she asked.

"Obviously," he whispered as he grabbed her hand and walked with purpose to one side of the church. There were three narrow doors on a beautifully ornate wooden structure. Michael looked about at the tourists walking around the building snapping photos. He opened the door on the far left. He quickly stepped inside and shut the door.

Jewel stood in silence for a moment.

"Michael?" she whispered.

He came out of the door quickly and went to the door to the far right, skipping the one in the middle. Once again he disappeared within the wooden structure.

"What are you doing?" Jewel asked.

Michael quickly exited the door. His brow was furrowed in confusion. He looked around the church and spotted what he was seeking. On the other side of the church there was another structure with three doors. He walked to the structure at a quick pace. There was a couple taking photos nearby. Michael stood waiting for the couple to pass then ducked into the door on the right.

Jewel waited until Michael returned to her side. He had a strange look on his face and something in his hand. Jewel tried to make out what the item was, but Michael folded it in half, grabbed Jewel's hand, and headed for the exit. Once outside he set off at a rapid pace. Jewel felt like she was being dragged. After a few turns through the streets, Jewel freed her hand and stopped in her tracks.

"Okay. Where are we headed?" she asked, slightly winded.

"Back to the hotel in Lido," he replied, assessing their surroundings. "I don't want to run into Chauvin or any of his men."

"Okay. I just needed to catch my breath."

Michael took her hand, but this time more gently.

147

"I will slow down for you," he said.

Jewel saw a brief smile cross his lips.

"I'm not wimpy or out of shape. I just wasn't prepared to sprint," she defended.

"I didn't say you were wimpy or out of shape."

"I saw that smirk."

Michael rolled his eyes. He took her hand and continued to lead her through the streets. Jewel allowed him to pull her along, but she continued to sulk.

"We will catch the *vaporetto*, and when we get to the hotel, I have a couple of phone calls to make," Michael said. His last word trailed off into silence. He stopped walking and Jewel ran into him.

Jewel could feel his grip tighten around her hand. She looked around him to see what he was looking at. The black clad figure of Landry was crossing a bridge up ahead and turning in their direction. Michael turned and began running, pulling Jewel behind him. He made a sharp turn and cut down an alley. He pulled Jewel into a recessed doorway. He pushed her against the wall and looked in the direction they had come from. His body was pressed against her, pinning her to the wall. She was grateful for her backpack full of clothes as it cushioned her back against the hard surface. Her face was pressed into his chest. She could smell the salt water on the fabric. She also could smell his scent. It wasn't cologne or after shave. It was his natural scent. It was a comforting wood smell. Jewel breathed in deeply for a moment, enjoying the sensation so much that she almost forgot the dangerous situation of the moment.

"I don't think he saw us," Michael said, still looking out into the street.

Jewel looked up as he spoke. She could see the worry in his face. He let out his breath with a sigh, and then looked down at her. They were so close. She could feel his breath on her lips. They stared into each other's eyes for several seconds. Michael licked his lips and looked like he was about to say something. His eyes flicked to her mouth. He slowly leaned down toward her when she spoke.

"Michael, what did you take from the church?" Jewel asked.

Michael looked confused for a moment, but then narrowed his eyes as a flash of anger danced upon his face.

"I will tell you about it when we get to the room," he said, turning and walking out of the doorway.

Jewel followed. She noticed that he didn't take her hand. He continued his quick pace until they reached the *vaporetto*. He was silent on the ride back to the hotel.

"I'll meet you in the room. I have to make a phone call," he said as they entered the lobby.

Jewel made her way to the room. She had just gotten out of the shower when Michael returned. She was towel-drying her hair as he entered and sat down on the bed. He leaned forward, rested his elbows on his knees and cradled his head in his hands. Jewel watched for a few minutes and wondered if he had fallen asleep in that position when he finally moved.

"What is it?" Jewel asked. "What did you take from the church? And why did you get mad at me?"

He reached into his pocket and pulled out a gray strip about six inches long and handed it to Jewel. She held it in her hand for a moment.

"Duct tape?" she asked in surprise.

"Yes. Brogan always feared carrying things of value on his person, like safe deposit box keys or information about the item he was after. He often had unscrupulous competitors after him. For as long as I can remember, he used the church confessional as his hiding place. If he needed to hide something he would choose the Catholic Church closest to him and put the items under the bench or kneeler in the confessional," Michael said taking the strip of duct tape back from Jewel.

"So the thing with the three doors was a confessional? That's where you go to confess sins. And you found a piece of tape in the confessional?"

"Yes."

"What does that mean?" Jewel asked.

"It means that Brogan was hiding something there."

"What do you think it was and where do you think it is? Was it the Danish Jubilee?" she asked.

"No. The Danish Jubilee wouldn't fit under the seat and be held with duct tape. I'm not sure what was there. I really expected that we would find something. So, either Brogan removed it before he died and the murderer got it from the hotel room or the murderer knew about it and removed it from the church. I'm not sure what it is; perhaps the location of the Danish Jubilee."

"Okay, now what?" Jewel asked as she sat down on the bed beside him.

"I need to go to Ireland," he replied, turning to look at Jewel.

"Ireland?" Jewel was confused how the search for the Danish Jubilee could lead them to Ireland.

"Yes. I've been trying to contact my aunt to tell her about Brogan. I have tried every avenue available to contact her, but she's not responding.

I even called the University. They said that she taught a class two days ago, but she didn't show up for her class today. I'm concerned about her. Also, we have to decide what is to be done with Brogan's remains. The police here still have them. I guess he needs to be shipped back to Ireland for burial. I need to discuss this with her."

"Oh," Jewel replied. The mood was very grim. The talk of burials and remains was very serious. "Do you really have to go all the way to Ireland to see your aunt? No one can go tell her to call you?'

Michael took in a deep breath then released it.

"You don't know my aunt. She's a bit different. Besides, I should tell her about Brogan in person. She helped raise us. My father died right after I was born. My mother moved in with my aunt and the two of them raised us. So, she was like a second mother to us."

Jewel silently watched Michael as she processed the information.

"I see. So, Ireland, when do we leave?" she said.

"You don't have to come with me, if you don't want to. I just need to see my aunt."

"Well, I'm certainly not going to sit around here waiting for Chauvin to show up and kill me," Jewel stated.

Michael nodded his head.

"Very well. I need to make some arrangements. It is going to take some work to get us to Dublin without being followed. I think we'll need to fly for part of the trip."

"You said we should stay away from the airports," Jewel said, as she stretched out on the bed.

"Yes, I know. We'll buy our tickets last-minute at the airport counter. They won't have time to trace us. As soon as we hit the ground we'll be on the run. I need to work out the details. I'll need to get some more money, too. We may need to pay a few bribes to get where we need to be," he said as he stood up. "We don't want to draw anyone's attention, including the police."

"I hope I still have a job when I get back to Texas," Jewel said.

"Do you trust your co-worker? Perhaps you should give her a call. I wouldn't tell her too much, but just let her know that you're safe," Michael said.

∞   ∞   ∞

Jewel used the phone in the hotel lobby to make a quick call to Mary. After speaking with her friend, Jewel felt better about her job security.

"I hope I didn't cause trouble by calling Mary," Jewel stated. "It felt weird calling collect."

"I'm sure Gruber has already checked her out. I wouldn't worry too much," Michael reassured.

"Why do you think that Gruber checked her out?"

"Because I'm fairly certain that he's the one who ransacked your house. Your friend is probably safe."

"She's one Latina that you don't want to mess with. She's a tough cookie," Jewel responded. "But why do you believe that Gruber was the man in my house?"

"He has the same build. And we know that he's been following us," Michael said.

Jewel processed this information. She sat in the chair beside the small table.

*Now I'm glad I whacked him on the head. He deserved it after what he did to my house. I needed to avenge my Hummel figurines.*

"Okay, but what about Suran? Who is he?" she asked.

"That, I don't know."

152

The pair sat in silence for a while, both entertaining their own theories.

"What about your job?" Jewel asked.

"I'm on summer break," Michael said. "I would like to check a few more locations here in Venice before we leave for Ireland." He paused. "Will you accompany me?"

"Of course," Jewel said. She gifted him a beautiful smile.

Chapter 13
A Heathen

The rest of their research in Venice led to dead ends. Michael called upon two of Brogan's friends, one of which Jewel felt certain was a prostitute. When she asked, Michael refused to answer. The evening ended with room service in the hotel. Michael insisted that they reduce the amount of time they spent in public.

The tiny table barely held their two plates. Michael also had purchased a bottle of red wine. He poured a glass for Jewel and himself.

"I thought you didn't drink," Jewel said as she sniffed her glass.

Michael dipped his head in a noncommittal response.

"This is a very good wine." He set the glass on the table and watched Jewel. She was busy looking out the window.

"Do you know a lot about wines?" Jewel asked.

"A bit."

"Do you drink wine often?" she asked, still gazing out the window.

"You know you ask a lot of questions, but you don't offer much information," he said.

Jewel turned and looked at Michael shocked by his statement.

"Is there something you want to know?"

She watched him swirl the wine in his glass, as she waited for his response.

"Why don't you wear trousers? When I asked you earlier you gave me a strange answer."

"It's nothing," Jewel responded.

"You said, 'The Wish Book'. What does that mean?"

Jewel hesitated as she chewed the inside of her cheek. She sighed heavily then began her tale.

"When I was a kid, my mother had all these old catalogues that used to be mailed out to people at Christmas time. I would get so excited when she would pull them out and let me page through them," she said.

He was doing his best Moai impersonation again.

"Perhaps you're not familiar with these Christmas catalogues. They were just gift catalogues."

"I think I understand what it was."

"Well, The Wish Book ruined my life," she said.

"Can you elaborate on that?" Michael said as he cocked one dark eyebrow.

"See, The Wish Book was a catalogue that had all these pictures of families—a mother, a father, a son, and a daughter. Sometimes they would even toss in a dog. But in these pictures, they were always happy. They were sitting around the Christmas tree, sipping hot cocoa, eating dinner, or having a picnic. They advertised that this is what life looks like, and built these unrealistic expectations of what my life was supposed to be. In those photos the mother almost always wore a dress, or a skirt and blouse. I guess I always wanted to be that woman and have a family and be surrounded by happiness."

Michael was silent. He studied Jewel. She couldn't detect a reaction, so she continued.

"I'm kind of pissed off. The Wish Book lied. You don't get a beautiful family. You don't get smiles around the Christmas tree. Hell, I can't even remember the last time I drank hot cocoa. My life has been more like pizza rolls in my pajamas on Christmas morning watching 'It's a Wonderful Life' and crying."

The last word trailed off. Jewel was feeling embarrassed by her revelation.

"So that's why I wear dresses. I just keep pretending that one day I'll get the life that was promised by The Wish Book," Jewel concluded, then took a sip of her wine.

"Do you still want those things?"

Jewel didn't look at him. She thought about the question. She never really reflected on whether she still wanted it or not. She had just grown accustomed to being pissed off that she couldn't live her life in The Wish Book.

"Yeah . . . eventually, I do," she replied then drained her glass.

"Interesting. You're a very complex person," Michael said as he poured her more wine.

They were silent for a full minute.

"Anything else you want to know?" she asked.

"Yes. When was the last relationship you had with a man before Brogan?"

Jewel stared at him for the count of six, and then looked into her glass.

"Two years ago."

"What happened?"

"I don't want to talk about it."

"I bared my soul to you on the boat. You do owe me."

Jewel noted that his Irish brogue was very strong and wondered if it was due to the wine. She took a deep breath and then let it out slowly.

"I was also engaged to be married. My wedding day came and he never showed up. While I was at the church waiting, he cleaned out a few rooms of furniture from my house and sent me a text telling me that he wasn't ready for marriage," Jewel said, staring into her glass. "I never heard from him again. He blocked all my calls and disappeared. I had no way of contacting him."

They both sat in silence.

"He was a coward. It sounds like you dodged a bullet," Michael told her. "Any man that juvenile doesn't sound like he would make a good husband."

"Yeah, you're right," Jewel said as she looked up to meet his eyes. "I think I'll go to bed." She stood and stretched.

"I'm glad you didn't let that business cause you to hate men," he said.

She stopped and turned to look at him.

"If it had caused you to hate men, then you wouldn't have had the opportunity to be in a relationship with Brogan," he said. "And I wouldn't have had the chance to meet you," he continued while nodding his head as if he agreed with his own statement. "I guess things work out for the best."

Jewel felt uneasy. She kept wondering if she would ever have a relationship, not a made-up one or a fantasized one, but a real one.

Michael's statement kept running through her head until she succumbed to sleep.

∞    ∞    ∞

Michael planned their journey with the precision and care that Jewel had come to expect from him. They traveled three hours by plane from Venice to Manchester, England, then an hour by train to Liverpool. Michael explained that he wanted to throw Chauvin off the track.

Once they reached Liverpool, Michael left Jewel in a café for several hours while he headed to the docks. He procured passage to Dublin, Ireland, on a working freight ship. The accommodations were rough, but they woke up in Dublin in the early hours of the next morning. Michael said that this method of travel would not leave a trail. Jewel was afraid to ask about the cost. When the topic came up, Michael quickly changed the subject.

∞    ∞    ∞

The taxi stopped in front of a large stone building. Jewel could tell that the structure was very old, but well maintained.

"Is this the University where your aunt teaches?" Jewel asked. "Shouldn't we go to her house at this hour?"

Michael avoided making eye contact with Jewel.

"This *is* her house," he replied as he approached the huge doors.

"This is her house?" Jewel asked in awe.

*Oh, she is loaded.*

"Yes, this is where I grew up. Jewel, before we go inside I need to warn you about my aunt. She's. . ." Michael paused trying to find the right words. "She's different. Please just ignore what she says to you." Michael knocked on the door, but there was no answer.

After a moment Michael went to a huge stone statue of a lion that was standing beside the door. He reached to the back, under the lion's tail, and searched with his hand. It was an odd sight and Jewel chuckled in response.

"Umm. . . . Michael?"

"Got it," Michael said as he produced a key.

"It was in the lion's butt?"

"My aunt does have a sense of humor," he said as he used the key and pushed open the door.

The entry hall was huge and exquisitely decorated. There was dark wood on most surfaces. It was very masculine, but beautiful. A suit of armor stood beside a large curving staircase. An ornate chandelier hung from the high ceiling in the center of a decorative plaster medallion.

"Hello?" Michael called. The house was still and quiet. "I'm sure she's awake," Michael said. He took Jewel's backpack and placed it beside his own on a bench in the foyer. "Come on," he said as he walked through a door past the stairs. The hallway led to a kitchen. This was no ordinary kitchen. It looked like it would be better suited to a restaurant than a house. Everything was stainless steel. Jewel noticed a cart with several upside-down wine glasses upon it and several plates on one of the long tables.

"Aunt Hannah?" Michael called, but there was no answer.

Jewel followed Michael as he passed through a butler's pantry and into a formal dining room. The table looked as though it would seat about twenty people. It was made of a beautiful cherry wood. The walls were adorned with a royal blue silk. Jewel, wide-eyed, continued following

Michael. They returned to the foyer and crossed the large entryway. Michael pushed open another door to reveal a library. Every wall was filled, ceiling to floor, with wooden book shelves. Books could be seen everywhere. Jewel noticed there were even books above the windows and doors. A huge desk sat near a diamond-paned window. Jewel detected someone in the chair behind the desk, but the chair was facing away from her. Her eyes followed the cord from a phone on the desk to the chair. She could hear a female voice.

"No," the voice said. "No. That sounds like a problem that you will have to deal with, Charles." Jewel was enjoying the beautiful Irish brogue. "You idiot," the woman shouted. She continued the conversation, but in Irish. Jewel couldn't understand what the woman was saying, but it was clear the person on the other end of the phone was getting a tongue lashing.

Michael stood in front of the desk. When the woman started speaking in Gaeilge, Michael shook his head and sighed heavily. The woman's voice rose in volume, and Jewel stepped behind Michael to be shielded by whatever might erupt from behind the desk.

To Jewel it sounded as if the conversation was over. She peeked past Michael in time to see the chair spin around and the woman slam the phone down on its base. The woman was in her early sixties. She had red hair and pointed features. Although she was very thin, to Jewel she looked fierce like a warrior. When the woman saw Michael her face transformed into a wide smile, displaying large teeth.

"Faolan, I expected you yesterday," she said as she stood with her arms open for an embrace. Before she reached Michael, she spotted Jewel and froze.

"Who is this?" she asked, the warmth disappearing from her voice.

"Aunt Hannah, this is Jewel Townsend," Michael said as he stepped aside so that Jewel was completely exposed. "Jewel, this is Hannah Scott, my dear aunt."

The woman looked at Jewel from head to toe slowly.

"Humph," was all she said.

"It's nice to meet you," Jewel said. She had the sudden urge to curtsy, but didn't.

"Townsend? That's English, isn't it?" Hannah said with narrowed eyes as she slowly turned to Michael.

"I'm American," Jewel said.

"Yes, but the name is English; Yorkshire, I believe," she said still looking at Michael.

"Jewel is American, Aunt Hannah. What do you mean you expected me yesterday?"

"Faolan, you know I can usually predict your moves," she said as a faint smile spread across her face. She stepped forward and grabbed Michael into a hug. Seeing them together, Jewel realized that the woman was quite tall. She was only a couple of inches shorter than Michael.

"Aunt Hannah, I've been trying to reach you," Michael said as he released the embrace.

"Have you?" she asked as she was moving strands of his hair and studying his face.

"Yes. I have phoned you several times. I called your office at University. I even called the art and architecture department. At first I was concerned, but the department said that you taught your class a few days ago, but not your last class. While we're on the subject: why don't you have a mobile phone like most people?"

"Oh, Faolan, why would I want one of those retched things? If I had a mobile phone then people would call and bother me," she replied, still studying her nephew. "How have you been, boy?" she said as she pulled him into another hug.

"I was worried about you, when they said you didn't show up for your last class."

"I didn't miss class; I cancelled it. I just forgot to tell anyone. I've been busy," she said with a defiant tilt to her head. "Enough about me."

"Aunt Hannah, I'm actually here to give you some terrible news," Michael said as he pulled away. "You may want to sit down."

"Nonsense, my ears work just as well when I'm standing as when I'm sitting. What do you have to say?" she asked, and then glanced at Jewel. Her eyes grew in size and Jewel wondered if perhaps the woman had forgotten that she was there. "Oh, Faolan, you didn't marry the English girl, did you?" she asked, pointing a long straight finger at Jewel. "Did you?"

"No, Aunt Hannah. I didn't get married and Jewel is not English," Michael said. "It is actually more serious. It's about Brogan," he said as he hung his head. "Brogan is dead, Aunt Hannah."

The woman displayed no emotion. The silence seemed to stretch on, but it was only a few seconds long.

"Don't be ridiculous."

Michael looked stunned.

"He is. He was murdered in Venice," Michael said.

"Those Italians contacted me, too, telling me that nonsense. Now I'm glad you're here. I will be very busy. The caterers will be arriving in a little while. I'm hosting a dinner tonight for the Irish League. I had your formals cleaned and they're hanging in your room."

Michael was shocked. He looked from his aunt to Jewel then back again.

"Aunt Hannah, how can you say this? Brogan is dead."

"Do you have a body you can show me?" she asked, eyeing him defiantly.

"No, but the Italian police have his remains. In fact we need to decide what's to be done with them. I suppose we should have them shipped here for burial," Michael said as he hung his head once more.

"I'll believe that Brogan is dead when you can show me his body. I have lost too many people in my life. Show me his body, and then I will believe it," she said with conviction.

Michael looked at Jewel and shook his head. Jewel was saddened by the woman's denial and speculated on her comment about losing too many people.

"Aunt Hannah, it is true whether you're ready to believe it or not," Michael said as he watched her with pain in his eyes. "Should I call Father Wendell to come talk with you?"

"I will see Father Wendell tonight. He will be here for the Irish League dinner," Hannah responded as she returned to the desk, picked up a tea cup, and took a sip. She eyed Jewel up and down again. "Perhaps he could take your confession while he is here, Faolan."

Michael looked confused for a moment, but followed his aunt's gaze.

"No, Aunt Hannah. You have the wrong idea about Jewel."

"Humph," she said as she took another long sip of her tea. "Perhaps Father Wendell could take *her* confession too."

"I'm not Catholic," Jewel quickly said.

Michael let out a pained groan.

"Oh," Hannah said, setting her tea cup down. "Then which religion are you?"

"I don't belong to any organized religion."

"A heathen? Faolan, you have brought home a heathen?" she questioned, her voice growing in volume.

"Aunt Hannah, please don't do this," Michael pleaded.

The sound of a doorbell rang in the foyer.

"Well, I mean. . . I believe there's a higher power," Jewel added.

"A higher power? That's not a religion, child, that is an AA meeting," the woman stated.

The doorbell rang again.

"Wilson!" Hannah called out. "Oh hell, I forgot Wilson is picking up the quails," she said as she headed for the door. "Faolan, I will send people to dress your heathen and prepare her for the dinner. Please make sure she is clean when they arrive," she said as she exited the room.

*Well, damn!*

Michael gave a heavy sigh. He plopped down in a large winged chair.

"I'm so sorry, Jewel. I'll try to talk to her a little later about Brogan. I'll recruit Father Wendell to help."

"She really doesn't want to accept it," Jewel said, taking a seat in the winged chair opposite Michael.

"I'm sorry that she was so rude to you. I know it's difficult to believe, but she's a good person. She's just a bit different from most people," he said.

"I found her kind of hilarious," Jewel said with a chuckle.

"You're very kind. If you don't mind, let's play along with this for a little while. I'll sit down with her and Father Wendell tonight. This is just a shock to her. I guess she's in denial. Brogan and I were like her own sons."

"So she's a widow?" Jewel asked.

"Yes. She had only been married a couple of years when her husband died. They had no children. He was also extremely wealthy as you can see," he said, gesturing to their surroundings.

"Jewel, I'm sorry for the horrible things she said to you. I feel guilty. I feel like I didn't prepare you well enough for meeting her," he added, sheepishly.

"That's not your fault. Besides I kept my mouth shut because I thought she might be lashing out due to grief."

"I wish I could tell you that she was acting out of character, but I can't. That was classic Hannah Scott," he said with a faint smile.

"Got it," she said with a nod of her head. "I'll just have to stay on my toes."

"You don't have to go to the dinner tonight if you don't want to. I'll be going so that I can talk with Father Wendell."

"Oh, I'll go to the dinner. I'm sure it's not every day that Aunt Hannah has a heathen Brit in her house. I want her to be able to show me off," Jewel said with a smirk.

"You're being a very good sport about this, Jewel," Michael said with a faint smile.

"It's nice to see you smile," Jewel said. She realized immediately that it was an odd thing to say. She had been fighting with this man for the past week, but now she cared about the way he felt. She genuinely liked to see him happy. An awkward silence followed her statement. They looked at each other. Michael had lost his smile. Jewel couldn't read his expression. He almost looked sad.

"I'm sorry. Did I say something wrong?" she asked.

Michael shook his head.

"No," he said, but his smile didn't return. "I'll show you to a guestroom."

He stood and walked to the door. Jewel followed.

"Michael? What is 'Faolan'?" Jewel asked.

Michael froze, hand on the doorknob, and turned to face Jewel.

"It . . . it's a term of endearment."

Chapter 14
He Will Always be Second Best

Jewel thought her room looked like something straight out of a gothic novel with the huge four-poster bed and velvet drapes that produced images of Scarlett O'Hara's fancy dress. The adjoining bathroom was covered in gray marble and had a crystal chandelier.

After her shower she returned to her room only to find her backpack empty of all its clothes. Her makeup, passport, and other personal items were left untouched. She opened drawers and checked the oak wardrobe, but all of her clothes were gone.

*Again! Why do people keep taking my clothes?*

She wore only the plush, white bathrobe that she had found in her room. She pulled its sash tighter, then opened the door, and peeked out into the hall.

She sprinted to the room across the hall which Michael had indicated as his, and gave the door a quick tap. No answer. She tried the elaborate knob and found it unlocked. Movement at the end of the hall caught Jewel's eye. In a panic she rushed into the room, pulling the door shut behind her. His room was large. It had no windows. The walls held several shelves and paintings. Jewel surveyed the first set of shelves which were adorned with model airplanes and books. On another shelf she saw tiny models of buildings. She recognized one to be Notre Dame Cathedral. She looked closer and was fascinated to find that it wasn't a plastic pre-designed model, but had been painstakingly constructed by hand with pieces of wood and toothpicks, and the windows were formed with colored cellophane. Jewel was examining the model in awe when she heard a sound behind her. She spun around to find Michael entering the room from a door she hadn't noticed before. Steam surrounded him and billowed out of the doorway. He wore a look of surprise and a robe that matched Jewel's. Neither one spoke for several seconds. Uncomfortable, Jewel reached up and felt the towel that she had wrapped around her wet hair.

"Umm. . . Hi. Did you make this?" she said pointing to the cathedral model. She turned and continued examining the craftsmanship. She felt Michael move beside her. "This is really amazing," she said, studying it more intently. She turned to look at Michael. Her breath caught at his stare.

"Yes. I did make it," he said stepping closer until he was looming over her.

"Oh . . . really? Wow, that must have taken a long time to build," Jewel said, stepping back a bit. Michael matched her step. "Umm . . . how long did that take?" she asked, taking another step back. Michael matched her step again.

"About three months."

"Three months? Wow," Jewel replied, stepping back again. She was becoming very uncomfortable.

Her progress was halted when she felt a hard, unmoving piece of furniture behind her. She glanced to find her legs against a mahogany desk.

"You must have worked very hard on it," Jewel said into Michael's chest. He was so close she could feel the warmth of her own breath as it bounced off his plush robe. She didn't want to look up at his face. He was too close for comfort. Her mind raced trying to remember why she was even in his room. "I don't have any clothes," she blurted out as she looked up into his green eyes.

*I am a grown woman. I am a strong woman. I am the architect of my life. Oh my God, he smells wonderful.*

"I don't have any clothes. All I have is this robe. My clothes are gone," she repeated, continuing to look at Michael's face. She detected a small twitch to his eyebrows and the corners of his mouth as his eyes slowly looked down at her robe-clad figure, then back up to her face. Jewel could detect the fire in his eyes. He leaned his head down closer to Jewel. He breathed in through his nose as if scenting the air around her.

"Miss Townsend, you really shouldn't make a habit of entering a man's room, uninvited, and wearing only a bathrobe. The assumption would be that you're here for something other than conversation," he said, his voice low and deep. He slid his arms around Jewel's waist and pulled her closer.

"Whoa, whoa, whoa," she said as she ducked out of Michael's arms and started backing away from him. "No. I just came here to see you. . . I mean to talk to you and tell you about my clothes . . . that I don't have any," Jewel sputtered. She backed away. Michael slowly followed.

"I see," he said, looking Jewel up and down.

"Yes. That's right. I came out of the shower and my clothes were gone," Jewel defended as she continued to retreat. She was regaining her composure and strength, but they escaped her when her path was once again impeded. She reached back to discover something soft and springy. She didn't need to look behind her to know she had run into his bed. The shock of the knowledge must have been evident on her face. She was struck completely silent as Michael closed the rest of the distance between them.

"Miss Townsend, as I said, a man could get the wrong idea of your intentions if you visit his room in such a manner," Michael murmured as his body pressed the back of Jewel's legs against the bed. He continued to lean toward her. In order to keep their bodies from mashing together, Jewel leaned the upper half of her body further back until she had nowhere else to go but down. She sat on the bed and was being pushed further back by the advance of his body.

He was so close. He was leaning in with his head slightly tilted.

*He's going to kiss me. He's going to kiss me. Oh gosh! But then what? No!*

Jewel ducked under Michael's arm and scurried away on hands and knees until she was sure she was clear of his reach.

"I'm sure I'll find some clothes somewhere," she blurted. She scrambled back onto her feet, and then darted to the door and pushed it open. She glanced down the hall, and then ran across to her room. She was about to enter when she heard an odd sound: laughter. The laughter was so loud that it was nearly a howl. Jewel froze. The fear she felt a moment ago was transforming into rage.

*This was a game. He was toying with me. That piece of dirt was just playing with me. I'll show him.*

Jewel steadied her courage. She pulled the towel from her head and smoothed back her hair. She was ready to give him a taste of his own medicine. She crossed the hall with confidence and swung the door open. Her determination fled at the sight. Michael had taken off his robe. His back was to the door. Jewel took in his masculine build. She saw the familiar sight of his Celtic knot tattoo on the back of his left shoulder. Her eyes traveled down his muscular back and to his shapely rear and well defined legs.

"Holy crap!" she muttered as she stood with her hand still on the doorknob.

Michael's laughter had subsided, but he turned his head just enough that Jewel could detect the smirk that still lingered on his lips.

"Jewel, did I not just tell you that you can't come into a man's room . . ." Michael started.

"I'm sorry," she yelped as she pulled the door closed and abandoned her attempt to 'play the game'.

Once she was safely in her own room she paced the floor. She felt embarrassed. She could feel the heat in her cheeks. She hoped that Michael hadn't seen her blush. She stopped pacing and felt anger rising once again.

*He did that on purpose. He knew I would return.*

Someone knocked.

"I am a strong, independent woman!" Jewel yelled as she opened the door as wide as it would go. But it wasn't Michael at the door.

A man and two women stood in the hallway.

"I'm glad to hear that. Strong independent women are in fashion this season," the man said as he entered the room. The two women followed carrying what looked like deep suitcases. They placed the suitcases on the bed. "Good, your hair's still wet," he said as he reached up and rubbed Jewel's hair through his fingers. "Now let's see what we have to work with," he added, reaching for the belt on Jewel's robe.

"What do you think you're doing?" Jewel demanded, slapping his hand away.

"Mrs. Scott told us to rush over. She said that she had a project that may have potential," he said as he circled Jewel like a lion looking for a weakness. "You're shorter than I expected. All right, bring them in," he told one of the women.

The woman went into the hall and retrieved a rolling rack with at least a dozen dresses.

"This is Girl One and Girl Two. I don't bother learning their names. They never last," he said indicating the two women. "And I am Ronald Buckley." He waited for Jewel to react to hearing his name. But she just looked at him.

"American?" he asked. Jewel nodded. "Figures. Well, let's get started."

∞    ∞    ∞

*Jewel Journal:*

*I look amazing. I totally feel like one of the women in the sappy romance movies. It's totally cliché, but I feel beautiful. Ronald Buckley worked miracles. I'm so giddy.*

*I'm not sure how long we will be here Ireland; probably long enough for Michael to convince Hannah of the reality that Brogan is dead. I'm also not sure where the search for this Fabergé treasure will lead us, but I will trust that Michael has a plan. He is so annoying, but he's a pretty smart guy.*

*My current emotions: Excited. I'm going to make a grand entrance down the stairs to a dinner party.*

*My emotions forecast: I'm feeling good about tonight. I haven't been to a party since my engagement party. Stop, Jewel. Push those negative thoughts out of your mind. Happy thoughts, happy thoughts and wine . . . let's get some.*

Jewel closed the crunchy, formerly saltwater-soaked pages of her journal. She tossed the book onto her bed and took one more look in the mirror. She couldn't help herself. She did look beautiful. She kept turning to view herself in every direction. She wasn't sure how they managed her hair, but it was a departure from her usual poufy frizz. The loose, smooth curls falling gently on her shoulders made her feel like a pin-up girl from the nineteen-fifties. Jewel normally didn't wear much makeup, but the deep red lipstick and bronze eye shadow were so expertly applied that it looked fantastic without being overdone. The gold colored dress fell just past her knees and was lifted by two petticoats. She thought its retro design was modest but with just the right amount of cleavage. Jewel made a last minute inspection in the mirror and headed downstairs.

As she descended the stairs, she could see Hannah Scott at the door greeting guests as they arrived. The woman was an imposing figure. Jewel could imagine her as a Celtic warrior running and screaming into battle. She wore a dark blue dress with a plaid tartan sash hanging from her shoulder and draped to her hip. Her red hair was pulled up into a French twist at the back of her head.

Jewel stopped a few steps from the bottom of the stairs, unsure of where she was supposed to go.

Hannah turned to speak to a tall man outfitted in a formal jacket and kilt. Jewel noticed the tartan of his kilt matched Hannah's sash. The man had a nice build and Jewel wondered if he was Hannah's escort for the evening—until he turned in Jewel's direction.

It was Michael. He looked very handsome in his jacket and kilt. He stared at Jewel until Hannah pushed him in her direction.

"Miss Townsend," he said as he offered his arm to Jewel. She took his arm with a smile. He escorted her through a doorway into a room where drinks were being served. "It would be best if you tell the other guests that you're my fiancée," Michael said, looking around the room.

"I will not," Jewel stated, giving Michael a look of shock.

"Suit yourself," he said as he turned to a man in his mid-fifties.

"Professor Burns, I would like you to meet Miss Townsend. She is our guest visiting from the United States," Michael said as he removed Jewel's hand from his arm and placed it upon Professor Burns' arm. Michael gave Jewel a short bow and walked away.

Professor Burns was a letch, as was Mr. Mullen, and Dr. Foley. Jewel slowly understood why Michael had told her to pretend they were engaged. When dinner time arrived Jewel was relieved to be seated as that would lower the chance of someone else touching her rear. She found herself between Professor Nolan, one of Hannah's colleagues, and Ms. Donnelly, the editor of the local newspaper. Michael was seated across the table and to the left of Jewel. As she sat down they made eye contact. He gave her a slight bow of his head.

"I have a confession," Professor Nolan whispered.

"Oh? What is it?" Jewel asked as she placed her napkin on her lap.

"I switched place cards with Donald MacKenna," he whispered. "I really couldn't bear another dinner seated beside Dr. Bell. He is such a bore and he usually has so much to drink that by the end of the meal he tends to start spilling things. I hope you don't mind."

"No, not at all." Jewel glanced to where Dr. Bell was seated. The man already looked like he had had too much to drink.

"Besides, I have been hoping to get a chance to meet you all night," he whispered again, close to her ear. "I should introduce myself formally. My name is Everett Nolan. I'm a professor of History at Trinity College Dublin. You don't need to introduce yourself. I asked around to find out about you. Your name is Jewel Townsend and you are from the United States. And you've caught the eye of every man in this room."

Jewel turned to her left to look at Professor Nolan. His icy blue eyes held a mischievous sparkle. He had a mop of blond curly hair and a boyish air about him, although he was at least forty years old.

"Professor Nolan . . ." Jewel started.

"Oh, please call me Everett," he interrupted with a large smile.

"Everett, thank you, but I'm sure you exaggerate the desire for my company," she said, sipping from her wine glass.

"Oh, not at all, Miss Townsend. I could point out at least four or five men that would give up their dinner if they could have the seat next to you," he said as he stabbed a prawn with his fork.

Jewel smiled at Everett, and then looked around the room. Professor Burns winked at Jewel from the far right of the table. Jewel looked down to the other end of the table where Hannah was dominating the conversation. Mr. Crane, a man that she had spoken to earlier, raised his glass to Jewel and drank.

Soon her eyes rested upon Michael. He looked at ease. Jewel thought back to when she had met him a week ago, and how different he was now. In the beginning, he was so stiff and tense. She could hear his conversation and noticed that his Irish brogue was very strong while he was around his countryman. She was so lost in thought watching him that she didn't realize that he, too, was looking her way. She smiled and was warmed by the smile he gave her in return.

"I'm sure you would agree, Miss Townsend," Everett declared.

"Umm . . . I'm sorry? I missed that last bit," Jewel said.

Everett entertained Jewel with stories of a photo safari he had recently taken. The conversation was lively. Everett truly liked listening to himself talk. Jewel had already had two glasses of wine. She was feeling relaxed and in high spirits.

"I would love to take you on my next trip, Miss Townsend, if you would be so inclined," Everett said.

"Oh. That is very kind of you."

"Do you do much travelling, Miss Townsend?"

"Not a whole lot. I did just return from Venice, Italy," she said as she took another sip of her wine.

"Really, that's exciting. What were you doing there?" he asked.

"Just visiting."

"Are you planning on any other trips in the near future?"

"I'm not sure. I'm traveling with Michael, so it's up to him," she said.

"Michael Walsh? Really? Have you met his brother, Brogan?" he inquired.

"Yes, I have."

"The Walsh brothers," he said. His voice sounded emotionless, but his face told a different story. Then he whispered, "Miss Townsend, I would love to take you to dinner tomorrow evening."

She was a bit surprised by the proposal. "Professor Nolan, you flatter me," Jewel responded, matching his low tone.

"Come on. Please call me by my first name. I'm trying my best here to romance you. At least tell me that we're past the surnames," he said with a flirty smile.

Jewel wasn't sure why, but the statement tickled her. She began laughing. She covered her mouth, trying to stifle the laughter.

"Finally, I made you smile," Everett said as he leaned his head down and touched his forehead to her shoulder as if in exhaustion.

Jewel looked around to see if anyone was disturbed by her laughter. No one appeared disturbed, but a pair of green eyes was staring at her from across the table.

"Oh my, I do believe we have angered Mr. Walsh," Everett said, looking at Michael. He didn't whisper and Jewel was certain that Michael could hear him. "He does look fierce, Jewel. Should we be frightened? I have heard that he has quite the temper," Everett said, baiting Michael.

Jewel was feeling good from the wine and the entertaining company, but the cold stare she was getting from Michael was starting to make her uncomfortable. She remembered their encounter in the bedroom and soon felt a spark of the rage.

*So what if he's angry. It serves him right, after teasing me the way he did.*

She felt a warm hand on her ear and turned to face Everett. He was extremely close.

"I like the way your hair falls, exposing just a tiny bit of your sexy ear," he said as he gently tugged her left ear.

177

*Sexy ear? That's bizarre. Is that some weird fetish?*

"What an odd thing to say," she responded. Jewel noticed Everett stole a quick glance at Michael. "Tell me, Everett, are you intentionally trying to do things to bother Mr. Walsh?"

"What? Why would I do something so underhanded?" he asked, with his hand on his chest in a gesture of shock.

"I'm not sure," Jewel said with narrowed eyes. "Do you have a history with Mr. Walsh?"

"I know him," Everett replied. "I think the attentions of such a beautiful, engaging woman are wasted on him," he said, loud enough for Michael to hear. "He will always be second best."

Jewel was startled as Michael abruptly stood up, still staring at the pair across the table.

"Quite right. Let's adjourn to the parlor for a nightcap," Hannah called out, right on cue.

"Jewel, would you join me?" Everett asked as he offered Jewel his arm.

"Actually, I need to visit the powder room."

The dining room began to empty as people migrated to the parlor. Jewel headed upstairs to her room. She knew she was going to struggle with her petticoats and didn't want people to hear her downstairs in the nearest restroom.

Jewel admired the work of Ronald Buckley in the mirror as she reapplied her lipstick.

*I wish I could remember all the makeup tricks to make me look this good every day. Who are you kidding, Jewel, you know you wouldn't put in that much effort.*

As she exited the bathroom she found Everett Nolan sitting on her bed.

He gave her a smile with his blue eyes flashing.

"What are you doing here?" Jewel asked, instantly uncomfortable.

"I just came to check on you," he replied.

"I'm done. We should go," Jewel said.

She headed for the door. Everett intercepted.

"Hold on. I just wanted to spend a few moments alone with you," he said, grabbing her hand.

Jewel felt a moment of panic.

*What kind of weirdo follows a woman to the restroom?*

"I would like to go back to the party," Jewel said, unsmiling.

"We will. I just wanted to talk privately for a moment. So what is your relationship with Michael Walsh?" he asked, grabbing her other hand. "You know I have always bested Michael Walsh in all things. It's kind of a hobby of mine. I was always better at sports, in school, and in love," he said as he pulled Jewel against him.

At that moment the door swung open. Michael stood unsmiling and slightly out of breath. He appeared taller than Jewel remembered. Dressed in his kilt, Jewel was reminded of the cover of a romance novel she had once read.

"Michael," Jewel said in shock.

Michael came forward, grabbed Jewel by the back of her arm and guided her out of the room without a word.

"Michael, what are you doing?" she asked, although she was relieved that he had arrived when he did.

"Please return to the party," he said, as he released her arm. He spun around, returned to her bedroom, and shut the door.

Jewel wondered what Michael was doing alone in the room with Everett. She leaned closer to the door, as she could hear the rumble of low voices.

"Jewel!" she heard through the door. "Return to the party," Michael demanded.

Jewel quickly went downstairs. She joined the other guests in the parlor, but kept a sharp eye on the stairs.

She noted that Michael returned to the party several minutes later. Everett, however, left the party directly after coming downstairs and he looked disheveled.

The party ended and the guests left en masse. Jewel kept her seat on a settee in the parlor.

After bidding the guests farewell, Hannah and Michael returned to the parlor and joined her. Everyone was exhausted and silent. Jewel could hear the caterers cleaning up the dining room and the clinking of dishes from the kitchen. She was staring into her cup of tea thinking of the evening's events.

Hannah began talking in Irish to Michael. He responded. The conversation continued. Jewel looked up to watch them. Hannah kept nodding toward Jewel as she spoke until it was clear to Jewel that they were talking about her. She continued to watch, but was too exhausted to care.

"Goodnight," Jewel said as she stood and headed for the door.

"I'm going to bed, too. Aunt Hannah, do you need anything before I go?" Michael asked.

She responded in Irish to which Michael gave a throaty scoff.

He followed about ten paces behind Jewel. She wondered why he looked so angry.

*Was he jealous, perhaps?*

A brief smile passed her lips at that thought.

*Doubtful.*

"You don't waste much time moving on, do you?" Michael said.

"Excuse me?" Jewel responded, turning around at the top of the stairs.

"Aye, my brother has been dead barely a week and you're moving on to the next man," he spat as he passed her.

An enormous sense of guilt passed over Jewel as the memory of Brogan sparked in her mind. All the pieces fit together. She understood now why Michael was angry. She thought about her interactions with Michael. He had continued to treat her like his brother's girlfriend. He had a brief moment of playfulness earlier in his bedroom, but he never made a serious attempt at flirting with her. She had completely forgotten that she had maintained the façade that she and Brogan were lovers.

"Michael, you have the wrong idea," she told him.

He was about to enter his room. He looked back at Jewel.

"Michael, Brogan and I spent one day together. That was all. We weren't lovers or in a relationship. I mean . . . I had hoped there would be a relationship, eventually. We just had that one day. It was the first date I had since I was jilted at the altar. He was the first man I had been even remotely interested in, after my fiancé. I know you thought that we were closer than that, but we weren't," Jewel said, looking down at the ornate carpet. "It's my fault, because I let you believe it. I just liked the idea of being in a relationship, even if it was all a lie," she said, feeling emotional.

Michael walked to Jewel until he was standing in front of her.

"I'm sorry that I let you believe that," she said. "You must think I'm a horrible person. I really didn't mean for this to go on as long as it has."

She slowly looked up at Michael. He was watching her—unsmiling.

*Crap! He's really mad. You should have come clean much sooner, Jewel.*

"I really didn't mean to deceive you. When you came . . ."

Michael grabbed Jewel with one arm around her waist and the other cradling the back of her head. He kissed her. It was not a kiss you would give your brother's girlfriend. It was a deep kiss. It was a steamy kiss. She closed her eyes and felt her entire body respond. Jewel didn't realize until Michael released her that he was holding all her weight; at some point during the kiss she had stopped supporting herself. Michael released Jewel slowly, allowing her to get her balance. She didn't open her eyes, but she felt her body sway as if the room were spinning. When she finally opened her eyes she saw Michael's retreating form.

*What the hell was that?*

Chapter 15

Bitch-Slapped

Jewel dressed for the day. She was pleased to find her clothes had been cleaned, pressed, and hung in the wardrobe in her room.

*I could get used to this. However, it's really creepy to think of Wilson, the butler, handling my underwear.*

Jewel entered the dining room for breakfast and was met with sudden silence. Hannah and Michael were seated at one end of the table. She heard hushed speech before she entered, but the pair sat silent as she took her seat. Jewel could detect a faint smirk on Hannah's thin lips.

Wilson entered with a plate of eggs, toast and sausages and set it upon the charger plate at Jewel's place setting. He poured some hot tea, and then left the room.

"Good morning," Jewel said.

Michael watched Jewel as Hannah watched Michael.

Neither one responded.

Jewel decided to ignore them and began eating.

"Did you enjoy yourself last night?" Hannah finally asked.

Jewel looked across the table at Michael. She wondered for a moment if Hannah knew about the kiss.

"Yes, it was a nice dinner."

"Yes. And an eventful evening," Hannah said to Jewel. But she was watching Michael.

"Did you enjoy the company of that pompous ass, Everett Nolan?" Michael asked.

Hannah laughed lightly.

"Everett has been trying to best the Walsh boys as long as I can remember. He has even been known to claim a victory here and there," Hannah said with a wry smile. "It's good to have a little competition now and then, son."

"Competition? Him? You can't be serious," Michael replied to his aunt.

"Did you make plans to see Everett again, Jewel?" Hannah asked, still smiling.

Jewel choked on the orange juice she was drinking.

"No!" She wondered why she felt so defensive about the question. Her eyes slowly rose to look across the table. Michael was slouching in his chair. Jewel noticed how this posture was so uncharacteristic of him. He watched as if he were waiting for her to do something.

"What?" Jewel asked.

"I have a class to teach this morning. I'm not sure why I agreed to teach a Saturday class. I should be home by lunch," Hannah said as she sipped her tea.

"Aunt Hannah, we need to make arrangements for Brogan's remains," Michael said.

Hannah winced briefly at the words. "You know we can't keep putting it off."

"Faolan, I cannot have this conversation right now. Do what you will. I have class," Hannah said as she looked at her watch. "Sweet Mary, is that the time?" She popped to her feet and charged out the room.

"I'm going to go see Father Wendell about the service," Michael loudly said.

"Do whatever you feel is necessary," Hannah called from across the hall.

A clamor of movement could be heard, followed by the door closing.

Michael stared into his teacup while Jewel finished her breakfast. She was enjoying the last of her toast when she looked up to find Michael watching her.

"I have to go see Father Wendell. I think I need to do this alone. Do you mind?" Michael asked.

"No," she replied in a small voice.

She studied his face.

*Typical Easter Island Moai man . . . Wait, is that a hint of emotion in his eyes?*

"You can stay here, or you can go downtown," he said.

"I may go for a walk."

"Excellent idea. There's a park nearby and if you walk a little further there's a small pub," Michael said. "But wherever you choose to go, I insist you take Wilson with you."

185

"No. I'm not having the butler take me around town," she replied.

"Yes, you will. It's dangerous for you to be alone."

"Michael, I doubt Chauvin knows we're in Ireland and I don't need a babysitter," Jewel replied and threw her napkin down beside her plate.

They stared at each other.

"Then I suggest you stay here and take advantage of my aunt's extensive library."

Jewel's face transformed. She bit her lip in excitement.

"Yes, well, then it is settled. I should be back well before afternoon tea," he said as he stood and headed for the door.

Jewel had a strange emotion as she watched him walking away.

"Michael?"

He stepped back into the room with a questioning gaze.

"Please be careful."

A small smile played at his mouth and he nodded his head.

Jewel tried to identify the feeling that she was having.

*I'm not really worried about him. I mean he can totally take care of himself. I've just gotten used to having him around.*

She heard the front door close. She stood, went to the window, and watched as Michael got into a taxi.

Jewel entered the library. She ran her hand along a row of books and loved the feel of the leather spines. She slowly walked alongside the shelves and wondered if Hannah had a filing system. The collection was large enough that an organizational system was necessary or she could never locate a particular volume. Jewel pulled a book from a shelf titled "The Art of the Irish Language". She walked to a window bench to read in the sunlight. As she approached the seat, she dropped the book. She bent down to pick it up and noticed another shelf beneath the bench. She sat on the floor and pulled a thick, tall book from the shelf. It was a photo album.

She opened it to the first page and examined a photo of two teenage girls. They both had long red hair. Jewel picked out Hannah in the pair. The other girl looked a lot like Hannah, but was a tad shorter. Jewel suspected that this woman was Brogan and Michael's mother. She turned the pages and picked both girls out in several photos. One page had a large professional photo of Hannah on her wedding day. She was very beautiful. There was a smaller photo of the other woman on her wedding day, but the photo was much different. The man wore a military uniform and the bride was dressed in a simple dress with a small bouquet of flowers. Jewel flipped the pages until she found what she was hoping to see—baby pictures. Brogan's baby pictures consisted of the usual fanfare; baby's first picture, naked baby on a rug, baby's first haircut. The one constant in all the photos of Brogan was the smile.

"Were you ever unhappy, Brogan?" Jewel said aloud.

As she turned the pages, another baby was introduced. Jewel laughed aloud. To say Michael was chubby would be an understatement. Jewel critiqued his baby pictures and marveled at his likeness to a walrus. The pictures told the story as he shed his baby fat and grew into a boy.

Jewel looked at a picture of the two brothers. Brogan was holding up what looked like an Egyptian Pharaoh statue as Michael stood beside him. Michael was not looking at the camera, but at his brother, with a look of pride. One picture caught Jewel's attention. A group of teenagers were all standing around a car. Jewel picked Brogan out immediately. He was standing in the center. It looked as if he was speaking and the others were watching. Michael could be seen a few feet away. He was also watching Brogan, but he wasn't smiling.

*Michael, you have been in your brother's shadow for a long time. But you sure did love him.*

She felt somewhat emotional looking at the photos of Brogan. It also made her miss her own sibling, Jane. She reflected that sibling relationships were different in every family. Jewel sensed the relationship between the Walsh brothers was often competitive. This was so different from her relationship with her sister.

The rest of the album read like a time lapse film of Brogan and Michael aging into adulthood. Brogan's pictures became fewer until only Michael was left. The last photo in the book was Michael's college graduation. He looked stern and business-like.

Jewel returned the album to its place on the shelf. She stood and looked out the window. The sun streamed in and Jewel made a decision.

*I'm not a prisoner. It's time for some fresh air. Michael will just have to deal with it.*

The park was a short walk. Jewel wished she had brought her sunglasses as she shaded her eyes from the glare. She walked to a duck pond and found a spot not covered with duck droppings to sit down. She had just opened the book when a voice startled her.

"Beautiful day," Everett Nolan said as he approached.

Jewel watched in shock as he took a seat beside her in the grass. She had a moment of panic as she thought of the last time she was alone with Everett, but she looked around and took comfort in the presence of other people.

"What are you doing here?" Jewel demanded.

"I was just out for a walk. I thought I was hallucinating when I saw you. You are a vision of beauty. You are the Lady of the Lake," Everett Nolan said as he took her hand.

"Okay," Jewel said with suspicion as she pulled her hand free. "So you just happened to be walking by?" she asked, then noticed a discoloration high on his left cheek. "What's that about?" she asked, tapping her own cheek.

"Oh this," he said as he rubbed the spot. "I got a workout at the boxing club this morning. You know . . . just me and the fellas, a little bob and weave. I took one to the cheek, but I was distracted. I was thinking about you," he said.

*Yeah, right. I bet that's where Michael bitch-slapped you.*

"Uh-huh," Jewel responded.

"What are you reading, my Lady of the Lake?" Everett asked, changing the subject, as he glanced at the book. "Are you interested in speaking Irish?"

"Is that what you call it? I thought it was Gaelic."

"We call it Irish or Gaeilge. If you want to learn, I could teach you," he said as he closed the book in her hand. "Let's go have a drink. Shall we?"

Jewel was surprised by the offer. She was trying to think of a reason to refuse when Everett reached down and pulled Jewel to her feet. The movement was abrupt and rough.

"It's a bit early for a drink. And don't you have a class to teach?"

"It's Saturday," he responded. "There's a small café down the hill. We can have some refreshments," he said as he took her hand and pulled her along.

Everything was happening so quickly that Jewel didn't know what to say. Before she knew it they were stepping into a small pub.

"This is a pub. I thought you said it was a café," Jewel said as she sat down.

"They serve food, so it's the same thing."

Jewel was about to correct him when he asked an interesting question.

"So will Michael be angry that you're on a date with me?"

"What? This isn't a date."

"Oh? A man and woman, who are attracted to each other, having lunch in a pub . . . that sounds a lot like a date to me. However, if you choose to deny what is obvious to everyone else, then I'll play along."

Jewel was dumbstruck.

"What can I get ya?" a young blonde waitress asked.

"Two pints, Guinness," Everett ordered.

"No, actually, I would just like tea," Jewel interrupted.

"Nonsense. A Guinness for the lady," Everett said.

Jewel folded her arms and leaned back in her chair.

*I bet this guy doesn't get many second dates.*

"So, my dear, tell me all about yourself," Everett said as the waitress set down two pints, followed by a cup of tea which she served Jewel with a quick wink. Everett looked annoyed.

Jewel launched into a brief, very vague description of her job and her life back home.

Although Everett watched Jewel as she spoke, she had the suspicion that he wasn't really listening to a word she said.

"So how did you meet the Walsh brothers?" he asked.

Jewel thought of telling him that Brogan was dead, but felt it was not her place to broadcast such news. She took a long sip of her tea as she considered how she should answer the question.

"I met Brogan in Venice, and then a week later I met Michael."

"I'm just surprised that a woman like you would associate with men such as that," Everett spat.

"What's wrong with the Walsh brothers?"

"Oh dear, the things that I could tell you would be too vulgar for your delicate ears."

*Why is this guy always mentioning my ears?*

Jewel chewed the inside of her cheek as she considered his words. She had a strong compulsion to defend Michael and Brogan, but at the same time she wanted to hear the stories that Everett might have about the brothers. Loyalty won.

"Professor Nolan, I think highly of the Walsh brothers. They are my friends. I would appreciate it if you didn't speak poorly of them in my presence," Jewel said.

Everett gave her a look of pity.

"You too, Jewel? You have been taken in by that dubious pair? Please don't be fooled by their good looks and charm. Those brothers have had the benefit of being raised with wealth and privilege. They never had to work for anything. Brogan Walsh is an absolute cad and Michael isn't much better. I have it from a reliable source that Michael cast his fiancée aside in such as callous manner that she was a ruined woman after that. But I considered it my duty to care for her and help her in that time of anguish."

"Elizabeth?"

Everett Nolan took a long sip of his beer while he watched Jewel.

"So you know of dear Elizabeth?"

Jewel's breath hitched at the question. Jewel was hungry for information. She wanted to get the details from Everett. She studied her blond companion and noticed the look of satisfaction that he wore. Jewel worked hard to keep her own face neutral.

"I would be very careful associating with someone who would use a woman and then toss her aside so cruelly," Everett added.

"I've heard a much different version of the events," Jewel said.

Jewel hoped that Everett couldn't detect that he had piqued her curiosity.

*Is it possible that Michael lied to me about what happened? What would he gain by lying? Well, he could lie to make himself look better. No, Jewel. Think about it. Would Michael, the modern day Dudley Do-Right, lie to you about this? No.*

"It's time for me to go," Jewel said.

"I apologize. I won't say another word about your friends. I understand you feel loyal to them, so we won't speak of them again. Please stay. We were just getting to know each other. So tell me more about your travels. Where are you headed to now? Back to the United States?" Everett asked as he reached over and placed his hand atop Jewel's.

"I'm not sure. Michael hasn't said."

Everett gave her an exaggerated look of pity.

"So you're at his mercy. You know, I'm planning to take a year's sabbatical for research in Greece. I would love to take you along. You could be my little research assistant," he said.

Jewel's eyes grew in surprise and interest.

*A year in Greece? That would be cool. Wait, what are you thinking, Jewel? Some creepy guy dangles a vacation in front of you and you're actually thinking about it?*

"I've got to go," Jewel repeated as she got to her feet.

"What? But we were just getting acquainted. Please, Jewel, have a bite to eat with me. I really want to spend time with you," Everett pleaded as he stood and took her hand. "Please give me a chance."

"I really need to get back. Michael will be looking for me."

"Very well, then. I'll respect your choice. I'll walk you back," he said as he dropped money on the table and offered Jewel his arm.

"No, thank you." Jewel turned and walked out of the pub.

*That's a girl, Jewel. Remember you are strong and independent. You call the shots. You are in charge . . . And you have no idea where you are.*

Jewel stood on the sidewalk for a moment. She looked down the street to the right, then the left.

Jewel felt a presence beside her. She turned to find Everett offering his arm again. She gave him a quick smile and accepted.

Chapter 16

A Witch

Jewel felt like a teenager coming home after curfew. She slipped into the house and quietly walked through the hall and to the stairs.

"Miss Townsend?" Hannah called.

Jewel let out a sigh and detoured to the library.

Hannah sat behind the large desk. Her fingers were laced and resting in front of her.

"Yes?" Jewel said as she stepped into the room. "You're back from your class?"

"Obviously, or do you believe you're hallucinating? Do you have a problem with hallucinations?"

"What? No. I don't have hallucinations."

*This woman is a fast talker. I really need to watch my step around her.*

"Please sit," Hannah said.

Jewel took a seat feeling like it was a command rather than a suggestion.

A long, uncomfortable, silence stretched on in which Jewel began biting her nails. Hannah watched her disapprovingly. Jewel rested her hands in her lap and began biting her cheek.

"What are you intentions regarding my nephew?"

A startled sound escaped Jewel's lips.

"Intentions? I don't know. I don't really have intentions."

"Are you always this irresolute? I can tell you that I'm fiercely protective of my boys," she said. "Is it the money?" Hannah leaned forward and placed her hands down on the desk.

"The money? What money?"

"No. You don't strike me as an opportunist. I still haven't quite figured you out, but I'll be watching you. Make no mistake. I'll be watching," she said. She looked down at her desk and began shuffling papers.

*I think I just peed myself a little.*

Hannah didn't look at Jewel again, which Jewel took to mean that she had been dismissed. She crept from the library and, finally out of Hannah's sight, she hurried up the stairs. The front door slammed and Jewel spun around. Michael stood in the foyer looking daggers up at Jewel. She gave him a tentative smile.

"Hi, Michael."

"And when did you get back?" Michael said with an edge to his voice.

Jewel started to respond, but Michael's questions continued as he joined her at the landing.

"Are you injured? Did he touch you?" he demanded.

"Who?"

Michael tilted his head and his brows shot up in annoyance.

"Everett?" Jewel asked.

"Yes, you little fool," Michael snapped. His eyes burned with rage.

Jewel swallowed hard. She hoped that the warmth she felt in her face wasn't visible on her cheeks.

*I have never seen him pissed off like this.*

"You can't boss me around. I can go wherever I want and with whomever I want," Jewel said with a defiant tilt to her head. "You can't control me."

"Control you?" Michael said. His voice calmed as he reined in his emotions.

"How did you find out, anyway? Were you spying on me?"

"I don't need to spy on you. That ass, Everett Nolan, was waiting outside for me so that he could tell me all about your *date*."

"Seriously?" Jewel asked as she glanced at the door.

"Tsk, tsk, tsk," Hannah's tongue clicked from the library doorway, where she stood watching.

"Aunt Hannah, please," Michael called. He turned back to Jewel. "Everett Nolan is a pompous ass and it's no secret I abhor the man. However, that is not why I'm disturbed that you went on a date with him."

"It wasn't a date," Jewel defended. He showed up at the park. I was just being polite."

"Jewel, I have tried to keep you safe. That was the entire reason you left Texas with me. Last night when you and Everett both disappeared, I didn't come to find you because I wanted to tell you what bad judgment you had in your choice in men, it was because Everett has a history of forcing himself on women. I wanted to protect you. I see now that I shouldn't have gone through the trouble."

"I didn't know. You didn't tell me about that. You just barged in, seeping with testosterone," Jewel said, but her voice grew small as guilt washed over her.

Michael said something in Irish and shook his head.

"Even Elizabeth . . ." Michael started.

"The whore of Babylon," Hannah interjected.

"Even Elizabeth rejected that slimy fool because she could see what he was. You are correct. I cannot and will not control you. You are free to make your own choices, but I cannot protect you if you continue to put yourself in danger," Michael said, then turned, descended the stairs, and left the house.

The slamming of the front door echoed through the foyer.

Jewel felt like she had been punched in the gut.

"Wow. Elizabeth rejected Everett? And here I thought her only requirement in a man was to have something that swings under his kilt," Hannah said then ducked back into the library.

Jewel dropped down to sit on the step and continued to stare at the door.

*Great! Now I have guilt. I thought perhaps Michael was feeling jealous of Everett, but he was trying to protect me. Of course he isn't jealous, Jewel. Jealousy would imply that he has some kind of non-platonic feelings. Crap! My brain hurts. One thing for certain, you owe him an apology.*

∞     ∞     ∞

"Father Wendell said he'll make the arrangements for Brogan's burial in the church's graveyard. I faxed a signed release to the Italian police so they can cremate the remains and then send the ashes to the church. The condition of his remains made cremation the best option." Michael pushed the food around his dinner plate. "And . . ."

"Faolan, this is not dinner conversation," Hannah said with finality.

"Yes, Aunt Hannah. I just wanted you to know that it's all taken care of."

"Jewel," Hannah said, changing the subject. "There is a book missing from my library. Please make sure it's returned to its proper place when you are through."

*How did she know that I took the book from the library? With such an extensive collection, there is no way she could identify one missing book.*

"Umm . . . yes, of course," Jewel said.

Michael and Hannah wore twin blank expressions.

*They are a pair of Moai statues. She's bluffing. She just assumed that I took a book. Think about it, Jewel. You've been in your room for three hours. She figured you were reading.*

"If you are interested in speaking Irish then Faolan would be an excellent teacher," Hannah said, then took a bite of her salmon.

Jewel dropped her fork onto her plate. Michael was startled, but Hannah continued watching her with stone-faced regard.

*What the hell? How did she know? She's a witch . . . or she has cameras.*

Jewel looked around the dining room. She was studying the crown molding for any sign of cameras, when Hannah began speaking in Irish. Michael responded, also in Irish. Jewel looked at them with suspicion.

"Are you unwell, Miss Townsend?" Hannah asked.

"No. I'm fine, but I think I'm . . . just going to go to my room," Jewel said as she stood.

Michael got to his feet as Jewel did as a display of good manners. *Did he always do that?*

Jewel made her way to her room, but surveyed every inch of the ceiling along the way, looking for cameras.

Once she searched her room and found no cameras, she plopped down on the bed.

*Yep, she's a witch, all right.*

∞   ∞   ∞

Jewel sat up as she heard her door snap shut. Her room was dark.

*When did I fall asleep? How long was I asleep? And who the hell was in my room?*

Jewel sprang from the bed only to get tangled in a blanket and fall to the floor. The thud could have awoken the dead. She heard quick footsteps before her door flew open and, with a pop, the room filled with light. Michael stood in the doorway.

"What was that noise?" he demanded.

Jewel crawled around the bed on her hands and knees.

"I fell out of bed," she said. "Were you just in here?"

Michael pulled her to her feet.

"Sit down before you fall over and break bones," he demanded. "Yes, I was in your room. I came in to check on you. I thought you might be reading."

Jewel's eyes were adjusting to the light. She looked at the blanket that caused her fall. She had never seen this particular blanket before. It was pale blue with a design of soccer balls. She was certain that the blanket was not part of her room's décor.

"Where did this come from?"

"I'm not sure originally where it came from, but I brought it from my room. You were asleep on top of your blanket. The temperature drops at night in this old house. I didn't want you to get ill," Michael said.

Jewel was touched by his concern, but avoided eye contact.

"Michael, I need to apologize to you. I understand that you were trying to protect me and that's why you were worried about me being alone with Everett. I mean . . . that's really nice, but wouldn't it have been easier to just tell me about Everett? That way I would know that he's dangerous."

"I thought there wasn't much chance that you and Everett would be alone. I didn't want to make you feel worried about what could have happened last night."

*Is it possible that I have been reading this guy wrong since the day we met? Does he actually care about people's feelings?*

"You do care, don't you?"

"Of course I care, Jewel. What kind of heartless man do you think I am?"

Jewel produced a huge smile. She began to giggle. The giggling started a laughing fit.

"I don't understand why that's so funny."

Jewel fell back onto the bed, laughing.

"I can see you have lost your mind, so I'm going to go to bed," Michael said as he turned to leave.

"Michael," Jewel called as she wiped her eyes. "I'm sorry. I hope you're not angry with me anymore."

Michael stepped closer. He reached out and held Jewel's chin.

"Do you have any idea how I would've felt if something bad happened to you? I would have been responsible. I'm supposed to keep you safe, but you make that very difficult," he said, then leaned down and gave her a quick kiss on the top of her head.

"Goodnight," Michael said. He turned and left the room.

She curled up on her pillow and noticed a sweet smell. She looked around and discovered a mug on her nightstand. She stared down into a cup of hot cocoa. It was still warm and smelled wonderful.

*I think the tin-man has grown a heart . . . or did he always have one?*

Chapter 17
Converting to Catholicism

Jewel arrived late for breakfast just as she had done the morning before.

"Good morning," she said as she took her seat. She looked across the table at Michael. He nodded his head in greeting.

Wilson came in with Jewel's plate and poured her some tea.

"Is tea okay with you, Jewel? Perhaps you would prefer hot cocoa," Hannah said.

*She's a witch.*

Michael choked on his toast.

"Careful, son, you need to eat more slowly," Hannah said as she looked at Michael and then Jewel. She continued to study them. "Now that you've made up you aren't nearly as entertaining. As fun as this is, I must be off. I have a meeting before Mass with the Rummage Sale committee," Hannah said as she got to her feet and headed to the hall. "The package that came for you is on my desk in the library."

"What package?" Michael asked, tossing his napkin onto his plate. He followed his aunt as she entered the library.

Jewel quickly drained the contents of her tea cup, and instantly regretted it.

*Hot, hot, hot . . . Jewel, you idiot.*

She grabbed her toast, and followed the pair. When she caught up to them they were in the library. Hannah was holding a small package.

"I opened it when I received it, but I repackaged it when I realized it was yours."

Hannah tossed the small package to Michael. He caught it mid-air and carefully opened it. Michael pulled out a box about the size of the toast that Jewel held. The box was tan and nondescript. He stopped and took another look at the outer envelope.

"This is addressed to you," Michael said to his aunt.

"Aye, that's why I opened it. But it's not mine." she replied as she sat in the chair behind the desk to watch.

Michael looked closely at the envelope.

"Germany," he said in a low voice.

He opened the box. The contents were wrapped in tissue paper. After he removed all the protective covering a small flat box lay in the palm of his hand.

"What is it?" Jewel asked, stepping closer.

"A cigarette case. Fabergé."

The case was not ornate like the ones Jewel had seen at the New Orleans museum, but it was lovely. It was silver in color and had a small enamel pattern in the corner of the lid. The pattern contained dark blue tulips on a white background.

Michael opened the cigarette case to find a note: "*Happy Birthday—B.*"

"Brogan sent you a birthday present," Michael said to his aunt.

"My birthday was four months ago. You should know that, Faolan," she said in a harsh tone.

"So, the present was late," Michael said, turning the note over to examine the back.

"No. Brogan sent me a brooch for my birthday."

"Then what makes you think it's for me?" Michael asked.

Hannah leaned forward, placing her elbows on the desk and clasping her hands together as if in prayer.

"Your birthday is in three weeks. Also, Brogan signs his missives to me differently," she said as a smile grew on her pointed face.

"How does he sign?" Michael asked as he studied the cigarette case.

"He signs; 'with love, your favorite nephew,'" she said as she leaned back in the chair.

Michael slowly turned to her with a look of disbelief.

"Don't look at me like that. I never said he was my favorite," she defended, with a smile.

Jewel picked up the envelope and studied the return address and postmark. Michael leaned toward Jewel and was looking at the envelope over her shoulder.

"When did you receive this?" Michael asked.

"The day before you arrived," Hannah replied.

"Aunt Hannah! Why didn't you say so before? Why am I just hearing about this now?"

"Because if I had given it to you when you arrived then you would have immediately left. I wanted you to spend a little time at home. I don't see you but once a year," she said, her voice rising in volume as she got to her feet.

Michael began a rant in Irish. Hannah responded, also in Irish. The argument continued to escalate until they were standing toe-to-toe in front of the desk.

Jewel sat down with the envelope. She was becoming accustomed to the outbursts and the volatile relationship. She studied the postmark and the return address carefully.

"Michael, this is postmarked on the day I met Brogan; the day he died," Jewel stated, holding up the envelope.

Michael immediately stepped away from his aunt and grabbed the envelope. He squinted as he studied the postmark.

"Frankfurt, Germany," he read under his breath. "How is this possible?" he asked as he sat down heavily upon one of the large overstuffed chairs.

"The return address is in Frankfurt, too," Jewel said. "I'm not sure what BKI Deutsche Industriebank is, but I suppose it's a bank," Jewel said with imperfect pronunciation.

Hannah swore in her Irish tongue then scurried around the desk to grab a large satchel.

"I'm going to be late," she said. She leaned down and gave Michael a kiss on his cheek. "I wish you would be here when I return, but I know you won't. Please come visit before Christmas."

She turned and looked at Jewel and sighed.

"I guess I'll have to call Father Wendell and cancel the meeting I made for Miss Townsend," she said as she headed for the door.

"Meeting with me? Why?" Jewel asked in surprise.

"To talk about your conversion to Catholicism," she said as she waved her hand as if to dismiss such a silly question. "I have to run," she said.

Jewel could hear the front door snap shut a moment later.

"Why would I need to talk to a priest about conversion? Who said I was converting to Catholicism?"

Michael was still studying the envelope. Then he sprang up from the chair and circled around to the back of the desk. He began typing on the computer keyboard.

"You're correct. BKI Deutsche Industriebank is a bank; a very large bank. Brogan must have had them mail this item." He shook his head. "But Brogan didn't keep money in banks. So he must have had other business with them."

"Maybe a friend of his works there," Jewel said.

Michael scowled at her from around the computer monitor.

"No. Doubtful."

"Maybe they were holding something of his," Jewel added.

Michael's face slowly transformed.

"You may be right."

Chapter 18
Frau Viessmann

*Jewel Journal:*

*So, my dear journal, this is what it has become of you. I am writing on your crunchy pages. Actually I believe this is like four pages stuck together with water from the Gulf of Venice, but at least I'm writing. My traveling companion warned me not to write anything revealing on these pages. He approved of the word Germany (I had to argue with him before he relented, but he agreed in the end). So, we are on a train headed to Germany, we boarded in Paris (I really had to fight to get the use of Paris approved). I can't believe I was in Paris, France and I didn't see anything. I have always wanted to travel. I'm doing a lot of traveling right now, but I'm not seeing any of the sights. Frankly, I'm exhausted and could use some downtime. My relationship and interactions with my companion change day-to-day. One moment we get along well and the next moment we just glare at each other.*

*I had a chance to call Mary again. She agreed that I needed two weeks off for emergency leave. So, I should still have a job when I return, if I return, if I don't die a painful death.*

*I had a huge realization this morning. I have been off of my anxiety medication for a few days. I didn't consciously stop taking it. I just forgot. This is very strange, because I'm in the most stressful situation possible. I'm going to hold off on taking the medication a bit longer to see how it goes. I'm feeling okay, with the exception of running for my life.*

*My current emotions: Tired. Yes, emotionally and physically tired.*

*My emotions forecast: That which doesn't kill us makes us stronger. I hope, if I don't get killed, I'll get stronger.*

"Couldn't we have taken a day off? We could have hung out in Paris and rested," Jewel said, as she slouched in the train seat. "I'm exhausted."

"This is the only lead we have. I want to know what business Brogan had with the bank. Besides, I believe it's best that we keep moving. Chauvin has resources. It's probably only a matter of time before he tracks us down. I didn't want him to find us at my aunt's house and put her in danger," Michael said. "Even though she can definitely take care of herself," he added with a grin.

"Okay. You've been making good decisions, so I'll trust your decision this time," Jewel said.

"Thank you," he said. "That is the first genuine compliment you've ever given me."

"Well, you deserve it."

Jewel started thinking about what Michael had said about his aunt taking care of herself. Aunt Hannah was definitely a force to be reckoned with. But, still. She had her vulnerabilities.

"Michael, your aunt never really came to terms with Brogan's death, did she?" She saw the pain caused by her words flutter across his face. "I'm sorry. I didn't mean to be so blunt."

"No. She wouldn't accept it."

"She strikes me as a very stubborn woman."

"You have no idea."

"I believe she would've had me converted to Catholicism by the end of the month if I'd stayed," Jewel said as she glanced toward the back of the train. Something appeared familiar, but she wasn't sure what it was. She studied the aisle and looked over the passengers, but dismissed it as her imagination.

"She's a very passionate woman. She has always wanted the best for me and Brogan. Which reminds me, we don't have to worry about money. When I went to pack I found an envelope with enough cash to cover our travel expenses. If she'd tried giving it to me outright, then I would have refused."

"That was generous of her. But I'm not sure how I feel about accepting her money," Jewel said.

A mischievous smile spread across Michael's face.

"Are you afraid of being in her debt?"

"Well . . . Yes. Actually I am," Jewel replied. "She's a scary woman."

"I don't blame you a bit."

"Besides, I suspect that she may be a witch."

"A witch?" Michael laughed.

Jewel had only heard his laughter once before—outside his bedroom door after her humiliating bathrobe incident. But today his laughter was deep and genuine, and it made Jewel instantly smile.

"I mean, I don't think she has a cauldron or anything. I doubt she dabbles with eye of newt, snakes, snails, and puppy dog tails, but she knows things that I can't figure out how she knows," Jewel said.

"Observation! My aunt has amazing skills of observation. When Brogan and I were young we used to test her. We would go into her office or bedroom and move an item about five inches from its position. You know, a pad of paper, or a notebook. Sometimes she would inquire about who was in her room, but then other times she wouldn't say a word. Brogan and I would think that she hadn't noticed until we snuck back in to find the thing we'd moved was back in its original position."

"It sounds like you and Brogan were mischievous boys."

"Well, it was more like a science experiment. We found that she had almost a ninety-seven percent accuracy rate at two and a half inches."

"What?" Jewel asked.

"Brogan and I began measuring the distance that we would move the item, the distance in relation to the other items in the vicinity, and the accuracy of the item returning to its original location. We analyzed the data and found Aunt Hannah had almost a ninety-seven percent accuracy rate at two and a half inches. The two and a half inches were the distance that we moved the object."

Jewel wasn't sure if she should be impressed by the boys' scientific acumen, or concerned that they would take such an odd interest.

"That's insane. How old were you?"

Michael closed his eyes in thought. "Oh, I remember Brogan was thirteen, because his birthday came and Aunt Hannah gave him two laboratory data collection books. So that would mean I was ten years old."

"Data collection books?" Jewel questioned.

"Yeah, they're just notebooks with grids for collecting data," Michael replied.

"So, she knew? She knew you were testing her?"

"Unfortunately she figured it out. Like I said, she has amazing skills of observation. So I guess our data wasn't as reliable because the test subject knew she was being tested. That's when we stopped measuring."

"Oh my gosh," Jewel said, laughing. "You were the strangest kid. Things are starting to make sense now. Thank you for sharing that story. It sounds like you and Brogan were close when you were young."

"Aye, we were close up until he turned nineteen, and went off on a college work study—an archaeological dig. When he returned he announced that he was quitting school. He began traveling a lot. We would arrange a visit every few months, and schedule our holidays together. This went on for several years, and then . . ." Michael's words trailed off.

Jewel felt certain that she knew what happened next. She didn't want to hear about Elizabeth, or about their fighting. She didn't want Michael to relive the pain.

"I wish I could have hung out with you guys. I bet you had a lot of fun. I bet you were always getting into trouble," Jewel said, trying to shift the conversation as she relaxed back in her seat. She stifled a yawn.

"Aye, Brogan was always in trouble. I was usually the one trying to figure out how we could stay out of trouble," Michael said with a laugh.

Jewel noticed Michael's Irish brogue. It was still strong. She anticipated that he would lose the Irish lilt once he had left his kinfolk, but she was enjoying the melodic tones when he spoke. As she relaxed, the gentle movement of the train lulled her to sleep.

Jewel was dreaming of Venice. She was looking down into the green water of the canal.

"It's a pretty shade of green. I never really thought about it," a warm voice said with a lovely Irish lilt.

Jewel looked to the side to find Brogan smiling at her. She noticed his crooked nose and it caused her to smile in response.

"I hate to say it, but I really have to go," Jewel said. "I have a plane to catch in the morning."

"I know," Brogan said as he pulled Jewel into his arms. He reached up and cradled her face as he gave her a kiss. Jewel closed her eyes and enjoyed the warmth of his mouth. The kiss was longer than she had expected and she could feel his longing as it grew with the kiss. Jewel became breathless and pulled away. She opened her eyes, but it was not Brogan that she saw. Michael was embracing her and she wasn't in Venice. She was standing at the top of the stairs in Aunt Hannah's house.

Jewel's head bumped something as she awoke with a start.

"Ouch," Michael said as he reached up and touched his lip.

"What were you doing?" Jewel asked as she pushed away from Michael.

"What was *I* doing? Nothing. You were resting your head on my shoulder while you slept. Why did you head butt me?"

Jewel's head cleared a bit. She looked around the train. Michael was sucking on his lip.

"I'm sorry. I was having a dream," Jewel said as she rubbed her eyes.

"A nice dream from the sound of it."

"Stay out of my dreams," Jewel snapped as she stood and headed to the restroom.

Jewel stayed in the restroom longer than needed. She was feeling self-conscious about her reaction to Michael and the memory of her dream. As she exited, a man quickly turned away from the door. She wondered if he was a pervert hoping to get a peek, and took note of his tan jacket and the gray baseball cap that hid his face. He turned and retreated down the aisle as she returned to her seat.

"So, I was in your dream? Was it the good part?" Michael asked.

Jewel felt her face flush. She was embarrassed, but she was also angry that Michael would tease her. She looked at Michael expecting to see his smug expression of satisfaction, but that is not what she found. He looked serious and somewhat hopeful. She didn't respond. She looked away and changed the subject.

"Are we almost there?" she asked.

"Yes. I'm glad you got some rest. I was worried when you said that you were exhausted. You were asleep for about three hours," Michael replied.

The train was slowing as it approached a station. Some of the passengers were getting to their feet. Jewel looked up and down the aisle and spotted the familiar gray cap at the back of the train. The man ducked down as if he were hiding from Jewel.

"Michael, either I have a creeper or we're being followed. There's a man in the back of the train with a gray baseball cap. I feel like he's watching us."

Michael tried to casually get a look at the man, but he wasn't successful. The train came to a stop.

"Come on," Michael said. "Let's get going."

Michael moved into the aisle and off of the train. Jewel followed. She glanced back and saw the man in the gray cap not far behind.

"He's following," she confirmed.

Michael took Jewel's hand and moved with the crowd along the train platform. The crowd swelled as more and more people exited the train.

"Stay close," he said, squeezing her hand then releasing it.

Michael stepped to the side, bent down, and began adjusting the cuff on his slacks. Jewel stood close to him. She saw the gray cap pass them and slow down. She was trying to see the man's face when Michael grabbed her hand and yanked her back on to the train. The doors closed as soon as she was inside. The action startled her, but also surprised the man in the gray cap. He stood on the station platform and looked directly at Jewel.

"It's Suran!" Jewel said.

She watched Suran as he took off the cap and slapped it against his leg in anger. Jewel sighed as the train started moving. She gave Suran a small wave.

"Don't taunt him. I had a feeling that's who it was," Michael said as he sat down.

"How did he find us?" she asked.

"I'm not sure, but he won't be far behind." Michael studied the posted map of train lines. "Only two more stops before Frankfurt."

"I guess that means Chauvin found us again," Jewel sighed.

"Maybe not," Michael said.

"What do you mean?"

"Suran might be working separately from Chauvin. I'm wondering if he's Brogan's killer. Remember, Chauvin said he was looking for the man that committed the murder. I wonder if that's Suran," Michael said.

"Oh," Jewel said. "So it's possible that we have more than one group after us."

"Correct," Michael replied.

"Maybe we should try to get off at a different station and then double back," Jewel suggested.

"I think we'll be fine getting off in Frankfurt. Our next obstacle is going to be finding somewhere to stay. I don't want to give up our passports at a hotel. Most hotels and even the bed and breakfast houses will ask for them. We'd raise red flags if we start calling around to hotels asking if they require passports. They will probably call the authorities," Michael said. He pulled out a guide book and flipped the pages.

"We haven't done anything wrong, so the police shouldn't have any issue with us," Jewel said as she began nibbling on the nail of her index finger.

"True, but we don't want our names out there," he said as he pulled her hand from her mouth and set it on her lap. "We need to stay hidden. If we talk to the police we would be advertising our arrival in Germany. By any chance do you read German?" Michael said handing the booklet to Jewel.

"No," Jewel replied. "You don't?"

"No."

"Great. So now we'll have to deal with a language barrier."

"It should be fine. We speak English. That's usually enough to get by. What languages do you speak?" Michael asked.

The question made Jewel wonder what she could contribute to this adventure. She really didn't have any special skills to offer, except her knowledge of literature.

"English . . . and Pig-Latin," Jewel replied with a smirk.

Michael gave a small chuckle.

"Let me know if that comes in handy."

"I know literature. I can talk about writers and books, and philosophy. I also have a wealth of knowledge when it comes to geography. That's about it."

"The American education system should focus more on language," Michael said.

"So what languages do you speak? I know you speak English, Italian, and Irish. Anything else?" Jewel asked.

"I also speak some Spanish. I only know Spanish because it's so close to Italian."

"I guess you know a lot of Latin, too, being Catholic," she said.

"Not as much as you would think. I wasn't as ….." Michael trailed off.

"That's really impressive. You're a smart man. You have a lot of knowledge. I bet you're a good teacher, too"

"You just gave me a brilliant idea. I need to call in a couple of favors when we get to the station," Michael said with renewed enthusiasm.

∞　∞　∞

The Frankfurt station was huge and crowded. Jewel was amazed by all the train tracks. There were trains below ground as well as above. For a moment she had forgotten that they were on a mission and running from crazed murderers. She was fulfilling a lifelong dream of traveling. She only wished she could savor the moment, but Michael pulled her through the crowd at an alarming speed. Once they were outside the station, Michael picked up the pace. Jewel was having trouble keeping up. After about three blocks she needed a break.

"Michael, your legs are a lot longer than mine. I have to take two steps for your one. Can you slow down?"

"I want to get us as far from the station as possible," he said, continuing his stride.

"Michael, I can't," Jewel said, yanking her hand free and stopping.

"Keep moving!" Michael demanded over his shoulder.

"I can't!" Jewel said, leaning over to catch her breath.

Michael stopped and looked back. Jewel's cheeks were flushed with exertion, or perhaps anger.

"We really need to keep moving," Michael said. "Come on!"

"You're a bully. You know that?" she said, between labored breaths.

He paused.

"I'm sorry," he said, softly. He came back and held his hand out to her. "Please?"

She was still trying to catch her breath. She nodded and took his hand. They continued at a slower pace.

"Look. There's a café over there," Michael said. "We'll get some tea. You can rest while I make my phone calls."

The café was quaint with a tiled floor and several small bistro-style tables. There weren't many patrons. They selected a table in the back of the café, away from the door. Michael ordered tea and biscuits. As the refreshments arrived, they sat quietly and Michael studied a map. He folded the map and set it beside his tea cup. He poured tea in Jewel's cup then his own. He watched her in contemplation.

"You're right," Michael said, breaking the silence.

Jewel glared at him, still angry about his inconsideration. She turned her attention to the other patrons and noticed a man at the counter, talking on the phone. She listened to his deep voice for a moment until she turned her attention back to her companion.

Michael shifted in his chair several times.

"When we first met, you commented on my lack of skill when it came to my interactions with others," he said. "I teach my classes, I go to the gym, I go to faculty meetings, I go to church, and I go home. That is about all the interaction I have. So, you are correct. I'm very deficient in my skills when it comes to personal interaction."

Jewel watched Michael make this confession. At first she was surprised, but she soon felt touched. This wasn't just a confession, nor was it an excuse for his behavior. He was baring a little of his soul. He was making an attempt to open up. This was Michael trying to improve his interaction with other, at least with her.

"I wasn't always like this, you know. I just slowly pulled away from friends and family, and then I moved to the U.S. to teach. I have stayed busy teaching and publishing scholarly articles. I just didn't have time for . . . relationships," he said, still staring into his tea cup.

"Was it because of Elizabeth?" Jewel asked.

Michael's eyes shot up to look at Jewel. She saw him swallow as if something was stuck in his throat. His expression changed. He looked defeated.

"Probably. I can't pinpoint just one thing that caused it."

Jewel didn't respond, but watched Michael carefully. His grip on his teacup was tight. She feared for the china.

"After Elizabeth, I refused to speak to Brogan. Aunt Hannah was not happy with me. She sided with Brogan . . . she always sided with Brogan," Michael said, as he started laughing lightly.

Jewel was shocked by this change, but said nothing.

"Brogan could always talk his way out of anything. Aunt Hannah said that he had the gift of Blarney. He was a silver-tongued devil. Everyone always loved Brogan," Michael said as he became somber again.

Jewel could detect a glisten in his eyes. She watched as he swallowed hard again. She looked away to give him privacy.

*Great, Jewel. You're a big fraud. Michael is truly mourning the death of his brother. You are sad that Brogan died, but you really didn't even know Brogan. You big faker.*

"Sorry that I called you a bully," Jewel said in a small voice.

"No. You had every right to call me a bully."

*Great, now I have guilt again.*

He gave her a brief smile then turned to look at the counter where the man was still talking on the phone.

"That guy doesn't look like he'll be off the phone anytime soon," Michael said as he got to his feet. "I'll see if I can find somebody who'll lend me a phone. You should stay here and rest. I shouldn't be too long."

Jewel watched Michael leave the café. She reflected on the conversation and considered how alike she and Michael were in their situations. Once again, she compared Michael and Brogan. She wondered if Michael had always been the serious one.

The volume of the German man, on the phone, grew to a disturbing level. He laughed loudly, hung up the phone, and exited the café.

Jewel was pouring more tea from the small pot on the table when she thought she heard someone say "Townsend". She looked up at a waiter that was holding the café's phone. He was covering the phone's mouthpiece and calling out something in German. She had no idea what he was saying, and the other patrons were ignoring him. He said the words again, loudly.

Now Jewel was sure he was saying "Townsend". She stared at the waiter, trying to understand. They made eye contact.

"Fräulein Townsend?" he asked.

Jewel just continued to stare.

"Fräulein Townsend?" he repeated.

Jewel slowly nodded her head.

The waiter began rambling in German. Jewel had no clue what he was saying.

"I don't understand," she said weakly.

He spoke again slowly. She understood her name, and the word telephone. The man held the phone receiver out to Jewel. She slowly stood and walked over. On the way she looked outside to see Michael talking on a borrowed phone. He wouldn't be calling her. Who would even know she was in Germany? She took the receiver from the waiter. He shook his head and walked away.

"Hello?" Jewel said meekly.

"Fräulein Townsend? I would like to speak with you. I'm sending a car for you. I would like to discuss a business arrangement," the female voice on the other end of the phone said.

"I'm sorry, who is this?" Jewel squeaked, as her throat tightened with panic.

"I am Frau Viessmann. I will explain who I am when you arrive. I prefer to speak face-to-face," the woman said in her deeply accented English.

Jewel felt the hairs on her neck standing up. She didn't know what to say. She felt a hand touch her shoulder and she spun around. Michael was looking at her with concern.

"What's wrong?" he mouthed.

Jewel shook her head. She put the receiver down in the cradle.

"We have to get out of here. I have a really bad feeling. We have to leave now," she said as she rushed to the table, grabbed her backpack, and darted out of the café.

Michael followed without comment, allowing Jewel to set the pace. She tore down the street, turning at every corner, her gaze swiveling back and forth as if she were looking for something or someone. She was exhausting herself. Michael stayed close behind her. She stopped at a corner.

*Where to now? Someone is watching. I know they're watching.*

"This way," Michael said as he pointed in the direction of a row of shops.

Michael continued to follow Jewel's lead without question. Jewel was panting and trying to keep up the rapid pace she had set, but her body was giving out.

"We have a place to go when you're ready. We can get a taxi," Michael said.

Jewel didn't answer, but nodded her head vigorously while gasping for air. She slowed her pace again. Across the street, about half a block away, Jewel could see a large hotel with two cream-colored Mercedes cars with taxi signs on their roofs. She waited as Michael darted toward them and spoke with the man standing beside the taxi. Michael turned and waved Jewel over.

The plush interior of the cab gave Jewel a sense of security for the moment. She had never been in this nice of a cab. Glancing at Michael, she noticed he wore a worried look. He reached over and squeezed her hand.

"You can tell me what happened, when you're ready," he assured.

Now that she felt safe again, she wasn't sure why the phone call had disturbed her so much. Yes, it was very odd to get a phone call from a stranger that knew who she was and where she was, but the woman didn't say anything threatening or scary.

*Why did you just hang up? You idiot. This was your opportunity to get some information. This was your opportunity to be useful. But you panicked.*

"I messed up," she said sheepishly. She described the call while Michael listened quietly. "I should have questioned her. She may have been able to shed some light on this whole thing," Jewel said.

"No. I think we should trust your gut instinct. We'll try to find out who this Frau Viessmann is, so next time we encounter her, we will know who we're dealing with," Michael said. "You didn't do anything wrong, Jewel," he reassured, giving her hand another squeeze.

"I guess I'm just freaking out," she said as she began to nibble on her thumb nail. "I've been on anxiety medication for two years, but I haven't taken it for the past few days. I was going to see how it all played out, but now I'm wondering if that's a mistake," she said, somewhat embarrassed by the confession.

"Whatever you think best. You know yourself better than anyone. However, I can assure you that a call like that would have bothered me, too," Michael said.

Jewel considered this statement. She gave him a brief smile. She looked out the taxi window as the driver navigated through the streets.

"Where are we going?" she asked.

"I got in touch with Father Wendell. He made a couple of phone calls. He spoke with a priest that has a parish here, and he'll be putting us up for a couple of nights," Michael said, pleased with himself.

"We're staying at a Catholic Church?"

"No. I truly doubt it's in the church itself, but I wasn't told the particulars."

"This will be interesting."

She took in the sights of the city through the taxi window until the cab pulled up to a large church. As the taxi drove away, Jewel began to feel uneasy once more.

"How are we going to communicate with these people? Neither of us speaks German," Jewel whispered.

"That won't be a problem."

They walked to the large double doors. Michael pulled, but the doors were locked. He stepped back and looked up at the building.

"Hello," a voice called.

Jewel spun around to find a small man in his fifties. He had short blond hair and a large smile. His green eyes sparkled behind gold rimmed glasses.

"Would you happen to be Michael Walsh?" the man asked with an Irish brogue.

Jewel noticed as he drew closer that he was dressed in black pants and shirt with a white-short collar that she had seen Father Wendell wear.

"Yes, I am," Michael said as he approached the man with his hand extended. "And you must be Father Albert."

"I am," the man said as he took Michael's hand and shook it firmly. "I heard from Father Wendell that you need a place to stay. He also said that you need to go to confession," the man said, maintaining his large smile.

Michael sputtered briefly. He looked as if he were searching his mind for something. "Actually… Yes, I do," Michael said. "Last Sunday, I missed Mass."

Chapter 19
Hey God, it's Me, Jewel

"You were in there for a while," Jewel whispered as Michael sat down beside her on the pew. She was watching the church fill up with people.

"Don't judge me by how long I was in confession," he said with a smile. He pulled the kneeler down and knelt upon it.

"What are you doing?" Jewel whispered.

"Penance. Penance for my sins. Stop asking so many questions." He bowed his head, closed his eyes, and became silent.

Jewel watched him for a moment. There was something attractive about this large masculine man bowing down and humbling himself to God. She looked around the church. It was beautifully decorated, but not as extravagantly as the cathedrals that she'd visited in Italy. More people filed into the pews. She noticed that many were kneeling and praying and wondered if she should perhaps do the same.

She slowly got on her knees on the kneeler beside Michael.

*Hey God, it's me, Jewel. I know that I don't really talk to you, but I'm kind of in some trouble. I guess you know that. I'm really scared. I'm trying not to show that I'm scared, because I don't want people to think that I can't take care of myself. I can take care of myself, but it's nice to have someone else looking out for me.*

She looked at Michael. He stopped praying, looked at her, and gave her a dazzling smile.

*So, thank you for sending Michael to look out for me, and thank you for sending Brogan to make me smile. So, if you can help us to survive this whole thing that would be great. That's all . . . I'm not sure how to end this.*

"Peace out," Jewel said, then sat back on the pew.

Michael sat beside her. He was covering his mouth to stifle laughter.

"'Amen' is sufficient," he said.

"Crap, did I say that out loud?"

∞    ∞    ∞

"What did you think of your first Catholic Mass?" Michael asked as they stood outside the church watching the last of the parishioners leave.

"It was interesting. I wish I could've understood what he was saying. I think I would like to go to a Catholic Mass in English," she said.

"Really? I'll let Aunt Hannah know. Don't worry, I'll leave out the part where you ended your prayer with 'peace out'," Michael said with a smile.

Jewel shook her head, but started laughing with Michael.

"I'm glad you can laugh with me. A few days ago I think you would have slugged me for making such a comment," Michael said, as he reached over and pushed one of Jewel's unruly curls behind her ear.

Jewel was a little surprised by his action, but smiled again.

"Well, a few days ago I wouldn't have caught you laughing."

"Did you enjoy the Mass?" Father Albert asked as he exited the church and locked the door.

"Aye, thank you. I don't speak German, but I followed along," Michael said.

"I used to have an English Mass, but the attendance was very low," Father Albert told them. "This way," he said as he led them to the rectory, a house beside the church.

When they entered the small kitchen, Jewel noticed the table held several dishes of food.

"Ah, my parishioners. 'Tis a wonder I don't weigh more than I do with all the good food they make for me," Father Albert said with a sigh. "Please sit down and we will have supper," he said, waving them to the table.

Father Albert pulled three plates from the cabinet along with silverware. He stood beside the table, bowed his head, and began saying a blessing and thanks for the food. Jewel glanced at Michael and bowed her head until the blessing was finished.

"So, tell me about your travels, Mr. Walsh," Father Albert said as he passed the bowl of beans to Michael.

"In my youth I did a lot of traveling, but now I'm tied to my teaching job and just don't travel as much," Michael responded.

"What brings you to Germany?"

Michael gave a quick glance to Jewel seeking approval to speak freely, but Jewel only shrugged.

Michael gave a brief account of the past week. Father Albert didn't interrupt nor did he comment. By the end of Michael's tale, Father

Albert's kind face held a smile and his eyes glistened like a boy's on Christmas morning.

"Every man and woman has a pleasure; something that gives them joy that they probably spend too much time doing. I have such a pleasure. I love mystery novels. This story sounds like it's straight out of one of my books."

"But this is real," Jewel said.

"Oh, I don't doubt it for a moment. I'm sure it's very scary," he said as he pushed his plate forward and rubbed his chin. "Is there anything I can do to help? I would be thrilled to be a part of this, even in a small way," Father Albert said with sparkling eyes.

"We don't want you in any danger," Michael said.

"Oh . . . oh, of course not, but if there is anything I can do then please ask," he said.

"It's a long shot, but does the name 'Viessmann' ring any bells?" Jewel asked.

"It's a common name. It's probably someone from the seedy underbelly of society," Father Albert said as his face took on a look of fascination.

"Possibly," Jewel said.

"Is there a Frau Viessmann in the art world in Germany? Perhaps she is an art collector," Michael added.

"Perhaps," Father Albert said. "Let me do some research tomorrow." He rubbed his hands. "This is so exciting!"

Michael smiled, and then covered his mouth as he yawned.

"You must be exhausted. Let me show you to your rooms. I'll clean up the plates. I insist. You both need to get some sleep," Father Albert said.

∞    ∞    ∞

Jewel was comfortable in the guest bedroom while Michael was given accommodations on the pullout couch in Father Albert's office. Jewel felt exhausted when her head hit the pillow, but she couldn't fall asleep. She wished she had her phone so she could at least play a game.

She made her way to the kitchen for a glass of water. As she passed through the living room she found Father Albert sitting in a chair, sipping tea, and reading.

"Having difficulty sleeping?" he asked as he scratched his blond head.

"A bit," Jewel said. "What are you reading?"

He sheepishly held up a worn paperback. The title read; 'The Case of the Smoking Gun.'"

"We all have our guilty pleasures," he said with a weak smile. "What do you like?"

"Books. I love books. I'm a librarian," Jewel said as she took a seat on the couch.

"Oh, a kindred spirit. What genre do you enjoy?" Father Albert asked, placing his book down on his lap.

"I enjoy all genres, but I love romance. I used to read romance novels all the time, like two or three books a week. Not the cheap romances. The long ones with substantial characters, ones you can relate to," Jewel said.

"You don't read romance anymore? Why?" he asked.

The question was simple enough, but the answer was far from simple. Jewel hung her head for a moment, but didn't respond.

"You know if you want to talk then we can talk about anything. It doesn't have to be about books," Father Albert said with concern.

"You know I'm not Catholic, right?" Jewel said.

Father Albert gave a small laugh.

"Yes, I know. I won't hold that against you."

Jewel wasn't sure why, but she felt very comfortable with Father Albert. He was such a benign man. Before she even realized she was doing it, she was talking about her past.

"A couple of years ago, I had my heart broken. I was to be married. The man never showed up at the church. It really destroyed me. I went into counseling and I had to write these stupid emotion journals. Before I was jilted, I loved reading romance novels. After my fiancé left me, every time I picked up a romance novel I would start crying. I really loved reading romance novels and he ruined it, forever. I haven't been able to read one in over two years," Jewel said.

"What kind of church were you to be married in?" Father Albert asked.

"My fiancé was Episcopalian," she said.

Father Albert nodded his head in understanding.

"Do you hate him for what he did to you?"

Jewel thought about the question. She had considered it many times.

"I'm angry with him. I'm pissed. I was hurt that he left me. I was confused that he never really explained why. I didn't know if it was something that I did, or something that I didn't do. I have spent a lot of money and a lot of time trying to sort out my emotions," Jewel said.

Father Albert nodded his head again.

"Emotions are out of our control. We think things all the time. We can try to redirect our brain to push the thoughts out, but our emotions . . . we really can't control how we feel. We can control how we react to our emotions or how we display our emotions, but we really can't control them," Father Albert said.

"True," Jewel replied.

The pair sat in thought for several moments.

"Do you hate him for what he did to you?" Father Albert repeated.

Jewel stared at Father Albert for the count of eight.

"No. Not really. I believe that I'm better off without him. I'm angry that I can't enjoy romance novels," Jewel said with a smile.

"I'm glad you don't have hate in your heart for him. Harboring hate is toxic. As for your love of romance novels, you need to try it again. Pick up a good romance and try reading it. Don't let the past rob you of your enjoyment of the future," Father Albert said.

Jewel smiled.

"Besides. You have a very nice man by your side that cares for you," he said.

"Oh, Michael and I are just two people thrown together by these crazy events. We're not together . . . I mean, we're not a couple or in a romance or anything," she said.

"I didn't say anything about being a romantic couple. I'm talking about building relationships with other people. That is what life is about. It's not about how much stuff you have, how many degrees you've earned, or how many silly books you've read," he said, holding his book up as example. "Life is about the interactions you have with other people. Life is about how you impact other people's lives. Michael is a good person and cares for you. So you must have made a positive impact on his life."

Jewel sat quietly thinking about how she impacted others' lives

*I have totally taken Mary and Jane for granted. They have listened to years of my whining.*

"Wow, I feel like I need to make up to my friends and family for my transgressions," Jewel said.

Father Albert laughed lightly.

"The people who care for you will understand. Just remember to be a positive impact on others. You are a good person. I should know, as I'm an excellent judge of character," Father Albert said with a smile.

"Are you sure?" Jewel asked.

"Absolutely. Just as I'm sure Molly Peterson is not being honest with Officer Diggs in this book," he said tapping the book with his finger.

Jewel gave a small laugh.

"I'll leave you to your book. Goodnight," Jewel said as she went back to bed.

Chapter 20
And Just like that We Trust the Crazy Guy with the Knife


*Jewel Journal:*

*Our adventure continues. As I have been forbidden to write anything revealing, "Our adventure continues" is all I'm allowed to say. We will follow our path and see this through to the end.*

*My current emotions: I am contemplative. I feel a little guilty that I have taken my sister and my friend, Mary, for granted.*

*Now for my emotions forecast: I'm feeling like I'm going to be more positive. I am a strong independent woman. I don't need a man to complete me, but if a relationship should fall upon me then I'll thank God.*


Michael studied Jewel at breakfast. She smiled as he passed the butter.

"You look well today," Michael said with a look of suspicion.

"Thank you, Sir," Jewel said as she lifted her orange juice in a mock toast.

"You must have slept well last night," Michael said as he continued his assessment.

Jewel and Father Albert exchanged smiles across the table.

"Actually I had a lot of difficulty getting to sleep, but when I did finally fall asleep, I slept well."

Jewel gave Father Albert a sweet smile. Michael looked at Father Albert then back to Jewel.

"I'm off. I have a few people to see, and I will make some inquiries about your Frau Viessmann. You have the key I gave you, yes?" Father Albert said as he stood and tucked a newspaper under his arm.

"Aye," Michael said.

Father Albert came over and placed a hand on Jewel's shoulder.

"Have a good day. Allow yourself a bit of happiness," he said as he gave Jewel a quick wink.

"Thank you. Enjoy your day," Jewel said over her shoulder as Father Albert left.

Michael continued to watch Jewel. His face suddenly took on a look of astonishment as he finally reached a conclusion.

"You can't flirt with Father Albert, Jewel. He's a Catholic priest."

Jewel choked on her toast. Her eyes were watering as the coughing continued.

"That is a sin. I'm not sure which sin it is, but I'm pretty sure that it's a sin to flirt with a priest," Michael said again as Jewel tried to recover.

"I didn't flirt with him!"

"You're behaving differently towards him," Michael said.

"Yes. Well last night, he and I . . . just connected."

233

Michael's eyebrows shot up.

"Jewel? That is definitely a sin," Michael said as he dropped his fork on his plate.

"No! We just had a good talk and I think it helped me. He made me feel that if I can survive being drugged, kidnapped, and framed for murder then I may be able to have a normal life," she said.

"Your life wasn't normal before this?" Michael asked, regaining his composure.

"Maybe normal isn't the right word. I can have a more fulfilling life," she corrected.

"Really? What did Father Albert say to you?"

"Not a whole lot," Jewel said then wiped her mouth. "Sometimes you're just too close to your own situation. Sometimes someone on the outside needs to give you a good shake and point you in the right direction."

Michael continued to watch her as she gathered their plates and carried them to the sink. After washing the dishes she turned to find Michael still watching her.

"So. Where to now, Professor?"

∞   ∞   ∞

The interior of the bank was modern and busy. The atmosphere was professional and reserved.

Jewel followed Michael as he approached the man behind a wooden desk. The man greeted Michael with a handshake and a large smile. He studied Michael's face, but didn't comment.

"Do you speak English?" Michael asked.

"Yes. I do," the gentleman replied.

He made eye contact with Jewel and gave her a nod in greeting. "Can I offer you some water, tea, or coffee?" he asked, while indicating they should be seated. "No? What can I do for you?"

"My brother is recently deceased," Michael blurted out.

"Oh, I'm very sorry to hear that," the man said, looking a bit uncomfortable.

"I received a parcel from your bank. I believe my brother may have had an account with this bank. I need some information about it," Michael said in his strong demanding tone.

Jewel gave a sigh. She knew Michael could be charming. She witnessed it with her own eyes. Today, however, he was neither tactful nor charming. He sounded like he was making demands. She watched the man behind the desk process Michael's statement for a moment.

"Our bank is well known for its customer care and the safeguarding of their information. Has your brother's estate gone through probate yet?" the man asked, still smiling.

"No . . . However, I am his closest relative. There shouldn't be any problems."

The man continued to smile. Jewel could see this was not going to end in Michael's favor. She leaned forward and glanced at the man's name tag.

"Felix. May I call you Felix?" she asked.

"Of course," he replied.

"This isn't going the way we intended. My companion is somewhat distraught over the death of his brother. We aren't trying to leave with anything that doesn't belong to us. We were just trying to get a little information," she said as she pulled the parcel that had been mailed to Aunt Hannah from her bag. "This package was mailed from this bank. Is there any way to find out who sent it?" she asked, handing the envelope across the desk.

Felix took the envelope and examined the addresses.

"This is a large bank. It could have been mailed by anyone," he replied, handing it back.

"Okay," she said, taking the envelope and returning it to her purse.

"What was the name of the customer?" Felix asked.

"Brogan Walsh," Michael replied.

Jewel noticed Felix's faint look of surprise when the name was mentioned. He typed on his keyboard briefly.

"Mr. Walsh is not our customer. I will offer you the information that he once had a safe deposit box with us, briefly, but it was cleared out."

"When?" Michael demanded.

"I'm sorry, but I have already given you more information than I should. Like I said, we are known for safeguarding our customers' information. That's all I can say. And since your brother closed his account before his demise then you shouldn't have further business with us, unless you would like to open an account yourself."

"Thank you," Jewel said as she got to her feet.

"Can you tell me what size?" Michael asked.

Felix and Jewel turned to look at Michael.

"What size box," Michael clarified.

Felix gave him a quizzical look. He typed briefly on his computer keyboard.

"He rented our medium-sized locker. The Dimensions are thirty-five centimeter by twenty-three centimeters by fifteen centimeters."

"Centimeters? Wait, how big is that?" Jewel asked.

"About the size of shoe box," Felix said, holding his hands out to the estimated size. "Perhaps a large shoe box."

"Thank you so much," Jewel said.

"You're welcome," Felix replied.

"I know you shared more information than you were supposed to. We really appreciate it," Jewel added, giving Felix a kind smile.

"I hope the information was helpful. I only gave you the information because it's very obvious that this is Brogan Walsh's relative," Felix said.

Michael and Jewel both looked at him in surprise.

"I remember Mr. Walsh. He was a very nice gentleman. You look a lot like him. I guess you could say that your face was your identification today."

Jewel touched Michael's arm. She recognized the look of hurt. He got that look every time someone mentioned that he looked like Brogan.

"Thank you," Jewel repeated.

They turned to leave.

"By the way, another man came asking about Brogan Walsh," Felix stated.

"Who?" Michael spat.

"I don't know his name."

"Do you remember what he looked like?" Jewel asked.

"Early forties . . . not bad looking. His German was horrible. I refused to give him any information. He didn't have your face or your charm," Felix said. "Actually the fellow was rather rude and demanding. He practically threw a tantrum when we refused to give him information."

"Can you give us any other description?" Jewel prodded.

"He wore a very nice suit. That is about all I can tell you," Felix said, shaking his head.

"Did he have an accent?" Michael asked.

Felix wrinkled his nose in thought.

"His German was so bad that it's hard to tell. Perhaps British."

A man stepped to the desk and said something in German to Felix. He responded rapidly.

"I'm sorry. I have to go. Good Luck," he said as he reached out and shook the hands of both Michael and Jewel. He then hurried behind the other man.

Michael grabbed Jewel's hand and they left the bank in silence.

"Well, that was interesting," Jewel said once they stepped out into the sunshine. The downtown area had motorized traffic as well as pedestrians.

"It was the Danish Jubilee."

"What was?" Jewel asked.

"He was keeping the Danish Jubilee here, in the safe deposit box. The dimensions that Felix described are perfect for the egg," Michael said in a low tone.

"Who do you suppose was making the inquiries?" Jewel said. "The description didn't sound like Suran . . . or Chauvin, either. I can't see him throwing a tantrum."

"No, it didn't. I suspect that there are other players invested or at least searching. We really can't trust anyone," Michael said. "And with such a vague description, it could be anyone."

"So, now what?" Jewel asked, stepping into the shadow of the building and out of the sun.

"I just don't know where to go from here," Michael said as he stared down at the sidewalk.

"Hey, you're not giving up, right? We just need to think harder."

Michael didn't move. He continued to stare at the ground. The helplessness that surrounded him was so thick that Jewel thought she could touch it. She suddenly had the urge to reach out and grab it, tie it into a ball, and punt it across the street.

"Hey, you," she said as she grabbed his arm firmly and stepped into his field of vision. "Michael, we can't give up. Our lives depend on it. Now you will need to work that huge brain of yours and come up with an idea, because I'm not ready to be gator food in some Louisiana swamp, or a pin cushion for some knife-wielding weirdo, or go to jail for a murder I didn't commit. I need you, smart guy, to come up with options. This is not where it ends. Do you hear me?"

Michael stared at her in wonderment.

"You think I'm smart?" Michael asked.

"That's what you got out of all of that?" Jewel said, and poked his arm.

Michael flashed a brilliant smile which quickly vanished as a long black limousine pulled up alongside them. The back door opened. Michael pulled Jewel behind him to shield her.

An elderly woman leaned into their field of view. She was dressed in a pristine white dress. Her silver hair was meticulously arranged and her limbs were decorated with sparkling jewels. Overall she reminded Jewel of a flocked Christmas tree.

"Mr. Walsh and Miss Townsend, I would like to speak with you. I am Frau Viessmann," the woman said with a smile.

Jewel peered around Michael at the woman.

"Should we run?" Jewel whispered.

Michael didn't respond.

"I will make it worth your while," Frau Viessmann said with her heavy German accent.

"What do you want to talk to us about?" Michael asked.

"The Danish Jubilee, of course," Frau Viessmann said.

Jewel looked up at Michael, but Michael was watching the woman.

Another head came into view inside the limousine. The dark hair and brown skin was instantly recognizable. Jewel gasped and took a step back, but Michael stood his ground as Suran nodded his head in greeting.

"Michael, let's go," Jewel said.

"I can promise that you will not be harmed," Frau Viessmann said. "There has been a huge misunderstanding."

"Michael, why aren't we leaving?" Jewel asked in a loud whisper as she pulled on Michael's arm.

"It's a lead," Michael whispered as he turned to look at Jewel.

"What? Are you out of your mind?" Jewel asked as she glanced into the interior of the car.

"Just a moment," Michael said. He pulled Jewel to the side.

"Jewel, we're at a dead end. This may be the lead that we need," Michael said.

"Or it could be a ride to our death. I mean it's a limo which is kind of like a hearse. You can't seriously be thinking of getting in that thing, can you?" Jewel asked.

"Not us, just me. I don't want to risk you."

"Are you out of mind? I know you're tall and the air is probably thin up there, but that is crazy talk. You're not going anywhere without me. You're stuck with me, got it?" Jewel said.

Michael's mouth gave a twitch of a smile.

"Got it," Michael replied.

They returned to the car.

"Please, get in. We have much to discuss."

"Why can't we talk here?" Michael asked.

"There are others after the Danish Jubilee. I can assure your safety as well as Miss Townsend's. I do understand that you had an encounter with Suran, but that was a misunderstanding," Frau Viessmann said. "I'm sure we can come to an arrangement that is mutually beneficial. Let's just discuss this privately," she said, as a pedestrian passed by. She casually covered her face.

Michael made a tentative step toward the car.

"Did you kill my brother?" Michael asked Suran.

"I did not," Suran said. "I swear. I had never even spoken with the man."

Michael stepped to the door.

*And just like that we trust the crazy guy with the knife.*

Michael got into the vehicle and sat in the seat opposite Frau Viessmann.

Jewel continued to stand on the curb.

"I really don't like this," Jewel stated.

"You don't have to come," Michael said.

She looked at Michael, then Suran.

"I'll come but not with him," Jewel said, pointing to Suran.

"Get out," Frau Viessmann ordered.

Without hesitation Suran got out of the vehicle. Jewel was shocked.

"Wow, I didn't know it would be that easy." Jewel climbed into the car. Michael leaned over and shut the door.

Frau Viessmann pressed a pearl colored button and spoke in German. The limousine pulled away from the curb.

Chapter 21
Where is My Egg?


The limo was filled with a floral perfume. Jewel pondered what it cost as she estimated the value of the jewels that Frau Viessmann wore.

"Let's get down to business. Something has been taken from me and I want it back," Frau Viessmann said.

"And what was taken?" Michael asked.

"Don't play games, Mr. Walsh. The Royal Danish Imperial Egg has belonged to my family for almost eighty years and I want it back."

"Belonged to your family? Are you a descendant of the Russian royal family?" Michael asked calmly. He gave his best Moai statue impersonation.

Frau Viessmann leveled him with a cold stare.

"Who writes the history books, Mr. Walsh?"

"The historians write the history books, but that's not the answer you're leading to," Michael replied.

"Quite so. The winners write the history books; the winners of wars, the winners of battles, the conquerors of cultures," she said.

"I'm assuming that the answer to my question is no, you are not a descendant of the Russian royal family. You state that the Danish Jubilee has belonged to your family for almost eighty years. May I ask how it came into your family's possession?"

Frau Viessmann studied Michael for a very long time. Jewel watched. The atmosphere was electrified by their tension. Jewel recalled having been told that in such situations, the first one to speak loses. She was fighting the urge to speak and dispel the silence.

"My family acquired The Danish Jubilee during World War II. It is useless to discuss how or when. I cannot tell you. I just know it has been in my family all of my life," Frau Viessmann said.

"And you do realize that the Danish Jubilee is one of the lost Imperial eggs?"

"Of course I do," the woman responded with a sneer.

"It's a treasure that should be on display for the world to see. You and your family have no claim to it," Michael said.

"The *winners* write the history books, Mr. Walsh. My family won. We have the Royal Danish Imperial Egg, acquired at a time of war. It is ours," she said as a flush of red crept up her neck.

"Your family acquired the egg. The word *acquired* leaves a lot of speculation, Frau Viessmann. Need I ask which side your family supported during World War II?"

"It doesn't matter! The Danish Jubilee has been ours for over three-quarters of a century," she repeated, her voice rising in anger.

"How did you lose it?" Michael asked.

The red that was creeping up her neck bloomed on her cheeks as a scowl marred her face.

"My foolish half-sister and your unscrupulous brother took it," she said with narrowed eyes.

A brief smile flashed upon Michael's face.

"This sounds like a family argument. I'm not sure how we play into it. If you are unhappy with your sister then you need to speak with her about it," Michael said, firmly.

"My *half*-sister. . . I thought you would be the sensible one. You are just as arrogant as your brother," she spat. "I want my egg back!"

"Frau Viessmann, you're not the only one after this treasure. There are other collectors that have gotten wind that the Danish Jubilee has resurfaced," Michael told her.

"Yes. I know," she said as her eyes searched out the window in frustration. "How much?"

"How much?" Michael echoed.

"Yes. How much do you want? Considering the egg is mine, I will offer you a finder's fee to return it to me. Three million?" she said.

Jewel choked, but Michael didn't look at her. His gaze was fixed on Frau Viessmann.

"Not even close," Michael growled. His tone took Jewel by surprise. She noticed the vein in his temple throbbing. His jaw muscles were so tight she was sure she could crack a walnut on his cheek.

"This is robbery. You and your brother are thieves. This is unacceptable. Where is my egg?" she demanded.

"Let me tell you something," Michael said in a low voice.

She leaned toward him, holding her breath.

"I will do everything in my power to make sure you never get your hands on the egg again," he said slowly, enunciating each word.

Frau Viessmann reached over and pressed the pearl colored button. "*Halte das Auto an!*" she barked.

The limousine came to an abrupt stop.

Frau Viessmann was so flustered that she couldn't form words as Jewel and Michael quickly climbed out of the vehicle.

"You bastard! You will regret this," she threatened.

She continued speaking, but Michael slammed the door. He grabbed Jewel's hand and took off at a brisk pace. Jewel struggled to keep up. They were still in town, not too far from the bank. Michael continued his rapid pace until Jewel yanked her hand from his grip.

"You know I can't keep up," she said, gasping.

Michael spun around to face her. He had a huge smile on his face.

"I'm so sorry. We'll take a wee break," he said, as he stepped to a building and leaned against the stone wall.

Jewel watched him suspiciously.

"Why are you smiling?"

"We have a lead," he said.

Jewel shook her head in disbelief.

"We have crazy people who want us dead, but you're happy because we have a lead?"

"Yes, you beautiful little Yankee, we have a lead, so we can continue our search and save our skins," he said as he patted her on the head. His words and actions were so unlike the man that she started wondering if a switch had been made that she hadn't noticed. He was acting much more like Brogan than himself. She glanced at his nose to make sure it was Michael.

"What has come over you?"

"We were at a dead end. But now we can move forward," he said, reaching out and pulling Jewel into a hug.

*Whoa! He has lost his mind.*

Jewel pushed him away.

"Michael, I don't see how we're any better off."

"How about some ice cream?"

*He has definitely lost his mind.*

"Michael, what has come over you?" she asked.

"The pieces of this puzzle are falling into place, *Mo chuisle*," Michael replied.

"Mu . . . what?" Jewel asked. "What does that mean?"

"Don't fret. It's not bad. Come on," he said as he took Jewel's hand again, more gently this time. "I want to get you some ice cream."

Jewel looked up into the dark forest of his eyes and was lost for just a moment. She physically shook herself out of the spell. Jewel turned away and noticed a horse walking toward her. She watched as the horse walked past. The other pedestrians glanced at the beast, but didn't appear shocked by the appearance of a horse, with no rider, and no saddle; walking down the city street.

*I am definitely losing my mind. What is going on?*

She spun to look at Michael.

"You see the horse, right? Please tell me you see the horse."

Michael nodded his head as he watched the horse pass.

"Okay, good," Jewel sighed in relief. "Good," she repeated, patting her chest.

Chapter 22
The Other Frau Viessmann

"So what you're saying is that we can find the other Frau Viessmann? The half-sister?" Jewel asked as she scraped the bottom of her ice cream bowl with her spoon.

"Exactly. The pieces are falling into place. We didn't know who Suran was, but now we do. We didn't know where the Danish Jubilee came from, but now we do. We even know where it was being kept," Michael said as he set his empty bowl on the table of the small ice cream shop.

"But that doesn't do us any good. We don't know where it is now."

Michael shrugged his broad shoulders, got up, and went to the counter. He was talking to the man that had served them ice cream. Both men began laughing. Jewel smiled to herself. Michael was laughing. She loved these unguarded moments.

"Good news," He said as he returned to the table. "We are not losing our minds. That horse we saw is named Jenny. She takes a walk by herself every day. She takes the same path that she used to take with her rider, but the rider has since passed away."

"Oh, that's kind of sad."

Michael handed Jewel a paper napkin and cleared his throat.

"I believe that our next logical step will be to find the other Frau Viessmann."

"What makes you think she'll talk to us?" Jewel asked. "She has no reason to talk to us. She probably won't even see us."

"Ye have little faith, *Mo chuisle*," Michael said. He gave Jewel a flash of a smile. "You forget the words of Felix: My face is my identification." He reached for her hand.

Jewel slowly pulled her hand free.

"You're behaving oddly," she said as she squinted at him.

"Is it wrong for a man to hold a woman's hand?" he asked, leaning toward Jewel. "Especially when they've just shared bowls of ice cream?"

Jewel was physically uncomfortable and got to her feet.

*What is he playing at?*

"We should head back. Perhaps Father Albert has played detective and uncovered some information about Frau Viessmann," Jewel said.

∞   ∞   ∞

"So someone else is looking for the treasure?" Father Albert asked with wide eyes.

"It appears so," Jewel said.

"Don't get me wrong. I'm very concerned for your safety, but things are getting more interesting. During World War II art collections that were owned by people sent to the concentration camps were confiscated.

I would have to assume that is when the Viessmann family came into possession of the treasure. We may never find out where it was once it was taken by the Bolsheviks," he said.

Michael entered the room and sat down on the couch.

"I was just getting Father Albert up to date," Jewel told Michael. Michael nodded.

"This came in the mail for you today," Father Albert said as he handed Michael a large brown envelope. "You also got a package in the mail," he said, handing a small package to Jewel.

Michael tore open the envelope and pulled out a folded newspaper.

Jewel looked at Michael to see his reaction. He had the two creases between his eyes; his trademark of concentration.

It was not a whole newspaper, but one section. The paper was written in German. While Michael rustled through the pages looking for clues, Jewel studied the envelope.

"This is local," she said. "There isn't a return address, but there is a postmark."

"Oh, please let me see," Father Albert said, holding out his hand.

Jewel handed him the envelope. He straightened his glasses and studied the postmark.

"This was sent yesterday," he stated, tapping the envelope. "From right here in Frankfurt."

"This newspaper doesn't have anything circled or highlighted. I'm not sure why it was sent to me," Michael said. "Father Albert, could you translate it to us? Just read it aloud perhaps?" Michael asked holding out the paper.

"I would love to, but I have Mass in twenty minutes. I need to head to the church to prepare. I would be happy to read it after."

"That would be very helpful," Michael replied.

Both men continued to look at Jewel. This prompted her to open her package.

Jewel removed a small box. The box contained a cuff bracelet. It was silver and held a large, turquoise-colored stone. It was a bit bulky and reminded Jewel of Wonder Woman's bullet deflecting bracelets. The bracelet wasn't very pretty. She looked at it thinking that she never would have chosen it for herself. Jewel held the item up for the men to see.

"There's a note," she said as she pulled a folded sheet of paper from the box and read aloud.

*Thank you for our date. I do hope we can meet again soon. Please wear this token and know that I am thinking of you.*

*Sincerely, Professor Everett Nolan*

Michael made a noise deep in his throat, but said nothing.

Jewel pulled the bracelet on and examined it.

"Is this an admirer of yours, Jewel?" Father Albert asked.

Jewel glanced at Father Albert then to Michael.

"I guess," she said.

"You aren't going to accept the gift, are you?" Michael asked.

"It's not that bad," she said as she continued to study it.

"Jewel, he signed the note 'Sincerely, Professor Everett Nolan'. You can't be serious?"

Jewel was feeling defensive. The last piece of jewelry she'd received from a man was her engagement ring.

"I'm keeping it," she defended.

"How did he even know you were here?" Michael asked.

"Maybe Hannah or Father Wendell told him," she said.

"Doubtful. I don't think you should keep it. The man is a pompous ass and he has ill intentions," Michael said then made a quick apology to Father Albert.

"Oh, don't mind me," Father Albert said as he got to his feet. "Will you be attending Mass?"

"Yes, I will," Michael replied, looking at Jewel.

Jewel held her chin at a defiant angle, but smiled as she turned to Father Albert.

"I will too, but I need to shower off first," she said. "I'l meet you there."

∞   ∞   ∞

Michael was on his knees, praying, when Jewel entered the church. She knelt beside him. She followed his lead and sat down when he did. Michael was looking at her bracelet. She followed his gaze then covered the bracelet from his disapproving glare.

Jewel tried to enjoy the Catholic Mass, but she could feel the icy chill coming from her companion. When Mass was over they waited outside the church for Father Albert.

*This is ridiculous. He can't stay mad at me.*

"So how often do you go to Mass?" Jewel asked.

"Once a week," Michael responded. "I have chosen to come to Mass the past two days out of respect for our host."

"Okay, I was just wondering," Jewel responded, hoping that initializing conversation would break Michael's critical stare.

"Are you going to continue wearing that ridiculous thing?" he asked, pointing to her arm.

"Yes, I am. Why does it bug you so much? Is it so unbelievable that a man would like me enough to give me a present? Is that the problem?"

Michael's face had a look of surprise which quickly turned into a brief smile.

"I never said anything resembling that. I believe he sent you that just to annoy me."

"Oh, so you don't believe a man would like me enough to send me a gift," Jewel said as she stormed off back to the rectory.

*I knew it. He thinks this is all about him.*

Jewel entered through the kitchen, walked to the guestroom, and shut the door. She studied the bracelet.

*It isn't very pretty, but I'll be damned if I'll allow that man to intimidate me into taking it off.*

∞   ∞   ∞

There was a knock on the guestroom door.

"Supper is ready," Michael said through the door.

Jewel's head popped up. She wasn't sure how long of a nap she had taken. She looked around the room in confusion.

The door opened slowly and Michael peeked into the room.

"Jewel, supper is ready," he repeated.

"Okay, I'm coming," she said as she rolled over and sat up.

Michael tentatively walked toward her, while she rubbed her sleepy eyes.

"Look, Father Albert spoke with me about the bracelet. He feels that I haven't taken your feelings into account. He's probably correct. I'm sorry if I offended you," Michael said in an official, command performance way.

"Okay," Jewel replied.

"Are we good now?" Michael asked.

Jewel looked up at Michael and considered his pathetic apology.

"We're fine."

"You don't sound fine."

"Michael, just leave me alone."

He turned and left the room.

*Okay, Jewel, now you're behaving like a brat.*

After a silent supper, the trio retired to the living room.

"So you need me to translate the entire newspaper?" Father Albert asked.

"Since you know the story of what we've been through and who we're dealing with, perhaps you can scan the paper and see if there's anything relevant," Michael suggested.

Father Albert nodded in agreement and silently began perusing the newspaper. Jewel sipped her tea, watching Father Albert. She looked up to find Michael watching her. He gave her a brief smile, but his eyes flicked to her bracelet.

"I do believe I have found the article of interest," Father Albert said, bringing Jewel and Michael to full attention.

"What is it about?" Michael asked.

"I will paraphrase it, line by line," Father Albert said.

"The well-known businessman and entrepreneur, Leopold Viessmann, has made news as it was discovered that he has had another family in France for several years. Viessmann is well known for his marriage to socialite Catharina Huber, who died in 2013. Together they had a daughter, Lydia Viessmann. It was only after the death of Leopold Viessmann that the truth surfaced, indicating that he had a mistress for over forty years. His mistress Alida Belshaw is of French descent and lives in Paris. The pair had a daughter together, Lisette Belshaw Viessmann. Lydia Viessmann was thought to be the only heir to the Viessmann fortune. Since the death of Leopold Viessmann, a new will has surfaced stating that his fortune is to be split, equally, between both of his daughters. This has been a shock to Lydia Viessmann as she was unaware that she had a half-sister until after the death of her father. Lydia Viessmann has refused an interview. Lisette Belshaw Viessmann, since her father's death, moved to Frankfurt and purchased Der Künstler luxury apartments," Father Albert finished.

"Interesting," Michael said.

"Of course I'm not an official translator, but that's the gist of what is written," Father Albert said.

"So, the Christmas tree lady that we met is Lydia Viessmann?" Jewel asked.

"Christmas tree lady?" Michael and Father Albert asked in unison.

"Yes, that's what she reminded me of," Jewel said, waving off their question. "She must be Lydia Viessmann. So, we need to find this Lisette Belshaw Viessmann."

"What is the date on this newspaper?" Michael asked.

"This is from last year, almost to the day," Father Albert said looking at the top of the page. "This is useful information, but I'm most curious about who sent this to you."

"That's what I'm wondering," Michael said, taking the newspaper from Father Albert.

"And who knew we were here? We need to find Lisette Viessmann," Jewel said.

"We will try to find her tomorrow," Michael said. "We will start at Der Künstler luxury apartments."

"One step closer to the solution," Father Albert said with a boyish smile.

Chapter 23
What is He Hiding?

Michael and Jewel stood in front of Der Künstler luxury apartment building. The doorman opened the door without question, but the security guard at the desk stopped them before they made it to the elevator. He addressed them in German.

"Hello, do you speak English?" Jewel asked as she eyed the expensive furnishings.

"Yes, I speak English very well," he responded.

"We are here to see Lisette Belshaw Viessmann," Jewel stated with confidence.

"I'm sorry, but Fräulein Viessmann is not here," he responded.

"Do you know when she will be back?" Michael asked.

The man looked at Michael for the first time. He flinched.

"No. I do not," the guard said, still looking at Michael.

"May I leave a note for her?" Michael asked.

The man nodded his head and handed Michael a sheet of paper and pen. Michael scribbled a note and handed it back to the security guard.

"Please see to it that she gets it," Michael said.

The man nodded his head, but stayed silent.

"Thank you," Jewel said as she tugged on Michael's sleeve and they left the building.

"Should we stake out the place?" Jewel asked once they were on the street.

"No. If we stand around a place like this the police will probably be called," Michael responded, glancing over his shoulder as they walked away from the building.

"How did you know for sure that she lived here? I know the article stated that she bought the place, but how did you know for sure?"

"Father Albert is connected. He made a few phone calls and reported that she lives in the penthouse," Michael said as he took Jewel's hand and began walking. "Come on, let's get out of here. I have the creepy sensation that we're being watched," he said as he looked around.

"I feel a little creeped out, too."

"Don't worry, *Mo chuisle*, I'll protect you," Michael said, and he gave her hand a squeeze.

*What?*

"Why are you suddenly being all chivalrous?" Jewel asked, pulling her hand free.

"What do you mean, suddenly? I've always been chivalrous."

"Dude . . . a week and a half ago you were trying to leave me alone after my house was ransacked, and then a few days later you were calling me an idiot for inviting Suran to join me for dinner, and like four days ago you kissed . . . me," Jewel said, the last words trailing off. "What are you doing?"

Michael stopped and faced Jewel.

"During confession, Father Albert talked to me about how I impact other people's lives. I've decided that I want to be a positive impact on your life," Michael said.

"You, too? He gave me that talk on the first night," Jewel said.

"Maybe he felt we both needed to hear it," Michael replied. "But I stand by my previous statement. I have always been chivalrous."

∞   ∞   ∞

Jewel didn't attend the evening Mass. She was asleep on the couch when the men returned. She awakened to Michael lifting her feet to sit down. She closed her eyes again as he put her feet on his lap. The men were talking quietly to each other. Jewel became aware that Michael was massaging her foot. At first she was going to pull her foot out of his grasp, but it felt nice. She continued to keep her eyes closed and feigned sleep because the situation felt too embarrassing. Michael, however, showed no sign of embarrassment. He was talking and rubbing her feet as if it were a natural thing to do, as if it was something he had done dozens of times.

The men were talking about the visit to Lisette Belshaw Viessmann's residence.

"I left a note for her, but I doubt that she responds. I put in the note that I could be contacted through the church. I hope that was okay? The only ones we need to stay hidden from are Chauvin and his goons," Michael said.

"No. Of course. My home is your home. . ." Father Albert said as he relaxed back in his chair.

"Ah," Michael said. "For I was hungry and you gave me something to eat, I was thirsty and you gave me something to drink, I was a stranger and you invited me into your home. Is that correct?" Michael asked.

"Close enough," Father Albert said with an approving smile.

"I just don't want to put you in danger. It is difficult enough trying to protect this one," Michael said, tapping the top of Jewel's foot. "I would have made further attempts today to see Frau Viessmann, but it felt like we were being watched. I just didn't want to risk it."

Jewel considered this statement. She felt badly about her comments to him about his chivalry.

"Yes, Michael, keep her safe," Father Albert said.

"Father, do you speak Irish?" Michael asked.

"Aye."

The men began conversing in low tones. Jewel tried hard to understand what was being said.

*Why? Why does he need to speak in another language? What is he hiding? He is definitely talking about something that he's hiding from me.*

Jewel was ready to jump up and call him out on this deception when Father Albert spoke again in English.

"Well, I need to get to bed. Sleep well," Father Albert said as he left the room.

Jewel stirred. She pulled her feet off of Michael's lap and curled into a ball, but kept her eyes shut. She could feel movement on the couch. She felt a blanket gently being placed on her body. She felt a warm hand touch her head and caress her curls.

"I'm sure your bed is much more comfortable, *Mo chuisle,* but if you insist on pretending then you can stay here," Michael whispered into her mop of brown hair.

Jewel fought an internal battle. She was torn between jumping up and accusing him of hiding things from her, and simply staying there and continuing to pretend she was asleep to prove him wrong. She didn't move.

"Good night, *Mo chuisle*," he said, and then left the room.

Jewel waited about ten minutes before retreating to the guestroom. She felt as if she had won a small victory by proving him wrong in assuming that she was pretending to be asleep. As she fluffed her pillow and rested upon it, she realized that she didn't win because she was pretending.

She started thinking about Michael speaking with Father Albert in Irish just so she couldn't understand. She wondered again what he was hiding, but knew she couldn't ask about it, as she was supposed to have been asleep.

*It is so hard to fall asleep when you're pissed off.*

Chapter 24
*Mo chuisle*

"I see you're still wearing that gaudy bracelet. Perhaps we should go shopping and find you a proper piece of jewelry," Michael said as he entered the kitchen and sat down for breakfast.

Jewel ignored his comment and took a bite of her toast.

*Ask him what he was discussing with Father Albert. Ask him, Jewel. Come on, grow a pair.*

"Did you and Father Albert have a nice evening?"

"Aye," Michael responded, pouring himself some tea.

"Did you discuss anything interesting?"

"No not really," he replied as he opened a newspaper that he picked up from the edge of the table.

"Nothing? No interesting information? Or insightful views? Or useful theories?" she prodded.

Michael peered over the newspaper at Jewel.

"What are you asking?"

*Abort mission! Abort mission!*

"Nothing," Jewel replied.

Michael continued watching Jewel. Something sparked in his memory and he fought back a smile.

"Come to think of it, we did have a nice conversation," Michael said as he lifted the newspaper again.

"About what?" Jewel asked.

"Oh, nothing really."

"I'm very interested," Jewel said.

Michael peeked over the newspaper at Jewel as she lifted her chin trying to see his face.

"It was somewhat of a confession," Michael said.

"Okay, so tell me."

Michael pulled down the newspaper and looked appalled.

"Jewel, Catholic confession is a sacrament. I can't discuss my confession with you," Michael said then lifted the newspaper again.

Jewel made a sound of frustration and poked her tongue out at the newspaper between them.

"Did you say something?" Michael asked.

Jewel could tell by his voice that he was smiling behind the paper and it added to her irritation.

"You don't even read German. What are you doing?" she said as she yanked at the paper.

Michael folded the newspaper and set it on the table with the tiniest hint of a smirk lingering upon his lips.

"Good morning," Father Albert said, as he entered the kitchen.

As he poured himself a cup of tea, a knock on the door brought everyone to their feet. Father Albert made his way to the door as Michael stood behind the door with a knife in his hand that he had taken from the table. Jewel couldn't see who was there, but Father Albert was speaking in German. The conversation was short and he shut the door, but was holding an envelope. Michael quickly hid the knife from Father Albert and returned to the table.

"It's for you," he said as he handed Michael the envelope.

"Me?" Michael asked as he studied the letter. It was addressed to him at the church.

Michael quickly opened the missive. Jewel watched his eyes move side-to-side as he read. He handed it to Jewel. She unfolded the paper and read it.

*Please meet with me tonight to discuss a particular artifact. I look forward to our visit.*

*Gros bisous, Lisette Belshaw Viessmann*

"Ask and it will be given to you," Father Albert quoted.

"So, that's it. We're just going to walk in and talk with her?" Jewel asked.

Michael re-read the letter and continued staring at the paper.

"So, are we going?" Jewel asked.

"No," Michael said.

"Why not? Isn't this the lead we were looking for?"

"What I mean is *we* aren't going. I'm going," Michael said.

"You're joking, right? You can't leave me out of this," Jewel said. "Michael, if you leave me behind, I'll never forgive you."

"If I bring you and something happens to you then I would never forgive myself."

"How is this different from what we've been doing for the past week and a half? I've been in danger the entire time. What's different now?" she demanded, her voice rising in anger.

"I'm different now. We're different."

"You aren't making any sense," Jewel said. "You're taking me with you. This is it. We could have answers to all of our questions with this single meeting."

"You're not going to the meeting," Michael insisted. "And that's final."

∞    ∞    ∞

Once again they stood outside the luxury apartment building. After passing the doorman, the security guard at the desk pressed a button which called the elevator to the ground floor.

"They are expecting you," the guard said as Jewel and Michael stepped into the lift. The doors shut.

"I don't like that," Michael said.

"What?"

"He said, '*They*'. There must be someone else besides Lisette Viessmann waiting for us."

"Well, there's no turning back now," Jewel said as she smoothed her cotton skirt. "This is it. Everything answered."

"Right. And then what?" he asked.

"Then we tell Chauvin where the egg is, and I go back to my life in Texas."

"Nothing has changed?" Michael asked with an odd note to his voice.

The elevator stopped on the top floor. The doors opened to a huge sign that read, "Le Penthouse".

"Well, here we go," Jewel said.

They went to the only door and knocked. A maid ushered them inside, down a long hall, and into a huge room with windows overlooking the city. One whole wall was made up of windows. The maid offered wine, but both declined.

Jewel took a seat on the white couch and Michael sat beside her. He nudged her and pointed to a painting of a man wearing a hat resting his head on his right hand.

"That's a Van Gogh," Michael said as he stood and went to the painting. "An original. This is incredible."

Jewel continued to study the room. Almost all the furniture was white as well as the carpet. She heard voices in the hallway and watched as another guest was led into the room by the same maid. It took Jewel a moment to realize the person was Lydia Viessmann.

*Christmas tree lady.*

Jewel got to her feet.

"Michael, Michael," Jewel said.

Michael moved to Jewel's side then stepped in front of her for protection.

"What in the hell are they doing here?" she said with her German accent. "Where is Lisette? I demand to see Lisette, now," she said.

"Mademoiselle will be out in a moment. She has instructed me to make everyone comfortable," the maid said with her light French accent then left the room.

"I don't know what you think you are doing, but I will not allow it," Frau Viessmann said to Michael and Jewel.

"And what would that be?" Michael asked.

Jewel let out a chuckle.

"You," she said pointing a finger at Michael. "You are playing the mouse and the cat, but I will win. I always win. I am a Viessmann," she said as she looked down her nose at the pair.

"Isn't she a Viessmann, too?" Michael asked, using his thumb to point to the hall.

The woman quivered with anger. She sputtered a few sounds, but was interrupted as new guests arrived.

Jewel went pale as Chauvin and Landry entered the room. Michael again pulled Jewel behind him to shield her.

Chauvin had a fleeting look of surprise, but played it off well.

"I don't get surprised often, but I must say I'm surprised to see you here," Chauvin said, his wry smile partly hidden by his mustache.

Landry closed the distance to Michael and reached out.

"Stop," Chauvin said. "We're here for a meeting. We'll have our meeting. Other things can wait," he said as he gave Jewel a wink and click of his tongue.

Jewel hoped she didn't look as terrified on the outside as she felt on the inside.

"Who the hell are you?" Frau Viessmann asked.

"Simon Chauvin," he said. "You must be Ms. Lisette Viessmann."

"I certainly am not," she said. "I'm leaving. This is ridiculous. I will not sit here with these criminals," she said as she stood.

Chauvin began protesting and Landry was looking confused about who he was supposed to squash. Michael still held his position in front of Jewel.

"Welcome. I'm so sorry that I am late," Lisette Viessmann said as she entered the room. She was in her forties and looked like she had just stepped out of a nineteen-twenties' movie. She was dressed in a beaded flapper gown that fit perfectly on her slender form. Her hair was in a short bob and she even wore a beaded headband with a feather flourish. The outfit was completed when she put a long cigarette holder to her mouth and drew deeply from the cigarette. Her black-lined eyes scanned the room.

"This is outrageous," Frau Viessmann stated.

"Please sit down, sister," Lisette said with her French accent.

"I'm so pleased to meet new friends," she added, walking to Michael.

Lisette kissed Michael on both cheeks.

"And who is this?" she asked peering around Michael.

"This is Jewel Townsend."

"Ah, she looks like a little doll. So cute," she said as she leaned over and kissed Jewel on both cheeks.

She turned away and approached her half-sister.

"Sister, I am glad to see you in good health," Lisette began, but stopped short as it was apparent her greeting was not welcome.

"I see you are into the nineteen-twenties today. Last week it was Madonna and the nineteen-eighties. What will it be next week, Ancient Egypt?" Frau Viessmann sneered.

"If I fancy it," Lisette said with a smile. "And you must be Monsieur Chauvin," she said as she approached.

Chauvin grabbed her hand and shook it firmly. He began speaking in French, but the woman held up her hand.

"Please Monsieur Chauvin, we will speak the language common to everyone here," Lisette said.

Chauvin looked put out by the statement. Jewel wondered if he'd thought he would have an upper hand using his host's native tongue.

"Can I get anyone a drink?" she asked.

"You can get me what I came here for," Frau Viessmann said.

"And what would that be, Ma'am?" Chauvin asked.

The pair started arguing again.

"You all received a letter indicating that we're here to discuss a particular artifact. Haven't you guessed? You're all after the same thing, the Danish Jubilee," Lisette said.

The room fell quiet. Everyone eyed each other.

Jewel and Michael had taken their seats again, but Michael held tightly onto Jewel's hand.

"The purpose of this meeting is to bring this *folie* to an end," she said as she ejected her cigarette into an ashtray. "All will be revealed shortly."

Voices were heard down the hall followed by footsteps. The maid came in offering apologies, followed by a man.

Jewel was taken by surprise as Professor Everett Nolan stepped into the room and glanced at each face as if looking for someone in particular. Jewel drew her breath as Michael leapt to his feet to shield her. Everett pulled out a gun.

The room stayed silent as he trained the gun on each person.

"This is who you're working with?" Michael asked.

"I have no idea who this man is," Lisette said as she moved away from Everett.

"I work alone," Everett spat.

He looked disheveled and manic.

"What are you doing here?" Michael asked.

"What are *you* doing here?" Everett countered.

"None of your bloody business," Michael said.

"Young man, put down that gun. We've had enough foolishness," Frau Viessmann said.

"Where is it? Where is the treasure?" Everett demanded.

"And what treasure are you talking about? I have many treasures," Lisette said.

"The Fabergé treasure," he said as he stepped closer to the group.

"You're going to need to be more specific than that," Chauvin said.

"I will win this time. Whatever it is, I want it," he said as he pointed the gun at Michael. "I saw the Fabergé cigarette case at your aunt's house. I saw in Jewel's journal that you were seeking a Fabergé treasure and that Brogan is dead. One Walsh down, one to go," he said as his lip curled.

Michael tensed at the statement.

"You don't even know what you are here for," Lisette said.

"I don't need to know. I just need to win," Everett said, his hand shaking with anger and frustration.

"Everett Nolan, you have never won against Brogan or me and you never will," Michael said.

"Don't taunt him, Michael," Jewel whispered.

"You think you're so clever. Do you even know how I found you? I'm the clever one. I'm the clever one," he said hitting his chest. "I put a tracker in that bracelet. So I'm the clever one," Everett repeated.

"He's mad," Frau Viessmann said. "Absolutely mad. These are the people you associate with?" she said to Lisette.

"*Nein bin ich nicht.* I am not mad," Everett said to Frau Viessmann.

Even to Jewel's untrained ear she could hear how awful his German was and realization struck.

"He's the one that was at the bank asking about Brogan," Jewel said.

In a movement so fast that Jewel barely saw, Landry grabbed the gun in one hand and Everett's throat in the other. He had the gun aimed at

Everett's head in a flash. Everett fought against the massive hand that was holding him.

"Get him, Lurch!" Jewel shouted.

The group all turned to look at Jewel, all except Landry and Everett.

"Just do away with the fool," Frau Viessmann said with a wave of her hand.

Landry looked at Chauvin waiting for a signal. Everett was whimpering, but had stopped fighting as he found it pointless.

"This guy is a piece of work," Chauvin said. "A friend of yours, Walsh?"

"No friend of mine," Michael replied.

Landry put the gun to Everett's temple. All eyes watched as a wet stain bloomed on the front of Everett's pants. The crowd said nothing, but watched as Everett sobbed.

Chauvin shook his head and Landry released him, but pocketed the gun. Everett fell to the floor in a wet heap. He wiped his face on his sleeve.

"Now get out of my house," Lisette said, looking down at the man with disgust.

Everett got to his feet.

"Jewel," Everett said as he held out his hand. "Come on. Come with me," he said.

Jewel looked shocked as all eyes turned to her once more.

"Absolutely not!" Jewel said.

"I will win at something," Everett said, his face contorted in anger, as he stomped his foot.

"I don't even know you," Jewel said, holding onto Michael's arm.

"Get him out of here, but don't kill him," Chauvin ordered Landry.

"Wait," Michael said. He grabbed Jewel's hand and pulled the bracelet off. He walked to Everett and shoved it into his jacket pocket. "Take this hideous thing and stay away from Jewel."

Everett made a pitiful sight as Landry yanked him from the room by the collar. The room was silent until the door slammed.

Lisette said something in French. The maid entered, and put towels on the urine puddle on the floor.

"This is not going as we had planned," Lisette said, shaking her head. "You are all here for the Danish Jubilee. It's time for us to discuss this treasure." She walked to an intercom on the wall and pressed a button. Footsteps could be heard, and then a bearded figure entered the room.

Jewel heard Michael's breath catch and felt his body go rigid. She placed a hand on Michael then looked at the bearded man again. She felt like her eyes were playing tricks.

*Could there be three of them? No. Not possible.*

"Brogan?" Jewel whispered.

Michael began speaking, but it was in Irish. He walked to his brother and continued speaking.

Jewel wished she could understand but needed no translation when the two men hugged and both had glistening, tear-filled eyes.

"You're supposed to be dead," Chauvin said.

"Brogan," Jewel said as her own eyes filled with tears.

Brogan walked to Jewel, picked her up, and spun her around in his arms.

"My wee woman," he said as he gave her a quick kiss.

Everyone started speaking at once. Brogan held up his hand.

"Where is my egg?" Frau Viessmann demanded.

"How are you not dead?" Chauvin asked.

270

"I can see you're very disturbed that I'm alive, Mr. Chauvin," Brogan said. "I would be too, because I know that's not what you planned. Obviously, I didn't die in Venice. The poor bastard that you sent to kill me was charred to a crisp. I didn't kill him, mind you. He knocked me out and was pouring fuel on me. It was actually the smell that brought me back to consciousness. The fool was about to light me when I awoke and jumped off the bed. I ran for the window to escape. The man fumbled with the match and blew himself up. I barely made it out of the window to safety. My arse got singed. Also you can imagine how difficult it is to not draw attention when you run through Venice naked as the day you were born. Won't you explain why you tried to have me killed?" Brogan said.

"This is ridiculous. I didn't send him to kill you," Chauvin said as his eyes flicked to the others present. "I just sent him to get the egg."

"Aye, you did. See, before he knocked me out, he explained. You wanted the Danish Jubilee, but you already had a lead on where it was. The reason you wanted me dead is because you knew that I had been collecting information about you. I have enough information on your illegal art ventures to have you wearing an orange jumpsuit for the rest of your life," Brogan said.

Chauvin showed no expression, but his left eye twitched. His face took on a smug look.

"I can buy my way out of any charges that you can come up with," Chauvin stated.

"Maybe . . . maybe, if the evidence ended up on the District Attorney's desk in New Orleans. It would be buried. But what if the evidence was sent to every major newspaper in the country? I don't think you could buy your way out of that one. Also your crimes are not just in the United States. You need to consider extradition laws," Brogan said. "All the evidence is safe and hidden. It'll stay that way as long as no harm comes to me, my family, or Jewel. See, I could cut a deal as a witness against you, so there isn't anything really stopping me from doing it. Do I have your word that you'll leave my people alone?" Brogan said.

Chauvin was grinding his teeth with anger. His fists were balled, but he stayed silent.

"I'm a very elusive man. I'll see your guys coming long before they ever see me. If I suspect that you're sending anyone in my direction, or in the direction of my loved ones, then you will be fair game in every country from which you have pilfered art," Brogan said.

Chauvin looked around the room. His mustache was quivering. He nodded his head.

"Done," he said, releasing a gust of air from his lungs.

"This is absurd. Where is my egg?" Frau Viessmann demanded once again.

"Ma'am, you are being hailed as a true patron of the arts," Brogan said with his trademark smile. "As of yesterday, you donated the Danish Jubilee to Museum der bildenden Künste. The newspapers are printing it as we speak. I'm sure it's already trending on the internet. It'll be printed and reported all over Europe since the Danish Jubilee is one of the lost royal eggs. This is big news and you're the one who made it happen. You're a celebrity," Brogan said.

"This is absurd. Where is my egg!" Frau Viessmann repeated, her voice growing in volume with each word. Her face was red with anger.

"I could have taken the credit, but Brogan thought it would be better to come from you, sister," Lisette said. "But you can't back out now. You need to just soak up the limelight."

Chauvin began laughing.

Jewel watched with amazement.

"And just like that, you give up the Danish Jubilee?" Michael asked Brogan.

"Faolan, haven't I already proven it. I'll do anything to protect you, brother," Brogan said.

"Fway-lawn? What is that?" Jewel asked.

"Faolan Michael Walsh," Brogan said as he clapped Michael on his shoulder.

"I prefer Michael," Michael said as he looked daggers at his brother.

"Aye, but your name is Faolan," Brogan said with a wink to Jewel. "Now. Does anyone have questions?" Brogan asked.

"I have questions, brother, but I don't think I can verbalize them all right now," Michael said.

"I will get my egg back," Frau Viessmann said. "Hear me. I will get it back."

"You could, but your name would go down in history as a synonym for avarice. Children will make nursery rhymes of your greed and wickedness. You will become a pariah in all the social circles that you hold so dear," Brogan said.

"Just accept the praise that will be heaped upon you, sister. We both know how you love being in the spotlight," Lisette said.

Chauvin laughed again.

"You are a son of a bitch and if I ever find a way, then you will be dead, but I must admit you had us fooled," Chauvin said. "Of course you will never work in art again."

"Oh, you would be surprised who is interested in my services," Brogan said, still smiling.

Chauvin shook his head as he took a step away from Brogan.

"Ma'am, would you be interested in selling that Van Gogh?" Chauvin asked Lisette.

"We might come to an agreement, but you would have to discuss this with my art acquisitions agent," Lisette said as she gestured to Brogan.

"Humph, I'll have my eye on you, Walsh," Chauvin said as he turned and left.

"Lisette, I will never forgive you for this," Frau Viessmann said as she followed behind Chauvin.

The group watched her leave.

"Brogan, I'm so glad that this is over. I'm going out for the night. Don't wait up," Lisette said.

Brogan spoke in French then waved to his patroness as she summoned the maid to call for her car.

The trio was alone.

"What's with the beard?" Jewel said as she scratched Brogan's chin.

"Aye, do you like it?" Brogan asked, turning his head to give her a view from the side. "It was part of my disguise."

"It kind of suits you," Jewel said.

"Why didn't you let me know you were alive?" Michael asked, his face dark.

"I needed to stay dead until I could work out a way for everyone to be safe," Brogan replied.

"You could have told me. I thought you were really dead," Michael said, his jaw tight.

"Aye, but you lived life a little over the past couple of weeks, didn't you, brother?" Brogan asked.

"Is that what this was for? So I would 'live life'?" Michael asked.

"No, but it's a nice benefit. I tried to help you out. I sent you the cigarette case and the newspaper article" Brogan said. "Although I was surprised that you got *Mo chuisle* involved," he added, sliding his arm around Jewel.

"What does that mean? Why do people keep calling me that?" Jewel asked.

"Oh? Someone's been calling you that?" Brogan asked with laughter in his voice and a quick look at Michael.

"Yes, Michael has been calling me that. Is it bad?" Jewel said.

"Michael? Really? That's interesting," Brogan said with his huge smile.

"What does it mean?" Jewel asked.

"Brogan, this is not the time," Michael said as he was visibly uncomfortable.

The brothers began speaking in their Irish tongue. Jewel watched them as the conversation went back and forth.

"I don't know, Faolan. I don't think I can give this one up," Brogan said as he kissed Jewel on the forehead.

"She'll have to choose," Michael said with his jaw firmly set.

"Choose what?" Jewel asked.

"*Mo chuisle* literally means 'my pulse,' but roughly translated means 'my darling' or 'my sweetheart' or 'my love'," Brogan said as he put Jewel at arm's length to study her face.

"Oh," Jewel said then looked at Michael. "Oh!" she said again then looked at Brogan. "OH!" Realization was apparent.

*This is some strange Irish love triangle.*

"Jewel, you can't string us both along. You will need to decide between the two of us," Michael said.

Jewel looked at Michael. His face was so hopeful. She thought of how he had changed over the past weeks. She thought of the moments that he had opened up and the moments that he had allowed himself to be kind. She thought about the powerful kiss he gave her in Ireland.

She looked at Brogan. He playfully winked at her then scratched his bearded chin. She couldn't help but smile at him.

Then she thought of herself and how she had changed over the past few weeks. She wasn't the same person.

"I think you're both wonderful people. You're both so different, but you both have your good points," Jewel said. "I care for both of you."

The two men stood side by side. Brogan wore his usual smile, while Michael was looking down at his feet. After a long pause, Jewel spoke again.

"Why do I have to choose?" Jewel said, looking side to side at the Walsh brothers.

"I like this one," Brogan said with a chuckle. "I never would have expected you to have both of us."

"You aren't suggesting what I think you're suggesting?" Michael asked Jewel.

"I doubt it," Jewel said. "You'll have to work a lot harder guys," she said as she walked toward the hall. She turned around to face them. "I am a strong independent woman and I don't need a man to complete me. I can enjoy life on my own," she said as she turned and left the penthouse.

The door shut with a thud.

"You scared her off," Brogan said.

"Me?" Michael countered. "You were the one making threesome references."

"Aye, you scared her off with your 'you have to choose'," Brogan said, mocking Michael's voice.

"You don't deserve someone like Jewel," Michael said.

The brothers stopped fighting when Jewel appeared in the room.

"I know I'm ruining my big exit, but I don't have any money for a taxi," she said.

"I knew you would be back," Brogan said as he headed for Jewel.

"I have your money, *Mo chuisle*," Michael said.

"I don't want either of you to get the wrong idea. I just need to get back to the church," Jewel said.

"Let's go, Jewel," Michael said as he took her hand.

Brogan slid his arm around Jewel as the trio headed for the door. They entered the elevator and hit the button for the lobby.

"You know we make a good team, Jewel, the three of us," Brogan said.

"I guess so, but I'm not sure what you're getting at," Jewel replied.

"Have you ever considered the treasure hunting business?" Brogan asked.

Jewel looked at Brogan then to Michael.

"Well," she said. "You never know what the future holds!"

The End

. . . for a wee bit

## Epilogue

Jewel walked the halls of the University of Florida with the books clutched to her chest. She had to ask for directions twice, but found Michael's office. She took a deep breath and knocked.

"Come," a familiar voice called out.

She opened the door to find Michael at his desk. The office was just as she had pictured it. It was very neat, very organized, and stacked almost to the ceiling with books.

He looked up. Then looked again, shocked.

"Jewel," he said as he sprang up and embraced her. "It has been months since I've seen you. What are you doing here?"

"What is this?" she asked as she reached up and tugged on a beard that, although matched his dark hair, had red strands throughout.

"A beard. You don't like it?" Michael asked, his face taking on a look of confusion. "I thought you liked beards. You liked Brogan's beard," he said, looking defensive.

"Michael, I'm not here to discuss facial hair," Jewel said as she sat down.

"Yes, I doubt you came this far to discuss my beard, although it took almost two months to grow out," Michael said. "Perhaps you're here because you have made your choice."

"Choice about what?" she asked.

Michael gave a stunned look.

"Oh, that, no," she said.

"Have you seen Brogan?" Michael asked.

"No. I haven't seen him. We've chatted on the phone and I got a postcard from him last week. But Michael, look," she said as she dropped three books on his desk.

"You chatted with Brogan, but you couldn't respond to my text from Tuesday?"

Jewel ignored his remark. She opened the top book which looked like a personal journal. It was old and the writing was badly faded.

"I found this journal from the eighteen-hundreds. It has information about Jean Lafitte," Jewel said, her eyes wide with wonder.

"Jean Lafitte, the pirate?" Michael asked.

"Yes," Jewel said with a smile. "So, Jean Lafitte supposedly sailed away on his flagship, the *Pride*. At least that is what history tells us. But this journal tells a different tale. It claims that Lafitte left of a different ship, and it gives hints about his treasure," Jewel said.

"What does that have to do with me?"

"Michael, if this book is authentic, it could lead to Lafitte's treasure," she said.

Michael picked up the journal and flipped through the pages.

"What are you suggesting, Jewel?"

"Remember when Brogan mentioned, that the three of us make a really good team? We all have talents to contribute. We can go find this treasure, Michael," she said.

"After all this time, do you really think the treasure is still there?"

"This book speculates that the treasure was broken up into caches and hidden in different places. At least one had to have survived."

"This is crazy," Michael said as he handed the book to Jewel.

Jewel's face took on a look of defeat.

"You came all this way for this? . . . We should have dinner," Michael said.

"Maybe," Jewel said as she slowly collected the books. She was staring down at the stack. "So, if I wanted to get in touch with Brogan, then how would I do that?" she asked.

Michael froze and eyed her with suspicion. He sat back in his chair and watched her until she made eye contact. He sighed heavily.

"Can you wait for the summer break for this adventure?" Michael asked.

Jewel's face broke into a smile. She lunged forward and hugged Michael.

"I told him you would help," she said.

"What? You told who?" Michael asked.

"Brogan. He said, 'if Michael is in then I'm in,'" she said as she collected the books.

"You deceived me," Michael said.

"No. I didn't deceive you. I just left some things out."

"So you have seen my brother?"

"No. But Brogan called me and I told him about the treasure," she said. "I have to run. I'm parked in a tow zone. I'll see you in June. Just come to my house when your break starts."

"You deceived me. I have half a mind to refuse," Michael said.

Jewel stopped and eyed him.

"Oh . . . Okay. Well, I guess it will just be me and Brogan . . . just the two of us . . . alone," Jewel said as she reached the door. "Bye Michael, let me know if you change your mind," she said as she slowly exited.

She shut the door and leaned against the wall just outside the office.

She was counting the seconds as she held her breath. After the count of six, the door swung open.

"Jewel?" Michael called in a panic.

"Yeah," she said, behind him.

He spun around to face her.

"June . . . I'll pack light."

"See you then, *Mo chuisle*," she said with a smile. She grabbed the front of his shirt, pulled him down, and gave him a quick kiss on the cheek.

Danish Jubilee

The 1903 Royal Danish Egg, also known as the Danish Jubilee, is one of two missing Imperial Easter Eggs that are only known to exist from a single photograph. The Danish Jubilee is still missing.

# Pronunciation Guide

Mi scusi: Mee skoo-zee

Brogan:  Bro-gan

Chauvin:  Show-van

Landry: Lan-dree

Suran: Soo-ron

Gruber: Groo-ber

Pepo:  Pee-po

Basilica dei Frari:  Bah-zil-lee-ka day frah-ree

Faolan: fway-lawn

Frau Viessmann: Frow veez-mon

Mo chuisle: Mu kooish-lah

If you enjoyed this novel, please leave a review at any of this author's affiliated sites:

KristelBeck.com

Goodreads

Amazon Author page

Facebook

Instagram

www.ingramcontent.com/pod-product-compliance
Lightning Source LLC
Chambersburg PA
CBHW030034180626
46810CB00001B/360